W9-AAE-209

CUPID, TEXAS: HOW THE COWBOY WAS WON

This Large Print Book carries the
Seal of Approval of N.A.V.H.

CUPID, TEXAS: HOW THE COWBOY WAS WON

LORI WILDE

Farmington Hills, Mich • San Francisco • New York • Waterville, Maine
Meriden, Conn • Mason, Ohio • Chicago

GALE
A Cengage Company

Thorndike Press® Large Print Romance.
The text of this Large Print edition is unabridged.
Other aspects of the book may vary from the original edition.
Set in 16 pt. Plantin.

LIBRARY OF CONGRESS CIP DATA ON FILE.
CATALOGUING IN PUBLICATION FOR THIS BOOK
IS AVAILABLE FROM THE LIBRARY OF CONGRESS

ISBN-13: 978-1-4328-5182-8 (hardcover)

Published in 2018 by arrangement with Avon, an imprint of HarperCollins Publishers

Printed in Mexico
1 2 3 4 5 6 7 22 21 20 19 18

To Bill, my husband and best friend.
Your kisses make my head hum.

CHAPTER 1

"Were I to fall in love, indeed, it would be a different thing; but I have never been in love; it is not my way, or my nature; and I do not think I ever shall."

— Jane Austen, *Emma*

"A toast to the woman who made this marriage possible!" The blushing bride, Susan Peoples Fant, resplendent in a white Vera Wang wedding gown on this special evening in May, raised her champagne flute. "My dear friend and awesome real estate agent, Ember Alzate. If she hadn't so stubbornly twisted my arm that Cupid was the place to find my dream home, I would not have found my dream husband!"

Enthusiastic applause erupted.

Across the horse barn turned cowboy wedding reception hall, Susan sent Ember a meaningful grin. "You really should consider matchmaking as a sideline career. You

7

broker relationships as easily as houses."

Ember gave a slight smile and tried not to look too proud of herself. While she did have a knack for hooking up other people, her own love life was a train wreck.

"Take a bow, Ember," someone shouted.

Ember stood and raised her champagne flute, putting the focus of the toast where it belonged. "All I did was open the door. Susan and Bryant were the ones who weren't afraid to walk through it. To the happy couple."

"To the happy couple!" echoed the guests.

After the toasts were completed and the champagne downed, the band struck up Michael Bublé's "Everything." The first dance between the bride and groom. As Bryant waltzed Susan onto the dance floor, they had eyes for only each other.

Aww.

Ember's heart swelled. She *had* done a great job. Maybe she should start a match-making business on the side. Real estate in podunk Cupid wasn't exactly booming, especially in the high-end properties that were her specialty.

Hey, why not? Her bank account was whining that it was time to move back to San Antonio and pick up her old career.

Yeah, about that.

8

As big as San Antonio was, it wasn't big enough for both Ember and her ex-husband.

She shuddered and decided she was not going to think about those three disastrous months where every single thing she'd done or said had embarrassed her social-climbing husband, Trey.

The final loose block pulled from their Jenga marriage came during a party their boss had thrown — she and Trey had both been real estate agents for the same company — and Ember had had a wee bit too much to drink. But with good reason. She'd been celebrating the closing of a twenty-million-dollar property to a famous Spurs basketball player, and she was flying high on the rush of achievement.

With her guard down, her passionate nature had come charging out, and she'd playfully yanked Trey into the wine cellar for an impulsive quickie. And they'd been caught by their boss, in flagrante, bent over a rack of Pinot Noir.

Mortifying? Oh for sure, but that wasn't the worst part. *That* had happened on the car ride home.

"I've never been so humiliated in my life," Trey fumed, and proceeded to berate her with vinegar and vim. "I should have known when we were dating that you were all wrong for me."

Her lungs had felt like balloons filled to bursting, and if she took one more breath she would explode.

His tirade was a train, rolling right over her. "When we were dating, I put your loudness down to enthusiasm."

Stunned, she'd just sat in the passenger seat, her mouth hanging open.

"But tonight has proven every reservation I've ever had about you."

He'd had reservations about the marriage? Why hadn't he said something? She'd had her own doubts that things had moved too quickly, but he'd seemed so sure that they would make a great team that she'd talked herself out of her cold feet.

"You're too sexual."

"But —"

"Too crude."

"I —"

"Too reckless."

"You —"

"Too headstrong."

Yeah, okay, guilty as charged on that one.

"Too playful."

What was wrong with being playful?

"Too everything. Face it, you're just too much, Ember. I've tried to get you to stop wearing clothes that showed too much skin, to speak more softly and less often, to pay attention to how you come across to others, but it's as if you haven't heard a word I've said during our entire marriage."

Of three months.

Right after their wedding, he'd asked her to wear dresses with longer hems and shirts with higher necklines, and pants cut more loosely. She'd done it to keep him happy. But he'd just criticized her more, slowly eroding her self-confidence to the point she started weighing each word that came out of her mouth, and that so wasn't her.

"You're hopeless." He snorted.

She could have pointed out that he hadn't protested when she'd pulled him into the wine cellar for sex, but she was too blind-sided, absorbing every hateful word like a sucker punch.

"Don't you even care what people think of you?" he asked.

"I . . . I . . . ."

"Finally you're speechless?" His tone sliced her to her core, a knife of words.

"I thought you *liked* that I was the life of the party."

"In a date maybe, but a wife?" He shook his head. "It's *vulgar.*"

"Trey, I didn't think —"

11

"That's just it. You *never* think."

Her stomach felt as if it had gotten dropped in the spin cycle of a washing machine, churned and wrung out. "What can I do to make this right?"

He'd frowned, gripped the steering wheel tighter, and clenched his jaw. His face going cold and stony. "It's too late for that. I want a divorce."

Numb, Ember had sat in the passenger seat struggling to process what was happening.

Part of her, the real *her,* had wanted to yell, *Projecting much, Trey?* But she was still so shocked, she'd been unable to dredge up a rebuttal.

What had initially attracted her to him was his gung-ho nature. Most of their romance had come from trying to outdo each other selling real estate. It had been fun and exhilarating, the rush of competition, and they'd quickly become a power couple in San Antonio's real estate market. What she hadn't realized was that while he loved competing just as much as she did, he cared far more about what people thought of him. He was more of a status seeker, while Ember had been more about taking calculated risks and setting trends.

That's what killed their short-lived marriage. Their clash of values.

He'd been terrified of looking bad in front of others, scared that he'd be judged and found lacking by his social group. Whereas Ember didn't give two figs what people thought about her.

Their brief marriage had ended eighteen months ago, but Trey's cruel words still stung, hung in her psyche. She'd gotten the message loud and clear.

You're unlovable the way you are.

If it had just been Trey's opinion, she might not have taken the message to heart, but throughout her life she'd received some version of the same rhetoric. *Bend, mold, toe the line if you want to be more pleasing to others.*

As the only Alzate sibling who'd inherited their Irish mother's wild red hair and sapphire blue eyes, she'd stood out among the four dark-haired, dark-eyed brother and sisters who favored their Native American father. She'd heard whispers from strangers when they saw her with the other children when her mother wasn't around. Absorbed the speculations that she was adopted or illegitimate.

Her parents had tried to soften the blow, assuring her she was neither adopted nor illegitimate and that they loved her as much

13

as they loved the other children, but she couldn't shake the feeling that she was the odd child out. Throughout her life, from teachers, neighbors, and the guys she'd dated, she'd often been rejected, chastised, or ostracized for being too exuberant or impulsive, for pushing boundaries or speaking her mind.

Shh, girls shouldn't be loud.

Don't be so bossy.

If you want boys to like you, let them win.

Beyond her family, the only person who had ever accepted her unconditionally was her best friend in the whole wide world, Ranger Lockhart.

She and Ranger had grown up together on the Silver Feather Ranch. Ranger was the elder, born June 15, to Ember's August 10 birthday. Ranger was the second son of wealthy Duke Lockhart, and Ember the oldest daughter of their ranch foreman, Armand Alzate. Even when she'd repeatedly gotten brainy, studious Ranger into trouble, he'd always been in her corner.

But when it came to the rest of the male species, Ember had learned she could either curtail her personality, essentially cutting off pieces of herself in order to be loved, or just be herself and lose the man.

Clearly, she was not the marrying kind.

And that was okay with her. It didn't mean she couldn't find joy in helping other people find their perfect matches. As for herself, she didn't want or need that whole happily-ever-after, shiny-bling-wedding-ring thing. She could take lovers for sex, and she had Ranger for companionship. What more could she ask for?

Except Ranger had been in New Zealand for the past year, elbow deep in postdoctoral studies in astrobiology at the University of Canterbury, and she missed him terribly. It was almost as if she'd lost a limb.

They stayed in contact for sure, but lately he'd been finishing up his research, and his texts and phone calls had grown fewer and farther between. She hadn't heard from him in almost a month. It was the longest they'd ever gone without being in contact.

Out on the dance floor, the music changed. Susan danced with her father under white twinkle lights strung from the rustic rafters.

The reception was being held at the Silver Feather Ranch, where Ember's younger sister Kaia lived with Ranger's older brother, Ridge, and their new baby daughter, Ingrid.

The Silver Feather had a chapel and reception barn they rented out for country-style weddings. Ember's youngest sister,

Aria, worked as a wedding planner. While her older brother, Archer, was the Silver Feather's ranch foreman, following in their father's footsteps. The Silver Feather was a family affair for both the Alzates and the Lockharts.

Honestly, it could get claustrophobic being around people who knew her so well. Which was why Ember lived in the artsy community of Marfa, twenty miles down the road from Cupid.

"May I have this dance?" a smooth male voice asked.

She glanced over to see Palmer Douglas, a dashing photographer from Alpine, who gave off a Zac Efron vibe. He'd been hired to record Susan and Bryant's wedding. At twenty-seven, Palmer was five years younger than Ember, overly handsome, and sexy as hell with straight white teeth and a light-bulb smile. But he was a bit shallow, something of a party hound, and had serious aspirations of leaving the Trans-Pecos in his rearview mirror.

Not that she was the least bit interested in him, but his attention was an ego booster.

"Thanks, Palmer," she said. "But I'm sitting this one out."

"C'mon," he coaxed, holding out a hand. "You know you want to let your hair down

16

and cut loose." He lowered his lashes. "I've seen you at Chantilly's whooping it up. You've got some serious moves, girl."

She did love to dance. Idly, she toyed with the idea of accepting his invitation, but she didn't want to encourage him. "Not in the mood. Why don't you ask Tara?" she said, referring to her sister, who was sitting with a group of older couples on the other side of the room.

"Tara's nice and all," Palmer said, splaying a palm on his nape. "But she doesn't have your spunk."

"She's a better dancer than I am," Ember corrected.

"I wasn't talking about your dancing skills." Palmer's voice took on a suggestive quality.

"Get out of here, kid." She waved him away with a laugh. "You're too young for me."

"Five years is not that big of an age difference, and I've been told women reach their sexual peak in their midthirties while men peak in their twenties —"

"Oh honey, don't even start. I'd make mincemeat of you. If I was going to take a lover, which I'm not, I'd pick a man not a boy. Now shoo." She waved him away.

Palmer grinned and shrugged impishly.

17

"Can't blame a guy for trying. You were sitting over here looking so hot and sexy, I just had to take a shot."

"Buzz off, little bee." She kept waving him away.

Palmer had no sooner glided over to the next table in search of a dance partner than Ember felt a tap on her shoulder. She looked up to see Zeke Tremont, a ranch hand on the Silver Feather.

Zeke was salt of the earth — loyal, kindhearted, and hardworking. Unfortunately, the lanky cowboy had two strikes against him. While his butt looked fantastic in a pair of jeans, he was rather plain, with clay-colored hair and weathered skin. And at thirty-one, he'd already been married three times.

Poor Zeke had the old-fashioned notion that he should get married before having sex, and he had a tendency to fall hard and fast for the wrong sort of woman. Women had happily taken advantage of his sweet nature to get their hands on the million dollars he'd won in the Texas lottery when he was eighteen. The women, and the money, were long gone, but Zeke owned his own home, free and clear, and he was good with kids and animals. Not a bad catch for the right woman.

The matchmaker in her started thinking about the single women she knew who would overlook Zeke's homeliness in favor of his winsome personality and gentle nature.

"Wa . . . wa . . . would you dance with me, Ember?" Zeke stammered, and she could tell it had taken an effort for him to work up the courage to come over.

She took pity on him, smiled, and took his hand. He followed her onto the dance floor like a well-trained puppy.

"Hey," Palmer said, two-stepping next to them on the dance floor with a peppy blonde on his arm. "You said you weren't in the mood."

"Zeke changed my mind." Ember laughed, and led her partner in time to the "Cotton-Eyed Joe."

When the song was over, Zeke escorted her back to her seat and asked if he could bring her a cold drink.

"Thanks for the offer, Zeke," she said, not wanting to risk him getting the wrong idea. "But I'm good. Thank you for the dance."

He bobbed his head and scooted off, leaving Ember feeling a little lonely. Loneliness was not a good reason to date someone. That's how she'd gotten mixed up with Trey. She'd been lonely in the big city, and he'd showered her with compliments and grand gestures and well, she'd succumbed. Being lonely alone was far better than being lonely in a relationship.

"*Psst,* Miss Alzate," a loud whisper came from behind her. It was a woman's voice this time. "Can I talk to you?"

Since there were three Alzate sisters attending the wedding, Ember wasn't completely certain that she was the one being hissed at.

She swiveled her head and spied a ginger-haired young woman in her early twenties. Ember's own hair was more Irish setter red, whereas this girl's hair was several shades more orange.

There weren't too many gingers in the Trans-Pecos, so most of them knew each other. This moppet was Chriss Anne Gossett, great-granddaughter of Millie Greenwood, one of Cupid's early settlers. Chriss Anne wasn't terribly sophisticated, but she was sweet as cherry pie and inordinately cheerful.

"Hi, Chriss Anne." Ember patted the bottom of an empty chair beside her. "Have a seat."

"Is it okay?" Chriss Anne glanced around furtively. "You don't have a date?"

"Nope."

Chriss Anne slid into the chair. "I feel so close to you."

"That's because you are."

"Huh?" Chriss Anne blinked.

"You're sitting right next to me."

"No." Chriss Anne giggled. "I mean 'cause we're both gingers."

"We're practically twins," Ember quipped.

"Oh no." Chriss Anne shook her head and her eyes widened. "You're like . . . *old.*"

Ouch. Although, she supposed when she was in her early twenties she viewed thirty-two as AARP eligible.

Chriss Anne cringed, lifting her shoulders up to her ears. "I didn't mean it the way it sounded. I just meant . . . well . . . that you know stuff."

"Is that so?"

"And you're smart and brave and different than most folks around here."

Okay, Chriss Anne was fast making up for the "old" comment. "Are you working around to something?"

"Mmm." Chriss Anne scratched her head. "You see, I heard you needed an assistant to help with the Chamber of Commerce movie you're directing."

Not a movie really. Rather a short film intended to promote tourism, centered around the history of Cupid and the role

21

the Camel Corps played in settling the Trans-Pecos. Ember was directing for free because she cared about her community, believed in the project, and quite honestly there wasn't enough real estate inventory to keep her busy at the moment, and Ember didn't do well when she had time on her hands.

"I have to tell you right up front, this is a labor of love. There's no pay at all on the front end," Ember said. "When and *if* the film makes revenue through ticket sales, the actors will get a small percentage of the take."

"Oh, I don't mind. I just want the experience of working with *you.*"

"Why?" Ember wasn't trying to be difficult; she was just a bottom-line person who liked knowing where she stood. "Are you looking to become an actor?"

"Confession time." Chriss Anne splayed her hands on the table, her fingernails painted chartreuse with pink seahorses on them. "You mentored my friend Kourtney, and she says you completely turned her life around."

Aww, that was sweet. One summer, back when she was in college, Ember had served as a mentor for an at-risk-teens program through her church. She remembered

Kourtney well. She'd been a disadvantaged young girl with a rebellious streak and a bright IQ who reminded Ember a lot of herself at that age.

"How is Kourtney?"

Chriss Anne beamed. "She's spending a year abroad as an au pair in Spain, and she said she would never have had the confidence to go for it without the life skills you taught her."

A warm glow lit the center of Ember's chest. She might have messed up royally in her own life, but if she helped an underprivileged kid like Kourtney, she'd done at least one good thing.

"Filming goes for three weeks, starting next Tuesday. Eight in the morning until five at night. Do you currently have a job?"

Chriss Anne shook her head. "I was looking after Miss Delia, but her Old Timer's got real bad, and my cousin had to finally put her in a home."

"I'm sorry to hear that about Miss Delia." Chriss Anne's great-aunt Delia was a town fixture and one of the founders of the group of women who answered the Dear Cupid letters that tourists left at the base of the Cupid stalagmite in the local caverns. At one time or another, almost every woman — and a few men too — in town had served

23

as a Letters to Cupid volunteer, Ember included. She liked volunteering. It made her feel like a larger part of her community.

"It's a shame about Delia." Chriss Anne fidgeted with her bra strap, which kept falling out from underneath the sleeve of her party dress. "But that means I'm free and can help with your movie. If you could use someone. I'll do anything. Be a gofer. Make coffee. Whatever you need."

Ember had a feeling she hadn't yet struck at the heart of the girl's true motive. "Wouldn't your time be better spent looking for another job?"

"Oh I have one," Chriss Anne said. "As a camp counselor, but it doesn't start until the middle of June."

"So that's it? You're just looking for a way to kill time until the camp opens?"

"Gain experience." Chriss Anne's smile was a bit over-the-top, like the latest trend to put way too much sugary frosting on cupcakes.

"And?"

Chriss Anne leaned in closer and lowered her voice. "I was hoping . . ."

Ah, here it comes.

"If you could . . ." Chriss Anne moistened her lips. "If you could . . . well, you know . . ."

"Know what?"

"Do that thing you do . . . for me."

Ember cocked her head. "What thing is that?"

"You know . . ." The girl seemed to love the phrase. "Hook me up with a guy."

Ember inclined her head and suppressed a smile. Now here was the meat of it. "You want me to find you a boyfriend?"

"Not just *any* boyfriend, but the right boyfriend. I want a *forever* man."

"Don't you think you're awfully young to be settling down?"

"I'm twenty-two. My mama got married when she was nineteen, and my gamma before her was only seventeen. I'm ready, but I've been through a string of guys who were all flash and no substance, if you know what I mean."

Oh she knew all right. *Trey.*

"Please, please, please." Chriss Anne pressed her palms together in front of her heart, a gesture of entreaty. "I want to be madly in love."

Hey, she thought, *so do I,* and that surprised her.

"Honey," Ember murmured, "here's where being 'old' comes in handy. You learn the hard way that sometimes the thing you

25

want the most is *not* the thing you most need."

"But sometimes, you *can* get what you want, right?" Chriss Anne looked like a kitten, all wide-eyed and huggable. "I mean, your sister Kaia got Ridge Lockhart, and she'd had a crush on him since she was knee-high to a grasshopper."

"Some people are luckier than others," Ember said. "You can't always bank on luck or chemistry. Chemistry is notorious for leading you astray."

Trey.

"I'm lucky," Chriss Anne bragged. "I've won six lotto scratch-offs this last year to the tune of three hundred and thirty-six dollars."

"That *is* lucky," Ember said kindly.

"See." Chriss Anne beamed. "There's hope for me."

"Sure, there's hope. But honestly, Chriss Anne, you don't need a matchmaker. If there's a guy that you like, why not just go talk to him?"

"Because the guy I like knows words that are longer than my arm, and when I'm around him my tongue gets all twisted up, and I can't put two sentences together. I've been reading the encyclopedia just so I can understand what he's saying half the time."

26

It sounded like a mismatch for sure.

"What do you guys have in common?" she asked, sincerely trying to help.

Chriss Anne paused, screwing up her mouth in thought and drumming her fingertips on the table. "Oh, I know . . . we both love stargazing."

Around Cupid, with the McDonald Observatory not far away and some of the clearest skies in the country, a lot of people enjoyed stargazing.

"What else do you have in common?"

"Hmm." Chriss Anne tapped her chin with an index finger. "Let's see. We both like Rocky Road ice cream."

So did Ember. What wasn't to like? Chocolate, almonds, and marshmallows. "That's a solid foundation to build a relationship on."

She was being sarcastic, but Chriss Anne squealed, "I know! So you'll help me?"

"Chriss Anne, I'm not a professional matchmaker. I introduced a few people to each other, and things just happened to work out for them —"

"You could at least introduce me to him."

"You don't already know your potential love interest?"

Chriss Anne shook her head and sent her carrot curls bobbing. "Not official-like.

Once, he held an umbrella over my head during a rainstorm and helped me to my car when I worked at the commissary at the McDonald Observatory, but I was too tongue-tied to even say thank you."

"How about you leave a note on his car telling him how much you appreciated his kindness?"

"I can't do that. It was over a year ago. He probably doesn't even remember me." Chriss Anne slapped her cheeks as if trying to wake herself up after pulling an all-nighter. "Although he did compliment my hair."

"And you've been carrying a torch for him all this time?"

Chriss Anne's nose crinkled. "What does 'carrying a torch' mean? Is it like in the Olympics?"

"Never mind the torch thing. It's just something older people say. Listen, Chriss Anne, if you're finding it that hard to talk to him, maybe he's not the man for you."

"Please don't blow me off. I really need help."

"I don't —"

"I can pay," Chriss Anne said, pulling money from the butterfly-shaped clutch purse. "I saved the lotto money."

"I can't accept your cash."

"I don't get it," Chriss Anne cried. "You help everybody else in town. What's wrong with me?"

"Nothing is wrong with you." Ember's heartstrings plucked at the desperate, love-struck expression on the girl's face. "You are absolutely perfect just the way you are."

"I thought you of all people would understand," Chriss Anne wailed, steamrolling right over Ember's comment, thrusting a fistful of dollar bills at her. "We're both gingers."

"Listen, listen, I can't take your money." Ember folded her hand over Chriss Anne's trembling fingers.

"If you won't help me, who will?" Chriss Anne shook her head like a long-necked goose, all sway and waddle. "You are so smart. One of the smartest people in town. And you don't take crap off anybody. You're bold and brave and gosh darn it, when I'm old, I want to be just like you."

The girl was so worked up her eyes bugged, and the three couples sitting at the table next to them were leaning in, obviously eavesdropping on their conversation.

Ember gave the Nosey Parkers a pointed stare, waved toward the crowded dance floor where people were shaking their feet to the "Hokey Pokey." "Why don't y'all go find out if the hokey pokey really *is* what it's all about."

On command, the three couples got up to dance.

"See?" Chriss Anne giggled. "See how you got those people to do what you wanted?"

Yes, and if Trey had been here, he would have chewed her out for being too "bossy." Good thing Trey wasn't here.

"All right," Ember said. "All right." Chriss Anne might need a lot of work, but in real estate agent parlance, the girl had good bones. She was earnest and sincere and kind. Ember could work with that. "I'll help you, but only on one condition."

Chriss Anne thrust the dollar bills at her again.

"Put the money away. I don't charge for helping you find your perfect match . . . ." But apparently, she could charge for her services if she wanted. Ember held up an index finger. "And you haven't heard my condition."

Chriss Anne stuffed the money back into her purse and sat up straight. "What is it?"

"If I decide this man is not the guy for you, you'll heed my advice and move on."

Chriss Anne started to whine. "But —"

"*Shtt.*" Ember held up her finger again. "I won't leave you high and dry. If he's not the one, I'll find you someone who will love you exactly for who you are, and you won't have to read the encyclopedia just to talk to him. Agreed?"

Chriss Anne bit her bottom lip and toed the leg of the table. "But I really, really like him."

Once upon a time, she'd really liked Trey too, back before she knew better.

"Keep in mind, you'll want someone who likes you back with as much enthusiasm as you like him. I'm speaking from experience here. There are some advantages to being old."

Chriss Anne sighed. "Okay, I agree. But will you try to match me with the guy I want?"

"I'm not making any promises, but tell me, where is this mysterious brainiac?"

"Right there." Chriss Anne pointed toward the open barn door, a dreamy tone in her voice.

Ember turned her head and saw her most favorite person in the whole wide world.

Ranger Lockhart.

Her heart surged.

A year in New Zealand and he was more handsome than ever. His hair was longer, his dimples deeper, eyes brighter, skin more tanned. Had he gotten taller? Or had she

31

simply forgotten what a compelling figure he cut?

No wonder Chriss Anne was head-over-heels for him. So were half the women in the building. What a sticky wicket!

Ranger caught Ember's eyes, grinned as big as Texas, settled his Stetson back on his head, and held his arms open wide.

Instantly, Ember was out of her chair and running straight toward her best friend.

CHAPTER 2

"Men of sense, whatever you may choose
to say, do not want silly wives."
— Jane Austen, *Emma*

Laughing, Ranger snagged Ember in his
arms and spun her around on the dance
floor. Skype and FaceTiming didn't cut it
when it came to best friends.

Her luscious red hair was pinned in a
fancy upsweep that showed off her high
cheekbones, creamy skin, and lively blue
eyes, and he couldn't stop staring at her.
He'd always known she was gorgeous, but
right here, right now, he could have sworn
she was the most beautiful woman in the
galaxy.

Ember threw back her head and laughed
that sweet laugh of hers, which was such
music to his ears.

He'd been gone for a year, fully submersed
in postdoctoral work, and truth be told he

hadn't even realized he'd been homesick until he held her in his arms.

She was what he'd missed.

Not the high desert plains of the Trans-Pecos, not his brothers who were all busy with their own affairs, not even the wide expanse of starry skies that had captivated his attention when he was a sickly kid suffering from scarlet fever, and its aftermath. There were starry skies aplenty in New Zealand.

Nope. None of that.

Ember, this flame of a woman, his forever best friend, was the only person, place, or thing he'd deeply pined for.

"I missed the hell out of you." He growled playfully and spun her around again.

"Ditto." She beamed.

People were staring at them, but that was to be expected. People always stared at Ember; she had that effect on everyone.

Including him.

Hell, especially him.

His best friend drew him like a moth to a candle, but he'd never felt the attraction as intensely as he was feeling it now. Damn, but she was sexy and bright and energetic. It was a bit confusing, this deep need to touch her, and to keep touching her, as if he couldn't believe she was real.

He *had* missed her so much. Missed her bluntness and her loyalty. Missed her verve and self-confidence. Missed her playful generosity and expressive laughter. Missed her bold cinnamon-and-anise scent.

He liked her take-life-by-the-horns approach, and how she slapped her cards on the table, direct and honest. He liked the almost constant twinkle in her eyes as if she were perpetually on the verge of mischief, and how her excitement was contagious. He liked the knowing smile that curled her lips over straight white teeth, and how that smile slipped under his skin, warming him from the inside out.

She was, in many ways, his complete opposite. She was an extroverted risk-taker who had a tendency to leap before she looked. The life of the party, easily bored with mundane activities. She was expressive and lively and filled with raw optimism. She hated phoniness and flattery, and quickly saw through people who tried to pull the wool over her eyes.

He liked to think they balanced each other out. Him getting her to think about things before she blindly jumped in. Her pushing him out of his comfort zone. The relationship had been going strong for thirty-two years and he couldn't, in his wildest imagination, picture a world without her in it.

"I'm getting dizzy with the spinning." She laughed. "Please put me down."

Reluctantly, he let go.

"Hey mister," Ember said, giving him a good-natured slug on the arm, the way they'd greeted each other since they were toddlers in the sandbox. "Why didn't you tell me you were getting in today? I would have picked you up at the airport."

He lightly tapped her shoulder with his fist. "I wanted to surprise you, and you had other things cooking."

"Paint me happy." She embraced him in a bear hug. "I was worried you weren't going to make it for Ingrid's christening tomorrow afternoon."

"Wouldn't miss it for the world," he said.

"Cut it pretty close. You were supposed to be home last week." She pretended to pout.

"Finishing touches on my research project."

"That's my Ranger." This time she tapped his chin with her fist. "Head in the clouds."

"You do know that time really is relative."

"Not here on Earth."

"Earth" — he laughed — "has always been my Achilles' heel."

"So New Zealand. Completely done?" She clapped her small hands as if she were thrilled at the prospect. "No going back?"

Ranger didn't have the heart to tell her that they'd offered him a teaching position at the University of Canterbury. It was plan B if he didn't get the job he really wanted — a directorship at the McDonald Observatory. Until he'd left for New Zealand, he'd worked at the observatory under various fellowships, but he had not been offered anything permanent. He'd returned to hold the director's feet to the fire. Either find him a permanent home at the observatory, or he was pulling up stakes and moving to New Zealand for good. The only qualm he had about the move was the woman standing in front of him.

But what if Wes told him, *Bye, have fun being a Kiwi.* What would he do about Ember?

Wes Montgomery had been Ranger's mentor from the first time he showed up at the observatory when he was fifteen, begging for any kind of work that let him be near the telescopes. Wes had finagled him a position in food service, but when he caught Ranger sneaking into the command center, he'd taken him under his wing and pulled strings to get him accepted into the University of Texas after Ranger graduated from high school at sixteen as the class valedictorian with a perfect 4.0 GPA.

"Have you seen your family?" Ember wrapped her arm around his waist, and he enjoyed the warmth and weight of her body against his.

He shook his head. "Dad and Vivi are in Vegas," he said, referring to his father and his third wife. "They're flying back tonight, and when I arrived, Ridge and Kaia were meeting with Father Dubanowski, going over the details of Ingrid's christening, so I came straight here."

To you.

"Remington?" she asked about his younger half brother who was Army Special Forces and deployed in the Middle East.

"He couldn't get leave."

"I hate that Remington can't make it home. He'll be missed."

For sure. Ranger hadn't seen his brother in over two years.

"And Rhett?" she asked.

Rhett was his youngest half brother, and a professional bull-riding star. "He's in town, but no telling whose bed he's in at the moment."

"Oh well, it doesn't matter. *You're* here, and that's all that counts in my book." She tucked her arm around his elbow. "It's an exciting time for our families."

"I'm still having trouble wrapping my head around the fact that Ridge and Kaia have a kid." He readjusted his Stetson. "And that you and I are in-laws."

"Yep. It's official. We're finally family."

"You've always felt like family to me." He beamed at her, and his chest tightened oddly. "Damn, but it's good to see you, Sparky."

"Good to see you too, Professor." She chucked him on the shoulder again.

A dancing couple bumped into them, apologized. "Oops, sorry."

"We better dance or get off the floor." Ember stuck out her hand, letting him know which option she preferred.

Ranger wasn't much for dancing. Because of his childhood ailments, he'd spent more time in bed with books than doing things with his body, but when they were teen-agers, Ember insisted he learn how to dance so they could go to prom together and they wouldn't have to — in her words — scramble for dullard dates.

Then he'd graduated high school a year early because he was bored out of his skull, went off to the University of Texas and left her to fend for herself. Which she still held over his head whenever she needed a favor. The woman had an elephant's memory.

It didn't matter. He would do anything for his best friend, including learn how to waltz.

He was rusty, and Ember had an endearingly annoying habit of trying to lead, but the minute he settled his hand on her waist and they glided across the floor in time to "I Won't Give Up," everything fell into place. With her, his two left feet somehow functioned the way they were supposed to.

Of course, Ranger didn't hold her close. She was his best friend. He might have experienced growing feelings for her over the years, but he wouldn't let himself think about her in a sexual way. He had never crossed that line, no matter how much he might have wanted to. He valued their friendship too much to ever let sex get in the way.

But God, she smelled good. Like cinnamon Red Hots, and licorice, and rich West Texas wind. It occurred to Ranger that maybe the reason, at almost thirty-three, he'd never felt the least bit inclined to get married was because he had Ember.

Sex, he could get any place, and if the urge arose, he would. And as for companionship, well, he couldn't find anyone who understood him better, who simply *got* him, the way Ember did.

He'd had several girlfriends over the years, but inevitably, they'd become jealous of his relationship with her. No amount of re-assurance had been able to convince his girlfriends that he and Ember were just friends, and that's all they would ever be.

"It doesn't matter that you don't have a physical relationship with her," his last serious girlfriend, Tonya, had said when she broke up with him over two years ago. "You're emotionally unavailable to me because you share all your secrets with her. *That's* what I'm jealous of."

He'd had to let Tonya go because, as much as he'd liked her, there was no way he could give up the one woman who'd helped him through the rough patches in his life — his biological mother abandoning him to his father in exchange for two million dollars; his stepmother's death from breast cancer when he was twelve; his own lingering ill-nesses, and his ups and downs with his brothers; all the various shit his ornery father had pulled over the years.

No matter what happened, Ember had been there for him, loyal to the core.

Always.

After Tonya walked out, Ember took him to Chantilly's to drown his sorrows. Laughing and tipsy, they ended up lying in the

41

bed of his pickup truck staring at the stars as he bemoaned his bad luck with women.

Ember had said rather sensibly, "Look, Lockhart, when we're sixty-four if we haven't found anyone else, we'll get married and take care of each other into our dotage. How's that?"

He'd stuck out his little finger. "Pinky swear."

They'd hooked their pinkies, grinned at each other, and returned their attention to the starry night sky. He'd considered that commitment enough, and then without warning Ember had gone off and married that fool Trey Sharpton.

Ember's marriage had been the darkest three months of Ranger's adult life, and he wasn't proud of himself, but he'd been relieved when Trey divorced her, and he'd gotten his best friend back.

If that made him a shitheel, then so be it.

Soon after that, he'd gotten the fellowship in New Zealand, and he and Ember had been apart again. On the flight home, he'd worried things might be awkward, since he hadn't had time to maintain their friendship the way he would have liked, but the minute she'd met his gaze across the crowded room, it was as if nothing had changed.

Ember was his rock. Always had been. Always would be. And whomever Ranger eventually married would have to accept that. In the meantime, he was home again and waltzing with his best friend.

Life was good.

"You *do* know that your boots don't match," Ember said as he waltzed around the room, finally getting it into her head that he was leading.

"Again?" He looked down at his feet, saw that his left boot was black, the right was dark brown. "Dammit."

"I've missed you so much, Professor," she said, her voice heavy with teasing affection.

"Um, why is that woman staring at me?" he asked. "Do you think it's the boots?"

Ember glanced over her shoulder. "Oh, that's Chriss Anne Gossett. She has a major crush on you."

"How does she even know who I am?"

"You held an umbrella over her head once."

"I did?"

"You really do strive to live up to the absentminded professor thing, don't you?"

"What can I say?" He shrugged, accepting who he was without qualms. "It's my shtick."

"Guess what? Chriss Anne wants me to

43

hook you up with her."

"Good God, why?"

"She thinks you're hot."

"No, I meant why did she ask *you*? Have you been playing matchmaker again, Sparky?"

She lowered her eyelids, sent him a side-long glance and an enigmatic smile. "I might have played a role in this current shindig."

"Susan and Bryant? That was you?"

Her smile widened; she was not the least bit humble. "Well, not *all* me."

"Ember, stay out of other people's business," he chided. "You know what happens when you pry. You're the one who ends up getting your nose caught in the door."

"Hey, they come to me. I don't go looking for it. And you know how I —"

"Love to control other people."

"Low blow! I was going to say how I liked helping people."

"Admit it, you like meddling in other people's lives."

She made a tsk-tsk sound with her tongue. "Didn't you hear the part where they come to me? What am I supposed to do? Turn them away in their time of need?"

"There's this word . . . it's two letters

long, starts with an 'n' and ends with an 'o.' "

"Were you actually invited to this wedding?"

"Nope. But hey, my father owns the property and my stepmother runs the venue. What are they going to do? Throw me out?"

"Wedding crasher."

"Admit it, you like rebels."

"So you came here tonight just to see me?" Ember's face was a rainbow of happiness, and he didn't have the heart to tell her, that no, she was not the only reason he'd shown up at the wedding.

But this was Ember, and she knew him so well he didn't have to say anything. She could ferret out the truth just by looking at him. She pulled back, wagged a finger in his face. "You came to see Wes Montgomery."

"I came to see *you*," he said, and fully meant it. "But it is an added bonus that Wes is also here. He's Susan's godfather."

"Go on with your bad self." She made shooing motions with both hands. "I know you can't wait to talk business. Find Wes. Crow about your accomplishments in New Zealand. Snag that job you've spent your life dreaming about."

"Wait, I —"

"You don't owe me all your attention. I'll

have you to myself soon enough. Catch you later, Professor." She waved at him over her shoulder as she sauntered away.

She was the most understanding woman in the world. Why couldn't his dates be like her? *C'mon, that wasn't fair. There was no one like Ember.*

"Wait," he said, and hurried to catch up with her. He stopped her, spun her around to face him. Those cobalt blue eyes, sharp as lightning, blasted into him.

"What?"

"You're not leaving, are you?"

"Tell you what. I'll meet you at our spot in thirty minutes." She winked. "Go out on the porch and hoot like an owl if you're going to be late."

"Mercury, Venus, and Mars," he said. "But you keep me on my toes."

"Someone has to."

"Later, Sparky." He touched her hand.

She laughed and headed across the room to the punch bowl. Ranger watched her go, his heart pumping strangely. It must be the dancing. He'd spent way too many hours in front of a telescope, and was surprised by how much he missed waltzing. Now that he was back home, he'd have to take Ember dancing more often.

The band took a break and the dancers

dispersed. It was the perfect time to find Wes. Ranger wandered through the crowd, greeting people he knew, pausing for a moment or two to catch up. Finally he spied the department head sitting at a linen-draped table with his wife and another couple.

His mentor was a balding man who sported a handlebar moustache and earlobes as long as saddlebags. Wes drove a Prius, lived in an adobe house on the grounds of the observatory, drank Corona with a twist of lime, and spoke fluent Portuguese. Ranger didn't know how or why Wes had picked up the language.

"Well, look what the mountain lion dragged in." Wes stood and pounded Ranger on the shoulder, drawing him into a one-armed hug. "How was New Zealand?"

"Stimulating."

"You remember Sally." Wes put a hand to the back of his wife's chair. "And Chuck and Mildred." Ranger did not remember Chuck and Mildred and barely remembered Sally. He didn't pay a lot of attention to names and small talk. His mind was usually tangled up with stars and galaxies and the possibility of life elsewhere in the universe. It was life here on Earth that he found a bit humdrum.

Sally was talking about the wedding, gushing over peonies and magnolia leaf wreaths and flameless tea candles in glass hurricane lanterns. Ranger tried not to let his eyes glaze over, but feared he failed miserably.

"Wes," he said when Sally paused to take a breath, "may I have a word?"

Wes, who appeared to be on his second or third glass of champagne, frowned. "Could it wait until Monday?"

Conceivably, but Ranger felt a pressing need to call dibs on the directorship that would be opening up when the current department head retired at the end of June. "It'll just take a minute."

Wes heaved a sigh and bussed his wife's cheek. "Be right back, sweetheart."

"Oh honey, do you have to talk shop tonight?" Sally reached for his hand, twisted her fingers with his.

"It's Ranger. You'll have to excuse him. He doesn't know how to talk anything *but* shop." Wes rolled his eyes.

"I'll make it quick, Sally," Ranger promised, and gave her his best grin.

"Ranger Lockhart, you're too damn handsome for your own best interest. Everyone forgives your lack of social graces because you're so good-looking." Sally narrowed her eyes, but then she smiled good-naturedly and waved Wes away. "Hurry back, my love."

"Always." Wes blew her a kiss.

Sally blew one right back.

"That's the kind of wife you want in your life," Wes said, picking up his champagne glass and following Ranger outside. "Gorgeous and forgiving."

Outside on the deck, a couple was making out in the shadows of the gazebo. Ranger moved as far from the couple as he could, and craned his neck to the expanse of stars overhead. The vast night sky always put things into perspective.

"I've missed this view," Ranger murmured.

"Welcome home." Wes's tone held a perfunctory let's-get-this-over-with note. "What's on your mind?"

Ranger lowered his head and met Wes's gaze. "I want Milton's job when he retires. I'm more than qualified. I'm officially putting my hat in the ring."

"Come in on Monday, fill out an application —"

Ranger scowled. He'd been working at the observatory on and off for the last seventeen years and Wes wanted him to fill out an application? "Seriously?"

Wes shrugged and held up both palms.

"You have to fill out an application to please HR."

"You can't tell me yes or no or maybe?"

"We have other applicants —"

"How many?"

"Okay, one other applicant —"

"Who?"

"We haven't yet opened up the application process to the outside —"

"Who?"

"Sheila Perez."

"You're kidding?"

Wes shook his head. "She's damn good."

"Sheila's not as qualified as I am, and you know it."

"Maybe not when it comes to education and experience . . ." Wes paused to drain his champagne glass. "But Sheila has something you don't."

"What's that?" Ranger felt the muscles in his neck tense and bunch.

"Sheila knows when to work and when to socialize." Wes's eyebrows crawled up his forehead like fuzzy caterpillars. "She knows how to schmooze and glad-hand, and she can bring in grant money. Can you say the same?"

"Bottom line, it's all about the money?"

Wes stared at Ranger as if he were a backwoods child wearing his clothes inside out. "Ranger, it's *always* about the money. Maybe not to you because you live with your head in the stars, and you came from one of the wealthiest families in the Trans-Pecos, but the rest of us here on Earth, we depend upon commerce to survive."

That went all over him in nine different ways, but he managed to keep his emotions off his face. Ranger wasn't an ace poker player for nothing. "I can raise money just as well as Sheila."

"Can you?"

"Sure."

"When was the last time you wrote a grant proposal?"

Mmm, never. Ranger jammed his hands in his front pockets, hunched his shoulders. "I've been focused on research."

"Research has to be funded."

"Isn't that what grant writers are for?"

"Fund-raising is a large part of the director's job."

"It shouldn't be."

"And children shouldn't be starving in Africa, but that doesn't change reality."

"You don't intend on giving me the directorship, do you?"

"Look, Ranger, you don't need it. You come from money. You've got a house because your grandfather left you land.

51

You're not interested in acquiring a wife and kids like normal folk. You live and breathe the cosmos, and you know what? There is absolutely nothing wrong with that. We need scientists like you."

"Glad to hear it." Ranger let out a pent-up breath. "For a minute there I thought you were going to tell me that my life's work is useless."

"Not at all. You're the kind of researcher who makes revolutionary breakthroughs. You are not, however, the kind of guy who would make a great administrator who can bring in the bacon to support the dreamers and revolutionary thinkers."

"I can learn the fund-raising part."

Wes sighed. "Accept who you are, Lockhart. Own it. Be proud of it. I don't get why you even want an administrative position."

Why?

Because from the time he was a little kid, stuck in that bed while the other Lockhart and Alzate children ran and played on the Silver Feather ranch, he would look out his window at the McDonald Observatory, situated high on the mountain, and imagine himself employed there, running the place. The dream was as much a part of him as the Chihuahuan Desert.

That same dream had sustained him

through a lot of toil and heartache, and he wasn't going to let it go without a fight.

"What do I have to do to convince you that I can handle the job?" Ranger asked.

Wes paused, studied him for a long moment. "You're really serious?"

"As a mortician."

"You're going to have to prove it."

"Tell me what you need."

"For one thing, get the hell out of your own head once in a while. Get involved in the community. Make new friends. Have some fun. Remember people's names. Show me you can be a regular human being."

"That's not fair. I volunteer for every star party the observatory throws."

"Volunteer for something that has nothing to do with the observatory. Broaden your horizons."

"I'll put it on the to-do list. What else?"

"You really want to steal this job away from Sheila?"

His competitive instinct, the one that drove him as a poker player, reared its head. *You betcha. I'm all in.* "Yes."

Wes got a gleam in his eyes, and before he even spoke Ranger knew without a doubt he was being manipulated. "All right, then. If you find a way to raise more grant money than Sheila, I'll back you with the board of directors."

"How much has she raised?"

"A million five."

Without a second thought Ranger did a mental fist pump. "It's in the bag."

"Not so fast," Wes said. "There are stipulations."

Ranger sank his hands on his hips, hooked his thumbs over the waistband of his dress slacks. "More hoop jumping?"

"You want it, play the game."

"Fine." Ranger snorted, not pleased, but determined to do what it took to get what he wanted. "Name the hoops and I'll jump through them."

"You have to raise the money before Milton retires at the end of June."

"That's barely a month away," he protested. "I can't write a grant and get it approved in a month."

"Your problem, not mine."

"Is ball busting your new hobby, Wes?"

"Also, you can't ask your old man or your brother Ridge for the money."

"Why not?"

"You have to raise it like everyone else does, the hard way. We need to know you possess the social skills necessary for fundraising before we can even consider giving you the job."

Dammit. There went plan A. But as unfair as this felt, Ranger's blood surged at the challenge. He did love a good mental game — chess, poker, finding ways around Wes . . .

"If I can't ask my family and there's no time to write a grant —"

"Then you'll have to find another way. An endowment perhaps? I hear Luke Nielson is close to making a decision on where he'll distribute two million of his grandmother's endowment money."

Wes, you son of a gun. His mentor knew Ranger and Luke were good friends. This whole damn thing was a setup to get at Luke's money.

"Anyway . . ." His mentor's smile was part disarming, part Machiavellian. "I'll leave the sourcing up to you."

Ranger glowered. "You expect me to fail."

Wes waved, turned, and headed back to the reception. Leaving Ranger wondering just how in the hell he was going to pull this off. And then he remembered his secret weapon.

Ember.

CHAPTER 3

"Success supposes endeavor."
— Jane Austen, *Emma*

A minute later, Ranger found Ember near the barn entrance scooping two longneck beers from a galvanized tub filled with ice. She was laughing with a younger, dark-haired man that he vaguely recognized. Her head was thrown back, exposing her creamy white throat, and a flirtatious grin lit up her face.

The other man was leaning into her, practically drooling, his eyes fixed on her cleavage.

Quick and sharp, a poke of jealousy stabbed Ranger's gut, and he had an inexplicable urge to punch the leering guy in the nose. Which wasn't him. He was normally the mediator, not the guy starting fights.

But right now? He'd roll up his sleeves for a full-on brawl if it stopped the guy from staring at Ember.

What was this? He knew Ember could take care of herself. She had no need for a chivalrous knight to protect her honor, but damn if he wasn't mentally searching for jousting armor and a white horse.

Confused, he blinked and shook his head, tried to figure out why he was suddenly feeling so possessive. She was Ember. No one could contain or control her. Nor had he ever wanted to, but right now? Watching this guy touch her shoulder? He felt positively Neanderthal.

Ranger knotted his fists at his sides, bit down on the inside of his cheek.

She caught sight of him and her eyes danced like a kid on Christmas getting the toy she'd long prayed for, and his jealousy vanished. "There you are!"

Her words were a caress, a joyous gift.

Cradling the longneck bottles, dripping with cold water, between her fingers, she reached out to take Ranger's palm with her other hand and called, "Bye Warren," over her shoulder to the other guy.

"Come with me," she said, guiding him out of the barn and across the dirt road to the cowboy wedding chapel. She opened the door into the empty building. At the back of the room, to the left of the altar, a wooden staircase led to an upstairs loft.

The place was quiet and dark. Music and laughter from the reception barn sounded muffled and faraway, and the only light came from the full moon shining in through the curtainless windows. The chapel smelled of hymnals and wedding flowers and Ember's cinnamon-and-anise scent.

It felt mysterious and secret, and Ranger found the place strangely erotic.

What was going on with him tonight?

Ember dropped his hand and hiked up the skirt of her formal gown, a sapphire blue that perfectly matched her eyes, bunching the material in her small fist. She kicked off her high-heeled shoes and climbed barefoot up the wooden ladder, somehow still managing to hang on to those beers.

Part tomboy, part girly-girl, she straddled both identities with ease. Poised and self-confident, Ember was one of those accomplished people who just naturally navigated any environment without having to think about it.

Agog, he stood in the darkness watching her as if seeing her for the first time, amazed at her agility and grace. He noted her delicate feet and toenails painted a pearly peach. Or at least they looked peachy in the moonlight. He admired how soft tendrils of red hair floated from her upsweep to trail against the nape of her long, swan-like neck. God, she was beautiful.

It was as if a year away had spritzed his eyes with window cleaner and rubbed them clear. How could he not have noticed before the ripe lushness of her breasts, the sexy curve of her hips, the pouty fullness of her bottom lip?

She's your best friend, Lockhart. Stop this.

"Earth to Professor, head out of the clouds," she called to him from the loft. "You gonna stand there all night?"

Sheepishly, Ranger scooted up the ladder behind her.

Once he joined Ember upstairs, she pushed open the wide barn door and walked out onto a ledge with roof access. Without missing a beat, and still holding the beers, she hiked up her skirt again, revealing those long shapely legs, and glided up a second, spindlier ladder that led to the roof.

Behind her, Ranger felt like a lumbering ape, the heels of his cowboy boots clinging sluggishly to each rung.

"Ahh," she said, sinking onto the shingles, her knees drawn up, her dress tucked around her legs.

Ranger's heart thumped oddly, and he lowered himself beside her. "Cowboy boots and roof shingles don't mix well."

"At least it's not tin like the barn." She shrugged, twisted off the top, and passed the beer to him before opening her own.

"True." He took a long swallow, tasted the familiar yeasty flavor of Lone Star.

With her knees still raised, she lay back on her spine and exhaled forcefully. "Ahh," she murmured again. "Ahh."

He doffed his Stetson, lay on his back beside her, resting his cowboy hat on his belly. Their shoulders barely touching, they stared up at the stars, resting in comfortable silence.

How many times had they climbed up on a roof to get away from the hubbub of their large families. A hundred? Two hundred? More?

"Look!" She pointed at the sky. "A falling star. Make a wish."

"You know stars don't have the ability to grant wishes. It's just —"

"Bits of dust and rocks falling into Earth's atmosphere and burning up. I know, I know, you've told me a million times, but I'll never give up trying to make a romantic of you."

"You're doomed to fail," he predicted. "I can't help being born with a scientific mind."

"Spoilsport," she teased, and dragged a

toe along the roof. "You could pretend once. For me."

"Sorry," he said. "I can't eschew a lifetime of education."

"And that" — she tapped his right knee with her left — "is why you're not married."

He didn't say anything. What was there to say? He'd never much been interested in marriage. His career, and helping his family out with the ranch, took up most of his time, and what was left he spent with Ember.

"So," she said after a few more sips of beer. "How did it go with Wes? Did you cinch the job?"

Ranger scowled at the sky and told Ember about his conversation with his mentor. Several minutes later, he ended with, "Basically, unless I learn how to be a fund-raiser there's no place for me at the observatory."

"Ouch."

"Yeah."

"Fund-raising is definitely *not* your forte."

"Tell me about it."

"So what will you do?"

He took a deep breath, gulping in the dry night air. He'd been dreading this conversation. "I've been offered a teaching position at Canterbury."

"The New Zealand Canterbury?"

"That'd be the one."

"And you're just now telling me this?"

"I wanted to tell you in person."

Ember grunted. "If you took that job, we'd never see each other."

"I know." He heard the anchor in his own voice, dead and leaden. Another long moment passed as they watched several more meteorites streak across the sky.

"That's five more wishes you've missed out on," she said on a lighter note.

"If wishes were horses . . ."

"I've got it!" She sat up like a jack-in-the-box, springy and unexpected. "You know what you need?"

"No, but I'm certain you're going to tell me."

She laughed, a deep, comforting sound that reminded him of a crackling fire on a cold winter night. "You, Ranger Lockhart . . ." she touched the tip of his nose with an index finger ". . . need a wife."

He groaned and sat up to join her. "Don't you dare start in with any of your matchmaking."

"No, wait, wait, hear me out." She raised a hand, solid as a stop sign.

He snorted, shoved fingers through his hair, and settled his Stetson back onto his head. "I'm not biting."

"Listen, listen, stubborn coot." She thumped on his chest with her knuckles. "If you married someone with social graces and people skills, someone practical and grounded and down-to-earth, someone who could sweet-talk investors into supporting your projects . . ."

Someone like you, he thought, and felt weird about thinking it.

"You would be free to keep your head in the stars and your nose in a book, and you could still appease Wes and make the board of directors happy as your charming wife keeps the grant money rolling in. If you marry the right woman, you could stay in Texas. That's the important part."

It touched him that she'd go to such lengths to keep him near her. "It sounds like a very unromantic proposition for a marriage. Marry me and be my career wing-woman."

"Unromantic maybe, but as we've already established, it would be the perfect solution for a scientific-minded person like you. Of course," she mused, getting a faraway look in her eyes and tapping her chin with a finger, "you'd have to find a woman without any illusions about soul mates and true love and yak like that. She'll have to be devoted to you, but also understand her supporting role in the grand scheme of things."

"Or I could just learn to raise funds on my own. That's a viable option."

"Your brilliant mind shouldn't have to worry about money." She patted his cheek. "Nope, you need a woman who is good at that sort of thing so you can devote yourself to saving the world."

"I'm not claiming I can save the world —"

"I am," she said. "You're a rare mind, Ranger Lockhart. You're not like everyone else. Your relationships shouldn't be like everyone else's either."

That, he knew. He'd always been the odd duck out, never quite fitting in with anyone except other astronomers . . . and Ember.

He wasn't quite sure why they were such fast friends; they were pretty much opposites, other than she'd taken a shine to him when they were kids and their relationship had been glowing ever since.

Fresh noises came from the reception barn. More laughter and a throng of people gathering outside.

Ember craned her neck, observing the goings-on. "Looks like the bride and groom are leaving. C'mon, let's go throw birdseed — or whatever it is people throw these days — at the happy couple." She reached for their empty beer bottles. "Oh, and might I just add, *I* was the one who matched them up."

"Yes, I know. Your matchmaking skills are renowned. Susan and Bryant, Archer and Casey, Kaia and Ridge —"

She swept her hand in a panoramic gesture. "Ranger and his witty new missus . . ."

"Stop it."

"That directorship at the observatory could be yours if you just let me have a shot at finding you the right woman."

"Thanks for the offer, but I'll muddle through on my own."

"Suit yourself," she said, then scooted down the ladder and out of sight.

And Ranger couldn't help thinking that Miss Ember Alzate was going to suit *herself*. She always did.

The bride and groom cut such a touching picture driving away in Bryant's shoe-polished and tin-canned-tied Ford King Ranch that it almost brought a tear to Ember's eyes.

Almost, but not quite.

After all, she wasn't a sappy sentimentalist moon-eyed over love. Rather, she was a pragmatic marriage broker, looking for core-values compatibility in the couples she introduced.

Well, except with Kaia and Ridge. They'd already been well on their way to falling in love. In their case, Ember had merely given her sister a shove in the right direction. But they'd both told her she was the reason they'd managed to work past their conflicts to grab their happily-ever-after, which was why she counted them as one of her matches made.

She stuck around to help clean up the barn and give the beer time to wear off before she got on the road. It was well after ten when Ember got home from the reception, her mind whirling with Ranger's news.

Bottom line, if he didn't develop fundraising skills, ASAP, he'd be off to New Zealand for good.

The thought of him living seven thousand miles away permanently struck her with bone-deep loneliness. A year without him in her life had been bad enough. Problem was, even if he could learn how to glad-hand and backslap for donations, he didn't enjoy such machinations. He was an introvert's introvert. The proverbial absentminded professor. If he couldn't remember to eat or check to see that his boots matched, how could he remember things like how many children a potential donor had, what their names were and where they went to school. Blah-de-blah.

But she wasn't one to give into despair. She had a few cards up her sleeve, a couple of strings she could tug on. She would do whatever it took to keep him home and happy.

Yawning, she poured herself a cup of chamomile tea and curled up on the couch with her gray tabby, Samantha, to watch a half hour of *House Hunters* to unwind before heading to bed.

She settled onto the cushions, Samantha in her lap, and glanced around at the small adobe house she rented in Marfa after her divorce. She'd kept the furnishings simple and understated. This arrangement was temporary. She'd come home with her tail between her legs to lick her wounds and figure out her next step in life. But that had been eighteen months ago, and she hadn't figured out anything. A few months of wound licking was okay. But for the past year — basically since Ranger had been gone away, come to think of it — she'd been in a holding pattern.

Rejoining the real estate agency where she'd first started out. The agency had three agents, including herself, and even though their business covered a wide territory — including Marfa, Alpine, Cupid, Fort David, Presidio — the senior agents got the bulk of the business, and there often wasn't enough inventory to keep Ember busy for more than ten or twenty hours a week, and most of that was spent showing houses on weekends, leaving much of her weekdays free.

She'd squirreled away money from her high-flying San Antonio real estate days, but she couldn't live on her savings forever. Sooner or later, she had to make a move in one direction or another. For now, however, she was happy to cool her once-overachieving jets and work this part-time real estate gig. She would soon be directing the Cupid Chamber of Commerce film for tourism — although they still hadn't cast the leads — and now, finding a proper wife for Ranger. Her life was full.

The doorbell rang.

Who was it this late?

Gently, she eased Samantha off her lap, slipped into her housecoat, and padded to the door in her socks. She flipped on the porch lamp, peeked through the peephole, and saw the new church secretary, Fiona Kelton, standing there in the circle of light.

Fiona had been at the wedding and she

still wore her tasteful beige dress, sensible matching pumps, and a strand of pearls, looking a bit like a 1950s-era housewife.

Ember didn't know Fiona well. The woman had moved to Cupid from Pennsylvania a few months ago. Quite honestly, such migrations didn't happen that often. Most of the transplants to the Trans-Pecos were either avant-garde artists, retirees, or social misfits.

The church secretary was none of those things. She was a rather ordinary, thirty-something single woman with a winsome smile, a talent for organizing things, and a knack for making people feel good about who they were.

Central question. Why had Fiona driven to Marfa so late at night when she simply could have spoken to Ember at the wedding?

Interest piqued, Ember posted her best real estate agent smile and swung open the door. "Hello there, Fiona. What brings you out to Marfa so late?"

"May I come in?" Fiona's hands were clutched around a simple beige purse, and her muddy brown eyes looked troubled.

"Sure." Ember waved her inside.

Fiona moseyed into the living room, scanned the clean, contemporary colors and lines of the airy decor, and sighed wistfully. "I should have known your house would be as elegant and put together as you are."

Elegant? Her? Not hardly.

"Have a seat." Ember waved Fiona onto the dove gray, Danish-design couch she'd paid way too much for.

Fiona perched on the edge of the couch, locked her knees together, and tugged down the hem of her dress to cover her legs. Samantha ambled over to eel around Fiona's ankles, which was surprising. Sammie was a one-woman cat.

Fiona leaned down to stroke her. "Coo, coo, kitty."

"Can I get you something to drink?" Ember offered. "Water, soda, hot tea, bourbon?"

"Oh no! I don't drink and even if I did, I'm driving."

"The bourbon thing was a joke."

"Was it?" Fiona hoisted a wispy smile. "I'm sorry, it went over my head. I don't have much of a sense of humor."

"It's not you. My wit leans toward dryness, and I tend to shoot from the lip."

"Is that another joke?"

"Uh-huh." Wow this was awkward. What now?

Fiona managed a halfhearted laugh. "I'll

take a cup of tea."

"Sure you don't want a shot of bourbon with it?" *For God's sake, shut up, Ember.*

"Ha-ha." Fiona forced a chortle. "Good one."

Ember was beginning to wish she *did* have bourbon in the house. "Be right back."

She returned with a teakettle of hot water, an extra cup, and tea bags. She gave the cup and a tea bag to Fiona, topped off both of their cups with hot water, and settled the kettle on a coaster in the middle of the coffee table.

"Thank you." Fiona took a polite sip.

Ember leaned back on the cushions and got straight to the point. "What's up?"

Fiona stayed perched on the edge of the couch, looked uneasy at Ember's direct approach. "I'm not really sure how to broach this."

"Just say it."

"I'm not —"

"Speak," Ember nudged as if trying to teach an old dog a new trick.

"Shoot from the lip?" Fiona smiled like she meant it.

"Yup. What do you need?"

"I need . . . I need . . ."

"What?"

"Help," Fiona whispered.

71

Music to her ears. Ember loved helping people. Her mother would laugh and say she loved telling people what to do. "How can I help?"

"I . . . mmm . . . well, I don't know how to start . . . I . . . er . . ."

"They're just words. Use them."

Fiona glanced over first one shoulder, and then the other, as if Edward Snowden was hiding behind Ember's couch taking notes of secrets to leak.

"It's only you and me here," Ember assured her. "Well, and Samantha, but she'll never tell. What's up?"

"I realize it's a bit rude dropping by your house so late, but I wanted to talk to you privately."

Good Lord woman, spit it out, Ember wanted to holler, but sat on her hands so she wouldn't.

Fiona moistened her lips. "I want . . ."

Ember leaned forward. Now they were getting somewhere. "Yes, yes?"

"To buy a home."

That was the big secret? What a letdown. Ember sank against the cushions again. "I can meet you at the office on Monday morning and show you some listings. I'd do it tomorrow except —"

"You have Ingrid's christening. I know,

I'll be there. Assisting Father Dubanowski."
She wriggled a foot, circling her ankle in
the unexciting beige pump. "Please bear
with me. This is a rather new development,
and I wouldn't have come by if I hadn't
heard Susan's toast."

Aha. At last. "This is about more than buying a house."

Fiona nodded, her chin tipping up and
down. "I want to make room for a man in
my life and buying a house feels like the
right move."

"What are you looking for?"

"In a house?" Fiona asked, paused, ventured, "Or a man?"

"Either. Or. Both."

"I want a ranch-style home. Not too modest. I need room for a man after all. But not
too big either."

"Say eighteen hundred to two thousand
square feet?"

"Perfect."

"Fixer-upper or turnkey?" Ember took a
notepad from the end table drawer and
started writing.

"Fixer-upper." Fiona paused, added,
"Like me."

"You have DIY skills?"

"No," she said. "That's why I'm here to
see you."

Ember clicked the ballpoint pen. "To be clear, are we talking about the house or your love life?"

"Cards on the table?" Fiona asked.

"Please."

"I do want a house, but I want love more. I feel so drab and boring and you're so vibrant and interesting and you know so many people and you hooked Susan up with Bryant and I was hoping . . ."

"What?"

"You'd give me some pointers."

"About what?"

"How to attract a man. Men buzz around you like honeybees. Teach me how to do that."

"You want me to give you a makeover?"

"I'll pay," Fiona said, reaching for her purse. "I know your time and knowledge is valuable —"

What was going on here? First Chriss Anne, now Fiona. Ember held up a palm. "I couldn't possibly take your money."

Fiona's face shattered like a china plate dropped on a concrete floor. "You won't help me?"

"Of course I'll help you, but I won't accept money. My matchmaking skills are a calling, not a vocation."

Seriously, Alzate, do you realize how ego-y

that sounds? Walk it back.

"What I mean," Ember quickly amended because she hadn't meant it the way it came out, "is that while I haven't had any luck in the relationship department myself, I do seem to have a knack for putting together people who click and stick."

"It's because you're a connector." Fiona nodded. "And you understand human nature. It's a rare talent."

Hmm, Ember wasn't so sure about that.

"Please, can you show me how to be like you?" Fiona pressed her hands together at her heart in a prayer pose. "I'd be ever so grateful."

"You don't want to be like me. Instead, you want to be the best version of yourself."

"Yes." Fiona's head bounced up and down. "That's it."

Ember rubbed her palms together. Hot dog, a project. "Do you still want to buy a house?"

"Oh yes, but maybe *after* I've found the man."

"Good choice."

Fiona sat up straighter, squared her shoulders. "Great. Thank you. Where do we start?"

"First things first. We need an assessment of two things. What do you want in a man

75

and what do you bring to the table?"

"I'm not sure what you mean. I have a good job and a nice inheritance, but beyond that . . ." Fiona hesitated again, tucked a strand of hair behind her ear.

"What are some of your interests?"

"I love to read." Fiona's face lit up like the Vegas Strip. "My house is stacked with books."

"You sound a lot like my best friend, Ranger. The man stores books everywhere, including a microwave someone gave him."

Fiona laughed. "I like the sound of him."

"Anything more active?" Ember prodded. "A date revolving around reading books doesn't generate many sparks."

"I see your point." Fiona shrugged, dipped her head, looked shy. "Well . . ."

"What?"

"I do enjoy acting in community theater." Fiona went on to list the dozen or so plays she'd been involved in.

Hmm. They still hadn't cast the female lead in the Cupid Chamber of Commerce film. Initially, the mayor's wife, Melody, was going to play Mary Beale, but then she got pregnant with twins. Anyone else in town who was right for the part either couldn't get the time off from work, or couldn't afford to perform for free.

"You didn't hear about the casting call for the Chamber of Commerce film?" Ember asked.

"I heard," Fiona said. "But I didn't think I was qualified."

"Around here? With those creds? You're *over*qualified. Would you be interested in auditioning for Mayor Nielson?"

"Really?" Fiona curled her fingers around the purse in her lap. "Oh wow. Oh yes."

Ember warned her about the three weeks of all-day filming, Monday through Friday and no pay until, and unless, the film earned something from showings at the Fort Davis theater and various other venues around the Trans-Pecos.

"It's actually perfect," Fiona said. "Father Dubanowski is going abroad for the summer on a ministry mission, and his temporary replacement is bringing his own assistant. This feels like divine timing."

Indeed, it did, almost as if the universe were one hundred percent behind Ember's endeavors. Her mind started walking an interesting trail. Ranger needed to start dating in order to find a potential wife who could be his partner in fund-raising, and Fiona seemed quite sensible and unassuming and she liked reading. Put a check next to her name in the possibility column. If

77

nothing else, Fiona could be his starter date.

"Tell me more about yourself," Ember urged.

Once she got talking, Fiona revealed she had a master's in business administration, but was drawn to the clergy because she loved helping people more than making money. She'd left Pennsylvania for a new start after her mother passed away, leaving her with a tidy sum of money, and she'd been drawn to the wide-open spaces of the Trans-Pecos after reading Edna Ferber's *Giant*.

Score! Fiona was business-minded and kind-hearted and she was on the hunt for a husband and she liked the Trans-Pecos. Win-win-win-win.

"What do you think?" Fiona asked. "Do you know any men who I'd fit with?"

"There's time to figure that out. Meanwhile, we have got to get you out of brown." Ember swept a hand at Fiona's clothes. "With your coloring, brown makes you disappear into the woodwork."

Fiona nodded. "I wear brown because it's understated. I don't *want* people noticing me."

"And yet, you like acting."

"I hide behind the costume."

Wow, low profile, under-the-radar, indistinct. Fiona would fit in nicely with academia. She was not the type to ruffle feathers.

"But now you want people to notice you. Or at least men." Ember studied Fiona, tapped her chin with an index finger. "I'm thinking red. It will play up your ivory complexion."

"Red?" Fiona crinkled her nose. "Red feels way too bold."

"There's a reason red birds catch people's attention, and the wren gets ignored."

"But red?" Fiona bit her bottom lip. "It's just not me."

"Your choice." Ember shrugged and lifted both arms, palms up. "You can keep doing things the way you've always done them, or you can take a step outside your comfort zone. You've got to ask yourself, is finding my perfect mate worth a little discomfort?"

Fiona nodded as if she could snag a man by the sheer force of head bobbing. "Red it is."

"Perhaps a new haircut . . ."

Fiona looked panicked, touched the bun pinned to the top of her head, clichéd librarian style.

"Comfort zone," Ember said. "Kick that envelope open. If not a haircut, at least wear your hair down more often."

"This doesn't feel like me."

"Just pretend that you're Diana Prince turning into Wonder Woman."

"Wonder Woman, huh?" Fiona pressed a palm to her chest as if she was unsure of Ember's plan, but a wild smile crept to her lips.

"Leave it to me." Ember rested a hand on Fiona's shoulder. "We'll transform you into Wonder Woman."

"A fantasy come true." Fiona sighed dreamily.

"Have you considered wearing contacts?" Ember reached over and plucked the glasses off Fiona's face. "Omigosh, you've been hiding under those dark frames. Time to let your light shine."

Fiona clasped her hands in her lap and squinted at Ember, but she looked pleased. "Do you really think I can catch the right man's eye?"

"When we're finished with you, your perfect mate . . ." This was where Ember mentally tried out the image of Ranger and Fiona as a couple and found it acceptable, if not entirely palatable. This wasn't about her. It was about finding Ranger a mate who could make him happy. "Is not going to know what hit him."

CHAPTER 4

"It is very difficult for the prosperous to be humble."

— Jane Austen, *Emma*

The next afternoon, Ember sat in the front pew of the First Episcopal Church of Cupid, squeezed in next to her sister Aria on one side and her mother on the other. Somehow the entire Alzate clan, also including her father, her brother, Archer, and his wife, Casey, and their twenty-month-old son, Tyler, her other sister Tara, and Granny Blue, had all managed to sandwich themselves into one row.

Ranger and Rhett, along with their father, Duke, and his wife, Vivi, sat on the other side of the aisle. It was just as it had been all their lives, the Lockharts, lords of the manor, opposite the servant Alzates. Ridge and Kaia's marriage had bridged that divide, and now, with Ingrid's birth and christening, the two families truly became one.

But they were still sitting on opposite sides of the aisle. Old habits died hard.

Ridge and Kaia waited at the front of the church with Father Dubanowski. Kaia was holding a wriggling, three-month-old Ingrid, dressed in a white lace christening gown handmade by Granny Blue and enthusiastically sucking on her sweet baby fingers.

If Ember was the maudlin type, she might have gotten a lump in her throat at the touching scene, but she wasn't, so she didn't. Instead, she shot a glance across the aisle at Ranger, who — no surprise because they were usually on the same wavelength — was grinning at her.

He winked.

She winked back. *Welcome home, my nerdy cowboy friend.*

Ranger smiled big, as if smiling only for her, and her heart did this peculiar swoopy thing it had never done before. Seemingly diving deep inside her chest as if searching for rare pearls.

"It's so heartening to see everyone gathered for the christening of our beloved Ingrid Blue Lockhart," Father Dubanowski said, and read a passage from the Bible. He explained the significance of the christening and then started the liturgy of baptism.

The liturgy went on for several minutes; Father Dubanowski's voice was a monotone drone.

Ember tried her best to pay attention and not get bored, but she found herself mentally listing off the lovers she'd had in her life, as she often did when she needed a time killer. There was Steve, who took her down to Lake Cupid at midnight when she was seventeen and officially plucked her virginity on a large flat rock underneath a half-moon. She'd loved his left coast smile and bohemian stride. There was Vic, who'd given Ember her first orgasm in the backseat of his father's Plymouth on a cold night in February. She still remembered the purr of that heavy engine when he'd started it up, felt the heat even now, low in her pelvis. And Pete, who'd taught her how to tie a cherry stem and do other wonderful things with her tongue. He'd tasted of the peppermint Altoids he'd kept in a tin in his front pocket. Bob, who —

"Godparents," Father Dubanowski said, cracking through her trip down memory lane.

Ember jumped, guilty. Surely thinking about past lovers in church reached some level of blasphemy. She slid another glance

83

over at Ranger, who looked as if he knew exactly what she'd been doing.

She crossed her eyes at him.

Ranger let out a short bark of laughter.

Father Dubanowski frowned and motioned to Ranger and Ember, cleared his throat in a testy *harrumph.* "Please join us."

She and Ranger got to their feet, reaching the altar simultaneously, and she caught a whiff of his scent — sandalwood soap, sunshine, and man. God, he smelled good. She tried not to think about that and positioned herself beside Kaia and baby Ingrid.

Ranger stepped over to join his older brother.

Everyone had gotten dressed up in their finest clothing for the christening, and it was only one of a handful of times in her life that Ember had seen Ranger in a suit. Normally, he was like everyone else around Cupid, all boots and jeans and Stetsons.

He cut a dashing figure in the navy, tailor-made cashmere blend suit and smart red tie. It looked like sangria, dark and sweet. He'd remembered to get his hair trimmed, although she was a bit partial to his shaggy, head-in-the-clouds, rumpled professorial look. He was wearing his favorite pair of bespoke Rocketbuster boots and yay! They matched. The vamp, toe box, and counter were a decorous black, but she knew if he were to lift the leg of his pants, it would show off a kitschy, brightly colored royal flush inlaid into the upper part of the boot.

Ember grinned, remembering the morning they'd strolled into Rocketbuster Boots in El Paso after an all-night, backroom poker game with some of the city's wealthiest clientele to order the boots with Ranger's winnings. He'd bought her a pair to match, although she rarely wore hers. She wasn't that good of a poker player, and the boots practically dared an impromptu poker game to break out.

Ranger was the rocket buster, not she. Ember shook her head. *Pay attention, dammit. Your first niece gets baptized only once.*

The solemn ritual continued. Ingrid was baptized in the name of the Father, the Son, and the Holy Spirit. Father Dubanowski gave a little lecture to Ridge and Kaia, and then to Ranger and Ember, detailing their sacred duties of raising a child to love and serve God.

It was serious stuff, and Ember couldn't help believing that Kaia might have been better served to have picked someone more pious to be Ingrid's godmother. Their sister Tara, perhaps, who was a pediatric nurse.

But Ember had agreed to do it, and she couldn't bail out at this late date.

Prompted by Father Dubanowski, she vowed to do her best, and by the time it was over, sweat ringed the collar of her white lace blouse.

Father Dubanowski presented a candle to Ingrid at the end of the service and said, "Shine as a light in the world to the glory of God." Once upon a time, *this* priest had said the same thing at *her* baptism. Ember couldn't help feeling she'd been something of a disappointment to Father Dubanowski. In the blister of the moment, she vowed to be a better person and put other people first and foremost.

Helping Ranger find a wife counted on that score, right? All she wanted was his happiness.

But the thought of seeing Ranger married was a knife to her spine. Selfish. She was such a selfish wench. As much as she loved her best friend, she couldn't keep clinging to him. He deserved the best that life had to offer. A true friend would let him go free.

Her heart slumped along the bottom of her stomach. Then again, maybe she should rethink this whole mission. Ranger hadn't asked for her help. In fact, he's expressly told her that he would handle it. Just because she had a knack for hooking people up didn't mean she had to do it, right?

She tilted her head, studied Ranger with a sidelong glance. He looked so serious. Eyes dark and lowered. Mouth stern. His default expression. She had an almost irresistible urge to reach over and ruffle his hair or tickle his ribs, anything to make him smile.

"And don't forget," Father Dubanowski said. "It takes courage to do God's will. Sometimes love demands a supreme sacrifice, and we must give up our humanly wants and needs in order to serve Him."

Yes, okay, she got the message loud and clear. By holding on to Ranger she was getting in the way of him having a fuller, richer life. Check.

"The Lockharts would like to invite everyone to the Silver Feather Ranch for a late luncheon to celebrate Ingrid's baptism. See Aria Alzate if you need transportation to and from the ranch," Father Dubanowski announced, and the baptism was over.

Ingrid was gumming the candle that Father Dubanowski had given her. While Kaia tried to wrestle it away from her daughter, Ridge went for the baby carrier. The rest of the family surged to the altar to hug, slap backs, and offer heartfelt congratulations.

"Wanna ride with me?" Ranger invited Ember. "I'll bring you back for your car afterward."

Ember was just about to say, "sure" when she spied Fiona Kelton talking to Aria and remembered what Father Dubanowski had said.

Sometimes love demands a supreme sacrifice.

"Offer Fiona a ride," she said to Ranger. "I have to swing back by my house first. I forgot the baby's gift." Okay, that wasn't true. The baby blanket she'd quilted for Ingrid was in the backseat of her Infinity, but surely God would forgive this little white lie in the grand scheme of finding Ranger a wife.

He jammed his hands in his pockets, the unconscious body language he used when he didn't really want to do something. "I don't mind stopping off at your place."

"Fiona needs a ride," Ember said. "I have my own vehicle. It would be a nice thing to do so she isn't stuck riding with Aria. The way Aria rides the brake could make a cast-iron skillet throw up."

Ranger shot her an odd look. "Are you trying to ditch me, Sparky?"

"Nooo."

His eyes narrowed and his dark brows

drew together. "What have you got up your sleeve?"

"Nothing, nothing . . . I've just, well, there's something I need to do before I go to the ranch."

"Is there a man in your life you haven't told me about?" He cocked his head, studied her for a long moment.

Her heart hopped out of her stomach and leaped into her throat. She'd already told one lie for his own good, she wasn't comfortable reeling out another one, not here in the middle of church, but that didn't mean she couldn't let him *assume* she had a guy. She gave him a Monty Python–style smile — nudge, nudge, wink, wink.

"So you'll give Fiona a ride?"

"Yeah, sure," he mumbled, jammed his hands deeper into his pockets. "But as soon as I get you alone, I want to hear all about this guy. I'm not going to let you make another mistake like you did with Trey."

"Don't worry about that," she said, speaking her truth. "I'm *never* getting married again."

Ranger shot her a troubled look that left her feeling out of sorts and she almost told him she'd changed her mind, but he'd already started toward Fiona.

■ ■ ■ ■

Fiona Kelton was not a chatterbox.

Which Ranger liked about her to some degree. By and large, chatty women drove him batty, but Fiona was so quiet he could hear himself breathing, and it was sixteen miles from the church to the Silver Feather Ranch.

Dressed in a plain brown dress, Fiona had her hands in her lap and was staring straight ahead. She was pretty enough, in an understated way, with soft brown hair and brown eyes. Not the kind of woman who stood out, and he couldn't help comparing her to bright, vivacious Ember.

What was Ember up to, by the way? Why had she stuck him with Fiona? Why hadn't she come along, as well? Where was she going? Who was she secretly meeting?

It set his teeth on edge to think that she was slipping off to meet some guy on the day of their niece's christening. It wasn't so much the idea that she had a man on the string, but rather it was because she hadn't told him about it. They were best friends. He told her everything — well, he hadn't told her about Dawn yet, but he hadn't had a chance — and he expected her to reciprocate.

Was that unreasonable?

Hell, maybe it was. She didn't owe him any explanations. Truth be told, he'd gotten his feelings hurt, and he wasn't used to Ember hurting his feelings.

Suck it up.

He needed to stop being a dullard and make conversation with his passenger. That was the way people who were good fund-raisers did things. They excelled at small talk. Ugh. "So Fiona . . ."

"Yes?" She exhaled as if she'd been holding her breath for miles.

"How long have you lived in Cupid?"

"Three months."

"You like it here?"

"The people are very nice."

"But it's pretty isolated country."

"Yes."

Was he going to have to get a dental license to yank a conversation out of her? "What brought you to town?"

"A moving van."

Ahh, that was better. Ranger chuckled. "Too many questions?"

"I just don't like talking about myself."

"Why not? You on the run from the law?"

"I did forget to return a library book when I lived in Pennsylvania, but I plan on mailing it back to them when I find it. I haven't gotten completely unpacked yet." She offered up a shy smile.

Hey, Fiona wasn't so bad. At least she could make jokes.

"You go to a lot of baby christenings?" he asked.

"This is my first. I've only been working at the church for three months."

"Mine too," he said. "I'm not a terribly religious guy."

"I figured," she said. "What with you being a scientist and all."

"True enough, but there is a whole lot that science can't explain about how the universe works. Everything is just a hypothesis until it's proven true."

"Good point."

Ranger tried to imagine them on a date. Fiona had a pleasant disposition, and was well put together. Everything on her matched, which was more than he could usually say for himself. She certainly wouldn't offend anyone, at least not what he'd seen of her so far.

"How old are you?" he asked.

Okay, that was blunt and probably a little rude, and it sounded far more like something Ember would ask. Usually he didn't give a good damn about someone's vital statistics.

But Fiona answered easily. "Twenty-five."

Seven years younger than he. Was he too old for her? He thought about what Ember had told him the night before. That he needed to find a wife who could navigate social situations. To be a partner in his career aspirations. Problem with that? He didn't *want* a wife.

Of course, Ember would claim that his lack of desire to follow tradition was the problem. Did he really need to get married to advance his career? Was she right about that? Should he get married just so he'd have a wife who could deal with social nice ties?

And leave Ember behind forever?

It didn't seem fair to anyone. Not him. Not the intended wife. Not Ember.

"It was very generous of you," Fiona said. "To donate so much money to Cupid's children's summer reading program."

"How do you know about that?"

"I volunteer at the library part-time. Your name is on a wall plaque."

Ranger winced. "I told them not to do that."

"They're proud of the donation," she said. "They're proud of *you.*"

Last year, before heading to New Zealand,

he'd sold off his livestock and donated the proceeds to the library. Growing up, the local library had meant so much to him. If it hadn't been for books, and Ember, he surely would have lost his mind those long months and years he'd spent recovering from rheumatic fever and his subsequent heart surgery. Things hadn't been easy for him as a kid, and he'd disappeared into books and daydreams long before he'd gotten sick. The ailment had just cemented his introversion.

He was the second son, but the first legitimate Lockhart heir. His older brother, Ridge, had been the product of their father's affair with a stripper, and she'd abandoned Ridge on the doorstep of the Silver Feather when Ridge was three and Ranger was eighteen months. Though he and Ridge had been close in age, there had always been an undercurrent of tension running between them. Things had improved greatly two years ago when Ridge had returned to the ranch, married Kaia, and took over day-to-day running of the Silver Feather.

Ranger had been surprised that he wasn't the least bit jealous about his father turning the reins over to Ridge. Truth be told, he'd been relieved to have someone else shoulder the mantle. As much as he loved the Silver Feather, he wasn't a rancher at heart. His first and last love would always be the stars. Although, he couldn't deny that cowboy blood ran through his veins. Five generations of Lockharts dug into the Trans-Pecos saw to that.

"They love you at the library." Fiona turned and gave him a luminescent smile that seemed to say, *I think I love you too.*

The look stunned him. Holy extraterrestrial, did the woman have a crush on him?

That pumped up his ego a bit. He eyed Fiona up and down. Why not give her a chance? She wasn't bad looking in a rather ordinary way. Taken feature by feature, she was pretty, even if the total did not add up to a beautiful face.

She certainly didn't compare to Ember. Then again, who could compare to his best friend? In Ranger's estimation, Ember was the most beautiful woman in town. Hell, in the whole of the Trans-Pecos.

"Ember said you keep books in your microwave."

"I ran out of storage space and the microwave was just sitting there unused . . ."

"So you found a way to use it."

"Do you find that weird?"

"I find it endearing." Fiona clutched her hands in her lap and hazarded a quick glance at him.

All at once, it dawned on Ranger why Ember had pushed him to give Fiona a ride. She wasn't sneaking off to meet some guy. The sly minx was playing matchmaker.

He was both irritated and relieved.

He should pretend to fall in love with Fiona just to teach Ember a lesson. It would serve her right. But of course, he wouldn't do that to a sweet person like Fiona. Wouldn't turn her into an unwitting pawn in a mental chess game with his best friend.

"You've just come back home from a year in New Zealand," Fiona said.

"Yes, I was at the University of Canterbury, doing advanced research on the possibility of intelligent life elsewhere in the universe."

"Sometimes," she said, "it's hard finding signs of intelligent life in this town, much less the universe."

That struck his funny bone and he let loose with a laugh. "For sure."

"So did you find E.T.?"

"Not yet. He must be hiding in a closet."

"Eating Reese's Pieces."

"That's a pretty archaic reference for a twenty-five-year old."

"*E.T.* is iconic. I bet you watched it a hundred times when you were a kid," she said.

He grinned. "Probably more like a thousand."

"Me too." Fiona's smile was a flashlight on a moonless night, bright and welcoming.

Ranger could see why Ember was trying to hook him up with her. Fiona was a nice woman . . . for someone.

"May I ask you a question?" she asked.

"Depends."

"On what?"

"If it's embarrassing enough to cut off my circulation."

She laughed again, a soft sound of enjoyment. "You don't have to answer."

"Fire away. What would you like to know?"

"Are you and Ember . . ." She didn't finish the sentence. Just let it dangle.

"Best friends? Yes, we've known each other since we were babies."

"Oh . . . good."

"What does that mean?"

"I ask because there's rumors around town that you two are much more than just friends."

"Look, Fiona, gossips are going to gossip. It doesn't matter what the truth is. Some people can't believe that a man and a woman can be just friends."

"So you and Ember have never —"

97

"God, no." He cut that off short and quick.

"Are you involved with anyone else?"

"I'm concentrating on my work at the moment." That was the truth. Then again, he was always concentrating on his work. The right woman could sway his interest, but so far, he hadn't found anyone who interested him as much as his job, except of course for Ember, but she was off-limits.

"Oh," Fiona said, her voice sounding like Humpty Dumpty after he fell off the wall. "So you're not interested in —"

"E.T. takes up most of my time."

"And your friendship with Ember takes up the remainder?"

"Pretty much."

"I see."

Silence filled the pickup.

Ranger couldn't think of anything else to say, and Fiona wasn't holding up her end of the conversation, and he was mighty relieved when the elaborate wrought-iron gates leading into the Silver Feather came into view.

The main house, where his father and Vivi lived, sat dead center in the middle of the hundred-thousand-acre spread that sprawled across Presidio and Jeff Davis counties. His grandfather, Cyril Lockhart, had left his four grandsons two-acre parcels of land on each of the four quadrants of the ranch, with the stipulation that none of them could sell their plots without approval from the entire family.

Ranger's acreage lay to the north. Three years ago, despite his father's ridicule, Ranger had built an off-the-grid, sustainable earthship house by hand, using reclaimed and recycled products, and he was damn proud of it. Most people thought it an odd house, but then those same people thought Ranger odd, so it fit. They were a headstrong lot, the Lockharts.

Cars packed the driveway.

He blotted his brow with his arm, dampening the sleeve of his suit jacket. He was tempted to drive over to his house before going to the luncheon and change clothes, but he had Fiona in the truck, and he didn't want to take her to the earthship.

Ranger parked and helped Fiona out. She gave him a shy smile when he offered her his elbow, and she eagerly slipped her arm through his. His stepmother, Lucy, had drummed good manners into his head. If it hadn't been for Lucy, he and Ridge would have turned out rank heathens. He still missed his stepmother. Except for Ember's mother, Bridgette Alzate, Lucy had been the only maternal influence in his life.

"Where's Ember?" Kaia asked the second he and Fiona came through the front door.

"I dunno," he said. "It wasn't my turn to watch her."

"It's always your turn to watch her," Kaia said.

"Oh really?" He lifted his eyebrows. "Says who?"

"Me. Without you around to keep her on the straight and narrow, no telling where my sister would end up. You should have seen her this past year while you were in New Zealand."

Huh. Ember had been struggling? Ranger dropped Fiona's arm and stepped closer to Kaia. "What's been going on with her?"

"She's completely at loose ends with her life. Going around in circles, decorating her house and then immediately redecorating. Dating like mad, but never going out with anyone more than once. She's volunteered and overscheduled herself to keep from missing you, and she kept roping me and Tara and Aria into helping her. I'm making a rule. You can't leave the country again unless you take Ember with you."

"Really?" He absorbed that, processing it slowly like he did most things. As a rule, he did not rush.

"Here." Kaia plopped Ingrid in his arms.

"Hold your niece while I mingle. Fiona" —
Kaia linked her arm through the other
woman's — "let me show you where you
can put your purse."

Fiona went away with Kaia but cast a
longing gaze over her shoulder at Ranger.
Yipes. He was going to give Ember an ear-
ful about this match-making nonsense.

Speaking of his best friend, where was
she? And why hadn't she told him she was
struggling?

Ingrid stared at Ranger and started whim-
pering.

Panic took hold of him. "Shh, shh, don't
do that," he pleaded with the baby and went
in search of his brother. He found his older
brother talking to Father Dubanowski in
the dining room.

"Here, here, take your kid." Ranger depos-
ited Ingrid in her father's arms.

"Scared of a baby?" Ridge teased.

"I'm not scared of her. I've just . . . er . . .
got something I need to do."

"*Riii*ght."

"I'm not scared of a baby."

"Better not be. You're her godfather."

"We'll bond more when she's older, and
I'll teach her how to find the Big Dipper."

"You're missing out, buddy." Ridge
grinned and rocked his daughter in his

arms. "One of these days you're going to want one of these. Mark my word."

"Yeah, yeah." Ranger scooted out the back door, breathed deep and whipped his cell phone from his jacket pocket to text Ember. Where R U?

A few minutes later, his phone dinged. En route.

Ranger texted: Hurry. It's boring without U.

EMBER: Talk to Fiona.
RANGER: About that . . .

He texted her a gif file of a man in a coma.

EMBER: Behave. She's nice.

Ranger texted the coma gif again.

EMBER: Haha.
RANGER: Get over here, ASAP.
EMBER: Keep U'R shorts on. Deputy Greenwood has it out for me and I can't afford another ticket.

Ranger grinned and wrote: Speed Racer.

Ember sent a gif of a girl sticking out her tongue.

God, he'd missed their easy camaraderie. Their natural way of teasing each other.

This was the main reason he didn't want to take that job in New Zealand. He couldn't be that far away from Ember again.

"Ranger!" said Bridgette Alzate, who looked so much like her daughter that it was uncanny. She gave him a glimpse at just how beautiful Ember was going to be at fifty-five. "Come in, come in. Don't be shy. Lunch is buffet style, get yourself a plate and get in there with the rest of them."

"I'm waiting for Ember."

"Where is she, by the way?" Bridgette frowned.

"Right here, Mama," Ember said, breezing into the room, bringing sunshine in with her smile.

Ranger grinned, and all was right in his world.

CHAPTER 5

"This sweetest and best of all creatures, faultless in spite of all her faults."
— Jane Austen, *Emma*

"Have you forgotten how to throw elbows around this bunch?" Ember shoved a plate in Ranger's hand and trotted him over to the kitchen table laden with a Mexican food buffet — chili-powder-laced hamburger meat scramble, chicken strips marinated in fajita seasoning, refried pinto beans, black beans, pico de gallo, shredded cheddar cheese, guacamole, homemade corn and flour tortillas, salsa, and sour cream.

She wanted to ask how the ride over from the church had gone with Fiona, but didn't dare. What if they hadn't spoken at all? Fiona could be pretty quiet, and Ranger wasn't a big talker either. Had she screwed up pairing them together?

"Beer?" Ember held up an iced Tecate.

104

He nodded. Ranger had loaded up a plate and was standing around looking for a place to sit. All the seats at the dining-room table were filled.

She balanced her own plate and drink, and gestured toward the living room. Ranger followed.

In the living room, Fiona was sitting on the couch bouncing a cooing Ingrid on her knee.

Fiona didn't look up at Ranger, and he had turned in the opposite direction to say something to his brother Rhett who was sitting on the love seat beside Aria, regaling her with stories of the PBR.

Granny Blue Alzate sat in one of the two La-Z-Boy recliners with her feet propped up and a plate settled in her lap.

Ember plunked right down beside Fiona.

Ranger hesitated and shifted restlessly. He tried to take the cushion beside Ember, but she inclined her head toward the other side of Fiona. He shot Ember a look that said, *I don't wanna.*

Ugh. Things must have gone really badly on the drive over. Okay, so not an instant love match, but that didn't mean there wasn't wiggle room for a developing relationship.

Fiona scooted over so Ranger could slip

between her and Ember, her eyes glazed glassy with baby love. Tentatively, she peeked through her lashes at Ranger.

He kept his attention locked on his plate.

Uh-oh. Ember could read the signs loud and clear. Fiona was interested in Ranger, but Ranger was not interested in Fiona. At least not yet.

What should she do about that? Help Ranger see Fiona's sterling qualities? Find another way to get them together? Find someone else for Fiona? Write Ranger off as a lost cause?

Fiona baby-talked to Ingrid, her plate of food untouched on the coffee table in front of her.

"Isn't she beautiful," Granny Blue said of the baby. "From the minute Kaia told me she was pregnant I knew she would be a girl."

"Really?" Fiona leaned forward, looked intrigued. "How did you know?"

Granny Blue waved a hand. "I read the signs."

"Which one?" Rhett chortled. "The sonogram?"

Granny Blue glowered at him.

Rhett gulped, and sweat beaded his brow. He mumbled, "Sorry, just kidding."

"Granny had a fifty-fifty chance at guessing right," Ember answered Fiona's question, trying to head off some of Granny Blue's more eccentric beliefs. Her mysterious talk of reading signs and listening to one's intuition could jolt the uninitiated.

"Don't disrespect your grandmother," Ranger said solemnly. "She has her ways, and there's more things in the earth and sky than man can understand."

Granny Blue lowered her eyelids, and sent Ranger a ghost of a smile.

Hey, what was this? The scientist taking up for Granny Blue's woo-woo?

"She's always been a skeptic, this one." Granny Blue's sharp, dark eyes settled on Ember. "She's afraid to open her heart and mind. Terrified that if she does she will no longer be running the show."

Ranger laughed, not making fun, simply agreeing. "She's got your number, Sparky."

Ember turned to Fiona; she loved her grandmother to pieces, but sometimes her mystical stuff defied all logic. "The month Kaia got pregnant, a black widow spider built a web in the east corner of Granny's barn, and apparently that meant Ingrid was going to be a girl. I guess if the spider had built a web in the west corner, the baby would have been a boy."

"You're poking fun at me," Granny Blue

said mildly, her eyes amused. "That's okay. You don't have to believe. It's your life, live it the way you want. But don't come crying to me when you end up with the wrong man again."

Ouch! The elderly lady didn't pull any punches.

"She doesn't know what she's missing, does she, Granny?" Kaia asked, sweeping into the room to collect Ingrid from Fiona. She cuddled her daughter and plunked down in a rocking chair. "Poor old Ember hasn't a clue. If she'd listened to you, she wouldn't have married Trey and made such a mess of her life."

"Hey, hey." Ember tapped her fingers on her leg trying to release some tension. She felt like she was trying to climb one of the Davis Mountains during an ice storm, in high heels. "I didn't make a mess of my life."

Kaia clucked her tongue, acting as if she were the big sister. "You're divorced —"

"Gratefully."

"If you'd listened to Granny, you wouldn't have gone down the wrong road in the first place." Kaia sniffed her baby's head and looked more than a little smug.

"Oh, here we go again." Ember rolled her eyes. "Please no, not the glorious humming story."

Ranger edged his boot over and touched her foot. In solidarity? Or warning her to check herself? Was she being too opinion-ated? It was sometimes hard for her to tell when she'd crossed the line until it was too late and she'd hurt someone's feelings.

"Humming?" Fiona sat up straighter. "What humming?"

Ember suppressed a groan. Now they were going to have to hear the old wives' tale she'd listened to a thousand times.

Ahem, lectured her better self, *they are your family. Let them have their say. It won't hurt a thing. It costs nothing to be kind.*

To keep from saying something she shouldn't, Ember stuffed her mouth with a soft taco. Just because she'd had a bad experience didn't mean she had a right to take it out on the ones who loved her.

Granny Blue lowered the footrest on the recliner, set her plate of food on the end table, and met Fiona's curious gaze. "My granddaughter thinks the story is silly and boring. Are you sure you really want to hear it?"

"Granny, I truly am sorry." Ember really should keep duct tape in her purse for times like these. She didn't mean to step on toes, she just enjoyed lively debate and it often surprised her to learn other people did not feel the same way.

"You've done nothing to be sorry for. You simply are who you are." Granny Blue's words were kind, her tone even kinder. "One day, if you're lucky, you will understand."

To Fiona, Granny Blue said, "When the women in my family kiss their soul mate for the first time, they hear a soft, but distinct humming from deep inside the brain. It's a sweet steady sound that fills all the cells in your body. And they also feel a light pressure right here." Turning in her chair so Fiona could see the back of her head, Granny pressed two fingers against her skull on the same plane as the pineal gland embedded deep within her brain.

Fiona looked dubious. Yay for Fiona. "You mean like ringing in your ears?"

"No, not like that at all. For one thing it's not inside your ears. For another thing it's a completely different sound. Ringing in your ears is high-pitched and annoying. This is a low, comforting hum. More like sound emissions from a miniature power generator. It is as if the sound of the universe is inside your head, and you are inside of it."

"I gotta say, I'm with Ember on this one." Aria wrinkled her nose. "Seems pretty far-fetched."

"Clearly, because you've never kissed me, darlin'," Rhett drawled and puckered up. "I'll make you hum all over."

Aria threw a pillow at him. "In your wildest dreams, cowboy."

"Ye of little faith." Kaia kissed her baby and looked through the door into the next room where her husband was having an engrossing conversation with her parents. Kaia and Granny Blue shared a meaningful glance.

"I don't get it. How could a kiss cause someone to hear humming in their head?" Fiona looked perplexed.

"Ranger's the scientist." Aria turned to him. "What do you think?"

Ranger's smile was a shrug, light and casual. "The more I learn, the more I realize how little I know."

"That was diplomatic. Good dodge." Aria winked.

"I'm thinking it's just the power of suggestion." Rhett threw the pillow back at Aria. "You know, like when your manager tells you that you can ride the most cantankerous bull out there and you do because he made you think you could."

"I cannot explain the why." Granny Blue's eyes were cryptic, her shoulders lifting easily, then riding back down. She didn't care

111

if anyone believed her or not. "I can only tell you what I *know.*"

Kaia raised a hand. "I second that."

"Is it because you are Native American?" Fiona asked.

"Maybe it is, maybe it isn't. The origin is not important." Granny Blue held out both palms in an it's-beyond-me gesture.

"And it only happens to the women in your family?" Fiona picked up her plate but didn't eat anything. "Not the men?"

"Just the women."

"I wish I could hear it." Aria sighed. "I'm quite musical. I would like to hear music in my head all the time."

"Wanna kiss me and see if I'm your soul mate?" Rhett waggled his tongue at her.

Aria shoved him off the love seat. Laughing, he rolled around on the floor and stayed there.

"It's so fascinating," Fiona murmured. "The mind is such a great mystery."

"Beyond fascinating." Kaia kissed Ingrid again. "It's cosmic destiny."

What a load of baloney! Ember thought. *Don't say it, don't say it, don't —*

"Baloney. C'mon people, you aren't seriously buying into this?" Ember's tongue couldn't hold back. "Granny Blue tells a ridiculous tale of finding your soul mate by

112

hearing a humming in your head when you kiss him, and Kaia swallowed it hook, line, and sinker. That doesn't make any of it true. She's an elderly lady on medication for crying out loud!"

The entire room went silent.

Granny Blue's face was impassive. Kaia looked wounded. Ember shot a glance over at Ranger.

He slapped her with a chiding stare, and she sucked in her breath. Oh no. Message received. She was acting like a jerk, and he was disappointed in her. Once more her unfiltered mouth had gotten her into trouble.

Remorseful, she dropped her gaze. "I'm sorry, Granny, really sorry," Ember apologized. "Trey did a number on me, and I guess it all got stirred up again today with Ingrid's christening."

"You *think*?" Kaia said sharply.

"It's all right, child," Granny Blue said. "I understand the fear and your pain."

"If it makes you feel any better, I didn't believe in the humming either until it happened to me." Kaia's voice gentled.

The truth? The real reason she was such a skeptic? Once upon a time she *had* believed in Granny's humming story, believed it deeply, desperately, to the depth of her soul.

When she was seventeen, and looking for love, she got it into her head that the legend was one hundred percent true and that in order to find her Prince Charming she had better get to kissing the frogs. In the course of one summer she kissed two hundred and sixteen guys. In all that time, and in all those kisses, she hadn't heard anything.

Not a whisper.

Not a peep.

Not a whimper.

Much less a hum. Out of two hundred and sixteen men she should have heard *something* if she was going to. Right?

But she did get a cold sore if that counted.

There certainly had been no humming with Trey, but by then, she'd given up on the stupid legend, and had started operating like a normal person. In other words, absolutely clueless when it came to love.

You never kissed Ranger. That sudden thought seared into her brain like a brand, glowing red-hot and strangely urgent.

And why not? Why *hadn't* she kissed him?

There had been opportunities when she could have kissed him — under the mistletoe at Christmas, in the stands at a high school football game when his brother threw the winning touchdown to her brother, playing spin the bottle at age twelve and loudly declaring "yuck" when the bottle landed on him and running off. Any number of times they could have had a light, friendly brushing of their mouths, just to check it out.

But she hadn't ever seriously considered it. Not even once.

Sitting here next to him, she realized with a start exactly *why* she'd never crossed that line. It had nothing to do with the fact they'd been best friends since childhood — well okay, maybe it had a little bit to do with it — but that wasn't the whole megillah.

The down and dirty reason she'd never considered kissing Ranger?

Because what if she had kissed him and she *didn't* hear the humming? It would confirm once and for always that there wasn't a chance he could be her soul mate.

And that scared her most of all.

Thankfully, everyone finally stopped talking about the humming, and the topic shifted where it belonged: on the delicious food, the good company, and the beautiful, newly baptized baby.

Ranger glanced up from where he was sitting beside Ember, caught Granny Blue studying him with intense black eyes. He noticed she had a sprinkling of sawdust in her hair. He didn't ask why. He'd learned a long time ago that with Granny Blue, you'd most likely get an answer you weren't sure you wanted to hear.

The elderly Apache lady had always unnerved him a little. Often, it felt as if she had the uncanny ability to read minds.

He smiled at her.

She didn't smile back.

"Where have you been?" Granny Blue blurted.

Ember might have gotten her looks from her mother, but she'd gotten her directness from her grandmother. He admired the ability in both grandmother and granddaughter, but he couldn't say he was entirely comfortable with it.

Caught off guard, he simply said, "New Zealand."

"That's where kiwis come from," Granny Blue said.

"Yes."

"I never much liked kiwis." Granny Blue dipped a chip in the salsa on her plate, but just held it in her hand without eating.

"New Zealanders?"

"No, the fruit. They're too fuzzy and green."

He couldn't argue with that assessment. Kiwis *were* fuzzy and green, but still delicious. Ranger stared at the chip, fascinated, wondering how long she was going to hold it suspended halfway to her mouth.

"I like blackberries," he said for no good reason at all.

"Too many seeds."

"I can see how that would be a concern if you're not into seeds."

"Do you ever take a hard stand?" Granny Blue asked. "Or do you always try to play both sides of the aisle?"

"I try to piss off as few people as possible. Life is easier that way."

"And that's your endgame?" The sawdust in her hair shook when she bobbed her head. "Easy?"

"What's wrong with easy?"

"It's lazy. My granddaughter isn't lazy."

"Kaia?"

Granny Blue snorted. "Ember."

"I know that."

"Some people only learn when you piss them off," she said, circling back around and almost leaving him in the dust. "Ember knows that."

"If you say so."

"Grow an opinion, young man!"

"My opinion is that I want to keep out of this conversation."

"At last!" she cackled. "You owned it. Good job."

Um, okay.

More people crowded into the room carrying plates and looking for places to sit. Ranger was feeling hemmed in and wished he wasn't wearing his best suit. He also wished he could think of a graceful way to get out of there, but he didn't want to be rude and he had to take Fiona back to the church. *Thanks a million for that, Em.*

"So," Granny Blue said, clearly not done with him yet. "Are you finished with New Zealand?"

"I don't know."

She rolled her eyes. "There you go, taking the easy road again."

"That's not true."

"Then what is true?" Her eyes were obsidian marbles, dark and shiny. "Are you going back to New Zealand or not?"

"It depends."

"On what?"

The woman was a tough customer. He liked that she didn't suffer fools, but at the same time he worried that she considered him one of those fools.

"I've applied for a permanent job at the observatory, but I might not get it."

"Why not?" Granny said. "You're the smartest man in Jeff Davis County."

"Hey!" Rhett protested, thumping his

118

chest with a fist. "I'm sitting right here."

Granny Blue barely flicked a glance Rhett's way, kept her eyes trained on Ranger. "Well?"

"Don't worry." Aria giggled to Rhett. "You don't need smarts. You're the handsomest Lockhart brother."

"I ain't dumb." Rhett glared. "Just 'cause I dropped out of high school to go on the rodeo circuit."

"I might be book smart," Ranger explained to Granny Blue, "but they want someone in the position who also has people smarts."

"Then marry a woman with people smarts. She can handle that for you." Granny Blue nodded like it was a solid plan.

Why was everyone trying to marry him off? He angled his head toward Ember, but she was tucking into her taco and pretending not to pay any attention to the *get-me-out-of-this* looks he was shooting her way. He supposed he deserved it for not backing her up when she was knocking that humming malarkey.

"I appreciate the advice," he said, being polite.

"Well, then, take it. Get a good woman so you can get the damn job, and you can stay home where you belong." Granny finally

119

crunched into the chip.

Ranger let out a sigh and couldn't believe how grateful he was when Fiona bumped him lightly on the shoulder and said, "Could you please give me a ride back to the church?"

The minute Ranger and Fiona left the house, Ember tracked down her parents and told them goodbye. Kissed the baby. Thanked Kaia and Ridge for entrusting her to be Ingrid's godmother and got out of there as fast as she could.

It was just after four in the afternoon when she walked into the house, fed Samantha, and plopped down onto the couch. She loved her family with all her heart, but sometimes she longed for the freedom — and the proximity to a Starbucks — she'd had in San Antonio.

Then she remembered how lonely she used to get without her family close by, and erased thoughts of San Antonio from her mind. And speaking of her stupid mind, it was still reeling from her realization about the real reason why she had never even tried to kiss Ranger. Not even that night in college they'd gotten drunk and slept in the same bed together. In a tiny area, tucked deep inside her, she wanted to believe in soul mates and even more important, desperately wanted to believe that *he* was The One.

It was unsettling to say the least.

Her cell phone dinged, signaling that she'd gotten a text. Idly, she reached over and checked the message.

What the hell, Sparky?

Her pulse pounded. There was that never-fail telepathy thing she and Ranger had going on. She thought of him and poof, he texted.

??? Ember texted back.

RANGER: Don't play dumb? I know U threw Fiona @ me. Knock it off. I'm not 1 of UR projects.
EMBER: Who me?

Ranger texted an emoji of an upside down smiley face sticking out its tongue.

EMBER: Pizza and Netflix 2night?

Immediately after she sent it, Ember cringed. Aria had recently informed her that *Netflix and chill* was a euphemism for a casual sexual hookup. God, she was getting old. Hopefully, Ranger was just as clueless as she was. Besides, pizza and Netflix wasn't the same as *Netflix and chill.* But it was perilously close, and it did set up a certain image once you knew of the undercurrent meaning. Not that Ranger thought of her in *that* way. It was just awkward.

RANGER: Rain check? Rhett's got women problems and he needs 2 talk.
EMBER: Rhett needs 2 keep it in his pants.
RANGER: Undoubtedly.
EMBER: Tomorrow nite?
RANGER: Poker with Luke Nielson. Wanna come?
EMBER: Sure. Where & When
RANGER: Backroom. Chantilly's 9 P.M.
EMBER: Just like old times.
RANGER: Nothing ever changes with me & U.

He added a winking emoji.

Ember couldn't decide if that was a good thing or not. Her stomach dipped in a weird way. C U then.

CHAPTER 6

"Surprises are foolish things. The pleasure is not enhanced, and the inconvenience is often considerable."

— Jane Austen, *Emma*

Ranger arrived at Chantilly's Bar and Grill on Monday evening, surprised by the collection of folks mingling in the back room. Not the usual suspects with whom he and the mayor normally played poker.

The director of Perfect Buddies Animal Shelter, Angi Morgan, sat at the table shuffling cards. A few cards flew from her hands and scattered across the floor. Laughing, she scooped them up. "Oops. I'm not much of a card shark."

Cardsharp, Ranger thought. *Fish don't play cards.*

"You lost one." Andre Johnson reached down to pick up the queen of hearts, which had floated underneath the table.

123

Andre was a thirtysomething science teacher at Cupid High. He also served on the board of directors for Pinyon Pines Ranch, a summer camp in the Davis Mountains for underprivileged city kids. Andre had once been one of those city kids, and he'd loved the Trans-Pecos so much he moved to Cupid after he graduated from the University of North Texas. Ranger knew him from the observatory's stargazing parties, where the teacher often brought his young charges to learn about astronomy. Andre was well-respected and well-liked around Cupid, but poker was not his strong suit.

"Make that two," said Spencer Greenwood from the other side of the table, and passed Angi a red Joker card. Spencer was a fun-loving, former minor league baseball player with a cowcatcher mustache. He ran an adult day care center in Marfa with his sister, Alice. While he'd once been a hell of a ballplayer, he didn't know squat about poker.

"We don't play Jokers Wild," Ranger said kindly to Angi and hid his wince with an encouraging smile. Hey, she was learning. But he couldn't help wondering what Luke was thinking inviting rank amateurs to poker night.

Ranger shot Luke a sidelong glance. He didn't know Luke's motivation, but clearly their host had something besides poker up his sleeve.

And where was Ember, by the way?

The game was supposed to start at nine, and it was five after. He was eager to get her opinion on the odd assembly of players. He was just about to text her when the door opened and she walked in with a gorgeous brunette following close behind her.

Who was this new woman?

Ranger craned his neck to get a good look at the newcomer and did a double take. *That* was Fiona Kelton?

Gone were Fiona's heavy, dark-framed glasses. Her hair had been let loose from its ubiquitous bun, and it flowed silkily over her shoulders. She wore a red dress with a short skirt that he could tell had come straight from Ember's closet, false eyelashes, and an abundance of makeup.

Andre and Spencer, who were both single, sat up straighter, sucked in their guts and smiled as if they'd won the lottery.

Ember paraded Fiona around the room like a show pony, introducing her to everyone, and instantly, Ranger knew what was up. His matchmaking best friend had given Fiona a makeover and was shopping her around for a mate, but why had she brought the prim church secretary to a backroom poker game?

Thickheaded much, Lockhart? Ember was still trying to hook him up with Fiona.

Ranger swallowed a groan. It was going to be a long night — amateur poker players, Ember playing matchmaker. Ugh. If he wasn't in need of Luke's endowment money, he'd cash in his chips and go home.

Luke rubbed his palms together as if pleased with the company, and waved Ember and Fiona to the two vacant spots at the table. "Grab yourselves something to drink and have a seat, ladies. We're about to begin."

Once Fiona and Ember had settled in at the table with beverages — water for Fiona, bottled tea for Ember — Luke mercifully took the deck away from card-mangling Angi and began shuffling them.

Ranger breathed a sigh of relief. Maybe they could play some real poker after all.

"You're probably wondering why I invited this particular group to my weekly Monday night card game," Luke said.

Finally, they were getting down to it. Ember's bottom-line attitude was rubbing off on him.

"Four of you at this table are interested in

my grandmother's endowment money." Luke glanced at Angi, Andre, Spencer, and Ranger. "And Ember's here because she has her fingers on the pulse of the Trans-Pecos and she's a natural connector, and Fiona . . ." Luke smiled at the church secretary. "Well, she's our guest. Welcome to Monday night poker, Fiona."

"Welcome Fiona!" Everyone said it so unanimously the room momentarily took on the feel of a twelve-step meeting.

It was a bit strange having the church secretary at poker night, but it was a low-stakes game played for fun. Tonight, however, had a different flavor as Luke laid out what was quickly becoming a two-million-dollar stake.

"Rather than take four separate meetings where you all try to convince me that your cause deserves the money, I thought why not let you see who you're up against and make your pitches all at once." The cards made a smooth shuffling sound between Luke's adept fingers as the players at the table sized each other up.

"Texas Hold 'Em. Nothing wild," Luke said.

"Wait a minute." Angi made a "time-out" sign with her hands. "This isn't fair."

"What's not fair?" Luke dealt two cards

127

facedown to each player.

"Ranger is a crackerjack poker player." Angi tugged at her right earlobe, playing with the gold hoop earring nestled there. "He'll mop the floor with the rest of us."

"I'm not basing my decision on the winner of the poker game," Luke said. "Rather on the strength of your pitches, your passion for your projects, and your powers of persuasion."

"Oh." Angi brightened. "In that case . . ." Angi met Ranger's eyes with a steely gaze. "Eat my dust, Lockhart."

Fiona giggled. It was a pretty sound, much like the high tinkling of wind chimes in the breeze, and Ranger smiled at her.

Fiona blushed.

Ember cleared her throat. *Ahem.*

All eyes went to Ember. She had that effect. When the woman spoke or even cleared her throat, people listened.

"Do you have something to add, Ember?" Luke asked.

"No. Proceed."

She didn't meet Ranger's gaze, and he couldn't shake the feeling his best friend was up to something besides the Fiona hookup. He searched her face, looking for her tells — the way she'd scratch her chin with her index finger when she was trying to make up her mind, or the way her left eye twitched when she was stressed, how she'd pull one corner of her bottom lip up between her teeth when she was holding back on saying something she wanted to blurt.

He saw none of her typical giveaways, but the fact that she wouldn't look him in the eyes was "tell" enough. Hmm.

"Angi, would you like to start while we make our bets?" Luke asked.

"Absolutely." Angi launched into her needs for the no-kill shelter at a breakneck clip, as if the faster she spoke the more likely she was to get the money. Her pitch was compelling and heart tugging. Her animal shelter was the only one in three counties. They were bursting at the seams. They needed to hire more workers, needed more kennels, more medicines, more everything.

Ranger loved animals, and he was ready to whip out his checkbook and write the shelter a big fat check right then and there, but if he did, would that look like he was trying to buy off the competition?

Instead, he eyed his cards, felt his chances of getting the money dwindling. How could stargazing compete with homeless animals?

On the plus side, he had pocket aces.

Spades and diamonds. This hand was in the bag.

Angi kept up her pitch as they went around the table placing their bets. Ranger was cagey and only raised the pot a little. If he came on too strong out of the gate with this bunch of amateurs, they'd all fold.

Fiona raised his bet.

Surprised, Ranger grinned and met her bet with another modest raise.

Fiona glanced coyly at her two cards again and smiled a Mona Lisa smile. Raised again. Ooh, had he found a tell?

Spencer folded, but everyone else stayed in.

Once the bets were in, Luke dealt The Flop — three cards face up in the middle of the table that all the players would play off of. The cards in the middle of the table were: three of diamonds, three of hearts, ace of clubs.

Ranger had a full house, aces high!

When it was his turn to bet, he raised boldly and confidently, upping the ante to a sum that had Ember, Angi, and Andre quickly folding.

Leaving just Luke, Fiona, and Ranger.

"You know," Ember said to Angi, "a wealthy client of mine who loves animals is ailing and she has to downsize. She owns a huge house with acres of ranch land not too far outside Alpine, and she really wants the place to go to someone who will love it the way she and her husband did before he passed away. She used to raise cocker spaniels and already has kennels sitting empty. You should call her."

"What a sweet thought," Angi said. "But the shelter has no money to purchase property, unless Luke decides to grant us the endowment." Angi shot the mayor a hopeful look.

"Here's the thing . . ." Ember made a steeple of her fingers. "She's willing to donate the property as a charitable deduction if she approves of the cause."

"Really?" Angi sank her elbows on the table and leaned forward. "Tell me more."

"Let's not chat over the card game." Ember led Angi off to a corner to continue their discussion.

"Connector." Luke grinned. "Ember's got it going on."

Ranger followed Ember with his eyes, felt a helpless smile slide across his face. Ember did indeed have it going on, and he couldn't help feeling she had just taken Angi out of contention for Luke's endowment. God, how he loved that woman. Realizing he was slack-jawed with admiration, he shut his mouth before anyone noticed.

"Spencer," Luke said. "Your turn to pitch. Why do you need the money?"

Spencer launched into his tale. More heartstrings tugged as he talked about his elderly clients who desperately needed someplace to go during the day while their loved ones worked. He wanted to extend the hours of his adult day care, but he couldn't afford to hire more employees. He embellished and elaborated, provided details about specific situations. The man was a gifted storyteller. Ranger gave him that.

"Spence," Ember piped up from across the room, "you know who's looking for a new charity to support?"

"Who?" Spencer beamed at Ember as if she were his queen and he, her humble servant.

"Ridge," Ember said.

"If Ridge is passing around money, why doesn't Ranger just ask his brother to support his cause and leave Luke's endowment to the rest of us?" Spencer grumbled.

"Family thing. You know how it is. Shouldn't mix money and family. Tell you what, I'll talk to Kaia and see if she can persuade Ridge to fund your expansion."

Ember, Ember, Ember. You little firecracker. How had Ranger gotten so lucky to have her in his corner? The stars must have aligned on the night he was born. Not that he believed in astrology, but he'd done something right at some point to entice this fetching woman's undying loyalty.

"You'd do that?" Spencer's eyes widened like the Queen of England had just knighted him. Hell, Ranger certainly understood that sentiment. He felt that way every time Ember walked into the room.

"Consider it done." Her smile was as magical as a famous amusement park in Florida.

"You're straight up awesome, Ember. Thank you." Spencer bobbed his head.

Luke sent Ranger a weighted look and said, "Now for The Turn." Luke laid down the fourth card beside the other three in the middle of the table.

Five of hearts.

It did nothing for Ranger's hand, but he didn't need it. He had a full house, aces high. He was going to win. It would take a mighty hand to beat him.

Fiona raised.

Luke folded.

Ranger studied Fiona with new respect. With the cards on the table, she probably had a straight, but who would have stayed in during the first round with a two-four split? Was it beginner's luck? Or was she so green she didn't know not to play to an inside straight? Or, and this was what made him sit up and take notice, was she so confident in her abilities to bluff, she was just going for it.

You had to watch out for the quiet ones. He knew that because *he* was a quiet one. Quiet ones were always thinking.

Ranger met Fiona's raise and kicked up the ante.

Fiona checked.

One more card left to turn over. No matter what it was, the woman barely stood a chance against his aces high full house.

Luke laid the fifth and final card in the middle of the table with the other four. The three of spades.

Ranger studied Fiona's face, but she was as stony as the Davis Mountains. Could the woman possibly have four of a kind? He calculated the odds in his head. Slim chance. Very slim that she had four of a kind.

Did he fold or take the gamble?

Go big or go home, right?

He pushed his stack of chips into the middle of the table, kept his gaze trained on Fiona, delighted to have found some real competition here tonight. "All in."

"You have pocket aces," Fiona guessed. It

wasn't wild conjecture considering how he'd been betting; not for someone with a working knowledge of the game. With a ghost of a smile, Fiona pushed her chips all in to join his.

A sick feeling washed over Ranger. They weren't playing for money, but he couldn't help feeling like he was losing something important. He hadn't been knocked out in the first hand of a poker game since he'd started playing with his dad when he was no more than eight or nine. Poker was the one and only way he and Duke had bonded.

And before Fiona even turned over her cards, Ranger knew with nauseating certainty what he was going to see.

"Four of a kind," Fiona called out joyfully, and raked the huge pile of chips toward her. "My four threes beat your ace high full house."

Ranger grunted, sounded impressed, but looked gobsmacked. "Well played."

Ember glanced up from her conversation with Angi and Spencer to see Ranger sitting at the poker table, mouth open, eyes wide. She'd never in her life known him to lose a hand when he went all in.

And he'd lost to Fiona of all people. Who knew the church secretary would turn out

135

to be Matt Damon from *Rounders*?

Ember hopped to her feet, zoomed over to the table to see what she'd missed, feeling both proud of her protégé and protective of Ranger. What truly surprised her, however, was the way Ranger was looking at Fiona.

As if he'd dusted off a garbage rock to find a sparkling diamond. Ranger pushed back his chair and got to his feet, settled his Stetson onto his head.

"Where you going?" Luke asked.

"I've been cleaned out."

"At low-stakes poker?"

"She . . ." Ranger nodded at Fiona and grinned affably. That was one of the things Ember loved about him. He was a good loser. Probably because he so rarely lost. Maybe he was in shock. "Mopped the floor with my reputation."

Fiona blew on her knuckles, polished them against her chest, looked sublime. "But the floor's clean."

Ranger laughed, a bright bubble of a sound that made Ember's stomach hurt. Yesterday, he'd barely seemed able to give Fiona the time of day. Tonight, he was eyeing her like she was the blue-plate special.

"So you're gonna tuck your tail between your legs and head for the hills?" Luke clucked his tongue.

"Nope, I was hoping to take Fiona out for ice cream before the Dairy Queen closes."

Luke stroked his chin pensively. "Without ever giving us your pitch?"

"All three of them" — Ranger indicated Angi, Andre, and Spencer with a tip of his Stetson — "have more compelling charities than I do, animals, kids, senior citizens. I just want the same thing I always want, to study the stars."

"Psst," Ember hissed in his ear. "Outside, Lockhart. Now."

Ranger grinned and held up a finger. "Go ahead with the card game. We'll be right back."

Before he could linger over Fiona, Ember grabbed Ranger's hand and dragged him through the exit door. They ended up in the alley behind Chantilly's, breathing in the night air, the smell of refried frijoles from La Hacienda Grill over on Main Street, and the sweet rot of agave cactus blooms scattered across the surrounding desert.

"What are you doing?" she asked.

"Huh?"

"Don't be thickheaded."

"Honest, Sparky, I have no idea what you're talking about."

"You're practically giving Luke's endowment away, and after I worked so hard to think up alternative funding for Angi and Spencer. It was down to just you and Andre, and you threw in the towel without a whimper."

"I didn't throw in the towel. I lost . . . at *poker*."

"Yeah, how *did* that happen?"

"Fiona's damn good."

Ember folded her arms over her chest. "Better than you, apparently."

"I underestimated her." That same shiny light of respect and appreciation that had come over his face when she'd brought the new and improved Fiona into the poker game lit him up again. "I won't make that mistake twice."

"Meaning?"

"I'm going to ask her out."

"What? Yesterday you jumped my butt for trying to match you."

"Wasn't that why you brought her around tonight? To get me interested?"

Initially, but that had changed once she saw how interested he'd gotten. "You're not the only bachelor on the planet. Spencer and Andre are both single."

"Fiona's prettier than I first thought. She's quiet and she's good at poker. Three pluses in her column."

"What column?"

"The I-need-a-wife-to-help-me-further-my-career column."

Ember settled her hands on her hips. Everything was going according to her plan. Why was she feeling disgruntled? "Fiona is not a doll to be toyed with."

"No? Then why are you playing dress-up with her? You wanted me to ask her out, I'm asking her."

Ember's head was like a swivel, wagging back and forth. "That's not the best idea in the West."

"Why not?"

"She's not right for you."

"I thought you wanted me to date her," Ranger said, his tone taking on a cagey note. "Yesterday, you practically threw her at me."

"That's when I thought you were opposites. Today I find out she's a female version of you."

"And that's bad?"

"The worst."

"Why's that?"

"You need someone the opposite of you. A real go-getter."

"Fiona was go-getting after that poker hand."

Ember lifted both shoulders, felt a band of tension stretch her muscles taut. "Point made. Let's move on."

"To where?"

"Back inside the bar."

"What for?"

Ember leaned over to knock her fist against the side of his head. "To get your endowment money, numbskull."

Being this close to him affected her in a strange way. A way she'd never quite been affected before. She couldn't really put a name to it, but suddenly, she felt awkward and gangly around him. Not at all herself.

It wasn't the first time since he'd been back that things had felt different with him. Since he'd been away, it seemed Ranger had gotten handsomer, if that was even possible. His shoulders broader. His winsome smile deeper. His brown eyes darker. His cheekbones more honed. His jawline more chiseled. What in the hell had they fed him in New Zealand? She needed to order a warehouse load of it, ASAP.

Then again, maybe not.

The way she wanted to be near him was rapidly approaching conduct unbecoming of best friends.

She stepped back and tried not to look at him, turned her eyes to the stars, searching for the constellations she'd committed to memory because of him. But tonight, clouds shrouded her view, and it wasn't exactly a prime sky-eyeing situation. She peeked over at Ranger, and he gave her that endearing you'll-always-be-my-best-friend smile that generally made her feel all warm and cozy inside but tonight left her feeling off-kilter and out of sorts.

What if she wanted more than friendship?

Oh shit, oh damn, oh three kinds of lollipop hell. Where was this coming from and why?

Ranger reached for the door handle, brushing his arm against her waist in the process and setting innovative tingles firing across her skin.

What was going on? Maybe she was getting shingles. Because it surely couldn't be a sexual reaction to Ranger.

Could it?

No. No. Absolutely not. *Get those weird ideas out of your head right now, missy.* Ranger was not a romantic possibility for her.

But why not? whispered her recalcitrant inner monologue. *Why the yellow-mustard frig not?*

Ranger stopped and stared at her as if he was feeling something novel too. Was it her imagination? Were things shifting between them? Was he becoming as aroused as she

141

was? Ember's nipples tightened inside her bra.

He lowered his head. Licked his lips.

Holy chain-of-title, she was staring at his lips and he was staring at hers. They had to stop this. Right now.

"Inside," she barked in her best imitation of a drill sergeant.

"After you." Ranger held the door open for her, his eyes dark and hooded, giving away nothing, poker-faced and cool.

No. Nothing unusual or suggestive there. It had definitely been her imagination.

Snapping out of her bizarro trance, Ember breezed in ahead of him like nothing had happened, because, let's face it, nothing had.

And she was glad for that.

So glad.

Glad. Glad. Glad.

Uh-huh. Gladder than glad.

"Hi, Ranger," Fiona peeped like an Easter chick when they returned to the poker table. She gave him an I-wanna-have-your-babies-and-starch-your-laundry smile. "We're starting a fresh game. You in?"

With one makeover, meek little Fiona Kelton had become the belle of the ball and a cardsharp to boot.

Irrationally irritated, Ember jammed her

fingers through her hair. She should be patting herself on the back for Fiona's transformation. Instead, all she could think was, *I've created a monster.*

CHAPTER 7

"Indeed, I am very sorry to be right in this instance. I would much rather have been merry than wise."

— Jane Austen, *Emma*

"We heard Andre's pitch while you were gone," Luke said, an impish quality creeping into his voice. "It was quite compelling."

"Very persuasive," Angi added. "*I* was ready to give him money."

"You're the last one to pitch, Range." Luke cocked his chair back on two legs. "Let's hear it."

Ranger sank into the chair he'd vacated earlier, feeling strangely light-headed after talking with Ember in the alley, and he had no reason for it. He'd only had the one beer.

But for a crazy moment there, when he'd stared into her eyes and she'd moistened her lips with her pink feminine tongue, he'd had an overwhelming urge to kiss her and not in a *hey there, good buddy,* kind of way.

Now, he was having a hard time meeting her gaze.

It wasn't the first time he'd had an impulse to kiss her. But years ago, Ranger had chosen the high road with Ember. He'd done the honorable thing, the noble thing, and sacrificed his desires for the sake of their friendship. He might be a gambler at cards, but when it came to the possibility of losing Ember's friendship, he was as cautious as an actuary.

Whenever unwanted desires arose, he'd always managed to stuff them away — mainly by focusing on what he loved best, astronomy — but since he'd been back home, Ranger found himself drawn to Ember so strongly that he didn't know if he could keep resisting.

That new knowledge scared him more than he cared to admit.

So when Fiona batted her eyes at him, Ranger thought, *what the hell, why not,* and just went with it. If Ember thought Fiona was a good choice for him, he should give her a chance.

"We missed you," Fiona said.

"Because you couldn't wait to beat the pants off me again?" he teased, doffing his Stetson and setting it on the table.

"Strip poker!" Fiona said gleefully. "Now there's an idea."

"No one is taking their clothes off!" Ember snapped as if it had been a serious suggestion.

Ranger shot Ember a sidelong glance. What was going on here? Was she *jealous* of Fiona? That thought intrigued and delighted him.

Ember tacked up a quick smile and rushed to make amends. "This is a business meeting, after all . . . well, of sorts."

Nah. He had to be imagining things. Why would Ember be jealous? She was the one throwing Fiona at him. Then again, she had backpedaled on Fiona out there in the alley.

He tilted his head, eyed Ember, who was shuffling the cards and purposefully avoiding looking at him. Hmm. Yeah? Maybe?

"Or we could forget the game entirely and go for ice cream," Ranger suggested to Fiona.

"I'm game." Fiona reached for her purse.

"Really?" Ranger said, watching Ember.

"Oh absolutely," Fiona chirped.

"Dairy Queen closes at ten during the week," Ember said, her gaze firmly fixed on the cards she was expertly shuffling.

"I've got Blue Bell in my freezer." Fiona

was giving those false eyelashes a real work-out.

"You don't say?" Ranger drawled, toying with the label on his empty beer bottle.

"Is it Rocky Road?" Ember asked. "Because Rocky Road is his favorite."

"No," Fiona said. "It's plain vanilla."

"You know," Ranger said, never taking his eyes off Ember, noticed goose bumps popped up her arms and it was not cool in the bar. "Sometimes a guy likes his roads nice and smooth. No rocky nuts. No sticky marshmallow. Plain vanilla sounds mighty good."

"Since when?" Ember snorted.

"I've been down under for a year." Ranger grinned, loving that he was getting Ember's goat. "A lot of things have changed."

"Ahem," Luke said. "Tell us about the stars, Ranger. Convince me why the observatory deserves my endowment."

"Yes." Fiona sighed dreamily and peeked at the cards Ember had dealt, ice cream apparently forgotten. "Tell us about the stars. I'd love to hear all about it."

As much fun as he was having needling Ember, the pull of his favorite topic took over and Ranger found himself waxing about the wonders of outer space.

"Wow," Andre said. "Luke, you should

give Ranger the money. Everyone will donate to kids, but not as many will invest in something as intangible as space research, and he's making it sound so important for the future of our species."

"Andre is right," Ember told Luke. "I know at least two dozen people who'd be willing to donate either time or money to Andre's summer camp. I can get on the phone tomorrow morning and round up donations for him."

"Notice how hard she's working it for Ranger?" Spencer pointed out. "Ranger, I hope you appreciate what a gem you have in Ember."

No news flash there. Ranger studied his best friend; hell, he'd known she was special since he was eight years old and stuck in bed with rheumatic fever. She was the only one who'd consistently dropped by his sick room every day after school, loaded with stories of her adventures on the playground. She'd been his window to the world.

In all honesty, wasn't she still?

They kept playing. Spencer dropped out at eleven p.m., quickly followed by Angi and Andre until it was just Luke, Ranger, Ember, and Fiona at the table. This time, Ranger did not underestimate Fiona. He'd quickly learned her tells and bidding strategies and he was winning.

Marginally.

"Where did you learn to play poker?" he asked Fiona.

"My daddy was a degenerate gambler," she said in a tone so cheerful it was unsettling. "It's why I work for the church. Don't get me wrong, I love my daddy, but what he put our family through . . . let's just say it made me want to walk closer to the Lord."

Ranger had a wild urge to say, "Amen." He met Ember's eyes and could tell she had the same urge too. They burst out laughing.

"What?" Fiona asked, her eyes widening and her perky smile losing some of its starch. "What's so funny?"

"Ranger," Ember said at the same time Ranger said, "Ember."

"Don't pay them any mind," Luke soothed. "Those two can communicate with just a glance. They're like twins with their own secret language or something."

Fiona yawned, covered her mouth. "This is way past my bedtime. I get up at five-thirty every morning to pray and read the Bible before work. Rain check on the ice cream, Ranger?"

"Rain check," he agreed easily.

"Could you give me a ride home?" Fiona asked Ember.

"Sure, sure." Ember grabbed her purse, and ruffled Ranger's hair as she went past him.

"I had a very nice time," Fiona called to Luke.

"You can join Monday night poker anytime." Luke stood up and bowed gallantly.

"I don't think I'll become a regular. I don't want to end up like my daddy. In the poorhouse and sorry for everything on his deathbed. Good thing Mama divorced him before he could blow through all my inheritance." Fiona wriggled her fingers. "Good night."

Ember and Fiona left, and Luke sank back down into his chair, a Wile E. Coyote grin eating up his face. "And then there was one."

Ranger had a feeling the entire night had been orchestrated for this moment. "What's going on here, Nielson? Has this card game just been a setup?"

"Setup?" Luke said it so innocently, Ranger knew it was true.

"Cards on the table," Ranger said. "No more pussyfootin' around. What's the story?"

Luke splayed both his palms against the table. "Straight up?"

"Straight up."

"Ember already had donors lined up for the other causes. I'd planned to give you the endowment all along."

"Ember was in on this?"

Luke shrugged. "The whole thing was her idea."

He should have known. Ember thought she knew what was best for everyone. "And Fiona's card playing?"

"Fiona was a curveball. Neither Ember nor I saw those four threes coming."

"Why the subterfuge?"

Luke rubbed his chin, considered Ranger with a speculative stare. "There is a stipulation I didn't think you'd agree to unless you knew that other people were vying for the endowment."

An uneasy feeling crawled across his skin. He needed this money if he wanted the permanent position at the observatory, and he needed it fast. Luke was his only reasonable chance of achieving his goal. "What stipulation?"

"Just in case you didn't know, I'm producing a film about the Trans-Pecos and the founding fathers of Cupid."

"Huh?" He might have heard someone mention it at the christening, but he hadn't been paying much attention since it seemed galaxies away from affecting him. "What made you decide to go into the movie business?"

"I'm not in the movie business, I'm in the promoting tourism to our hometown business."

"What does Melody think about this?" Ranger said, referring to Luke's wife, who had a background in advertising and had once worked on Madison Avenue.

"She's the driving force behind the whole thing. Much as Ember is the driving force behind you."

"What's all this got to do with me?"

"For starters, more tourists to the Trans-Pecos means more tourists at the observatory. I'll make sure Wes understands how crucial your involvement is in my decision to donate money. Adds a feather in your cap."

"I wear a Stetson," Ranger teased.

"Cap. Hat." Luke's shrug was mayoral, a man accustomed to navigating obstacles with aplomb. "Same difference."

"It's a feather in *your* cap, Luke."

"Finish hearing me out, would you?"

Yeah, about that. Ranger wasn't sure he *wanted* to hear him out. "Just tell me what hoops I have to jump through to get the money."

"The role of Edward Fitzgerald Beale —"

Aww crap. Ranger knew where this was headed. "You want me to play him?"

"Yes."

"Why?"

"For one thing, you look a bit like Beale. For another thing, you're the only one around here besides Zeke Tremont who knows anything about camels. And we've got a lot of camels that need wrangling."

When Ranger was a freshman at Sul Ross, his father had decided he was going to raise exotic animals, including camels. That had been a short-lived endeavor, but it had given Ranger a year's worth of experience as a camel wrangler.

"Why not tap Zeke?" he asked.

"We did. He said he won't play Beale, but he'll help out with the camels."

"Why are you working with real camels and not some computer-generated magic?"

"We're going for authenticity."

"Lord love a dromedary, Luke. Camels? You're serious?"

"Hey, camels are part of the rich history of the Trans-Pecos, and they're essential to the founding of Cupid. Camels *have* to be in the film."

"You've lost your mind, you know that."

"Possibly, but we're making the film anyway. The camels arrive next week."

"Rhett knows as much about camels as I do, and he's better looking than I am," Ranger said, feeling the walls closing in. "Ask him."

"He's got the rodeo circuit. Besides, he's Rhett. Not the most reliable person in the West."

Yes, there was that; unless it had something to do with the rodeo, Rhett could be pretty flakey.

"This has disaster written all over it," Ranger mumbled.

"That's what Edward Beale said and yet, he did it anyway."

"Because he was ordered to do it by his commanding officer."

"Consider me your commanding officer. I have two million dollars dangling over your head."

"I can't act," Ranger protested.

"You played the lead in *Our Town* in high school."

"I was shanghaied into that role, and I hated every minute of it. Hire a real actor."

"We can't afford one. This is a volunteer project. Consider yourself shanghaied again."

"Spend the endowment money for the actor."

"I can't. It's got strings."

"Clearly for everyone involved. Twist Ember's arm to scare up the money to hire a real actor. She's wicked clever at finding money."

"Bottom line, Lockhart, this project means a lot to me and the town council. You want the endowment money, just remember either Angi, Andre, or Spence would be happy to accept it instead."

Ranger glowered. Luke had him sewed up. *You know,* whispered the voice in the back of his head, *you do have the job offer in New Zealand.*

Yes, but that was a last-ditch option. While he loved New Zealand, his home was here in Cupid. His house. His family . . .

Ember.

Ranger sighed. "Who is the director on this wacko project?"

"You were just sitting at the table with her."

"Fiona?"

"No. Fiona isn't commanding enough to be a director."

"Angi?"

Luke grunted and sent him a look that said, *boy are you dumb.* "Ember."

What? Ember hadn't said a word to him about directing a film. Why not? Then he remembered he'd had his head stuck in the stars the past month putting the finishing touches on his paper about fast radio bursts emissions of extragalactic origins.

"Ember's the one who wanted you for the role of Edward Beale. Me, I don't really care who does it as long as the movie gets made on time and under budget."

Ember was behind all this? He should have known.

On the one hand, he was miffed. But on the other, if he had to play the part to get the endowment money, he couldn't think of anyone he'd rather do it with than his best friend.

"You want the endowment, you play Beale. Will you do it?"

"Doesn't look like you've given me much of a choice. When does filming start?"

"Next Tuesday."

"All right." Ranger plunked his Stetson on his head, pushed back his chair with a loud scrape against the concrete floor, got to his feet.

"Where are you going?" Luke called as Ranger headed for the door.

"To pick a bone with my best friend."

"I can't thank you enough," Fiona said as Ember pulled into the driveway of Fiona's little rented bungalow. Ember knew exactly how she'd list it for sale. *Cozy, much loved Cape Cod situated in a desert oasis. Great garden room with full sunlight for artists.*

"For what?"

"If you hadn't let me borrow your red dress and given me a makeover, Ranger wouldn't have paid me one bit of attention."

"It wasn't the clothes or the makeover," Ember said, feeling weirdly sulky and having no clue why. "It was your mad poker skills."

"Really?" Fiona pressed a hand to her chest, but kept sitting in the passenger seat even as Ember mentally willed her to get out. "You think so?"

"Only two things impress Ranger Lockhart. The outer space and poker."

"Three things," Fiona corrected.

Ember crinkled her nose. For the life of her she couldn't think of anything that commanded his attention like the sun and the moon and the stars, other than poker. "What's the third?"

"You."

Ember could have modestly exclaimed, *who, me?* But she wasn't built that way. She knew that she and Ranger shared a special bond. Had known it since her earliest memory at three when she'd gotten swatted on the fanny by her mother for tracking

157

mud over the pristine white, freshly cleaned floor of the Lockhart mansion after she'd told them twice to stay out of the mud puddle.

Ranger had gotten so mad about that swat, he'd stood defiant with his little hands clenched into fists, his face turning red, and declared, "Don't spank Emba, spank *me*!"

Struggling not to laugh, Mom popped him one light swat on the seat of his pants, mainly because she didn't want him to feel excluded, not even from punishment. Bridgette had a soft spot in her heart for Ranger because he'd been so small and studious, and his biological mother had run out on him.

Bridgette felt that tenderness for his brother Ridge too, but Ridge hadn't let her get close the way Ranger had. Ridge's defenses had already been set in stone by the time he'd come to live at the Silver Feather.

"So you think I have a chance with Ranger?" Fiona asked, snapping Ember back to the present.

"Keep playing poker the way you do, and he'll stay interested," she heard herself say when she wanted to say the exact opposite. Ack!

Fiona shook her head and pulled her bottom lip up between her teeth, her face turning grim. "He's already caught onto my game play. I won't beat him again."

"Don't get defeated. Keep him on his toes. Change things up."

"I don't really like poker, even though I'm good at it. It reminds me too much of the way my daddy wrecked his life."

More than anything in the world, Ember wanted Ranger to be happy, and if Fiona could provide that happiness, Ember would see that they ended up together, even if it felt like a knife was stuck all the way through the fleshy part of her heart.

"Hang in there," Ember encouraged her past the lump in her throat. "It takes Ranger a while to warm up to new ideas. If you want him, I'll help you get him. Just make sure he's what you truly want."

And you, Ember, what do you truly want?

She pushed that thought aside. Her needs didn't matter. All that mattered was Ranger's success. He was the one with the brain to change the world.

CHAPTER 8

"It's such a happiness when good people get together."

— Jane Austen, *Emma*

Ember had no more gotten settled into her house in Marfa than a hard knock sounded at her door, and she knew without looking who was standing on her porch. She'd recognize that particular brand of *rap-tap-tap* anywhere.

Before she answered, she made a detour to the fridge and took out two beers. Ranger would need appeasing since he must have found out she'd been in cahoots with Luke to con him into playing Edward Beale.

She opened the door on the third knock, passed him the beer without even saying hello, and led the way into the living room.

Ranger grunted and followed her.

"Have a seat." She plunked down on the sofa and slung her socked feet onto the old trunk that doubled as an ottoman. Samantha sauntered over and hopped into Ember's lap.

Ranger loomed for a moment, looking like the Big Bad Wolf, but he didn't intimidate her. She knew everything there was to know about him, and he knew the same about her. They had no secrets between them.

She patted the cushion next to her and he sank down, his weight a comforting anchor. Samantha immediately traveled over to him. He scratched her ears. So much for the Big Bad Wolf.

"Tell me all your troubles, Professor," she coaxed, and took a sip of beer.

"You mean besides you?" His tone was as dry and barbed as the Chihuahuan Desert. "You know what? I was gone for a whole year and never once got mixed up in anything like your crazy schemes."

"Oh you mean the schemes that push you out of your comfort zone because you'd never willingly take that step yourself. You mean the —"

She stopped talking because Ranger had that look in his eyes. The look that warned her not to push him. He might be easygoing ninety percent of the time, but when he dug in his heels, he plowed them deep and there was no moving him.

Ember winked, trying to soften him up. "Bet you missed the old pebble in your boot while you were whooping it up in Australia, huh?"

"I was in New Zealand."

"Same difference."

"No, it's not. They're distinctly different countries."

"Whatever. They're both very far away from here." And her.

"You've never been a pebble in my boot." His tone softened along with his eyes. "But challenging? Woman, I'd forgotten exactly how much of a handful you could be."

Handful.

Trey had slung that word at her on many occasions, but always with a sharp sting in his voice. In Ranger's voice, the word was a feather stroke, light and ticklish. Playful.

She'd often wished she wasn't so hard to manage. It certainly would have made life easier, but she didn't know how to be anything other than what she was. She could pretend of course, had done so during her marriage. But sooner or later, the real Ember always popped out, and that's when things fell apart.

Hence, the reason why she'd decided to take herself off the market as far as marriage went, forget all about love, and make matches for others. She didn't want to be the cause of anyone having full hands.

"Luke offered you the endowment?" she asked.

"Don't be coy. It doesn't suit you."

"I didn't know for *sure* he was going to offer it to you."

"Woman, please. You had donors lined up for everyone else at that meeting."

Ember couldn't suppress her smile. She had. There was some benefit to knowing most everyone in the Trans-Pecos.

"But there's one question that's plaguing me about all this." He paused and drilled her with his stare.

"What's that?"

"Why didn't you have a benefactor lined up for *me*?"

"Their causes were easier to fund . . ."

"And?"

"Luke wanted you to play Beale. The film is important to him since his great-granddaddy was in the Camel Corps, and —"

"Ember," he chided.

He knew her too well. "All right, *I* wanted you to play Edward Beale. I wanted to direct you."

"Why?"

"You were so great in *Our Town.*"

163

His right eyelid twitched in bewilderment, or maybe it was stress. "No, why did you want *me* to play Beale? You know how I hated acting in *Our Town.*"

Why? After a year away, she wanted to be near him from eight to five, Monday through Friday. But there was no way she was going to tell him that. "You're distantly related to Beale."

"No, I'm not."

"Yes, you are. That's why you look a bit like him."

"Get out of here. For real?"

"When Kaia was pregnant with Ingrid, part of her nesting instinct included doing genealogy and spending an epic amount of time on Ancestry.com. Beale is your third cousin once removed or something." Ember flapped a hand. "Kaia knows for sure."

"On my father's side?"

"If it was on Ridge's mom's side, you wouldn't be related. Think about it, man."

"If you wanted me to play the role that badly, you could have just asked."

"And what would be the fun in that? Besides, you would have said no."

"I might not have."

"You would have."

"You think you know me so well."

"That's because I do."

"Yeah." He took a pull of his beer, propped his booted feet on the ottoman beside hers. "You're right. I would have refused."

"Are you mad at me?" She jostled his foot with hers.

"A little, but I'll get over it."

"That's what I told Luke. You don't nurse grudges."

He reached over to chuck her under the chin. "I can never refuse you anything, Sparky."

"I told Luke that too."

"Pretty damn sure of yourself."

She couldn't help grinning. "Pretty damn sure of *you.*"

"Am I that predictable?"

"Geese migrating south for the winter aren't as predictable as you."

"Luke must think I'm your puppet."

"No more than I'm yours. I'd fly to the moon and back if you needed me."

"Truth." He conceded and raised his beer bottle. "Best friends?"

"Forever and always." She bumped her beer bottle to his in a satisfying *clink.*

They drank simultaneously and fell into a comfortable silence, sitting with their feet touching.

Several minutes later, Ranger asked, "How

did you get lassoed into the directing gig in the first place?"

"I wasn't lassoed. I thought it would be fun. I had a blast making that real estate commercial last year."

"You made a commercial?"

"I sent you the link."

Ranger pulled a palm down his face. "I forgot to look at it."

Ember shrugged. She didn't take it personally. She knew how Ranger could get lost in his work. That's just who he was. The proverbial absentminded professor. She found it adorable . . . most of the time.

"I feel like a dick. I should have watched your commercial."

"Seriously, do not give it a second thought. I don't."

After a lapse in companionable silence, Ranger said, "I have one condition to playing Edward Beale."

"Oh?" Ember kept her voice mild. Ranger wasn't one to make demands, and as such, when he had a request, he expected it to be carried out.

"If I'm going to do this damned film, I want you to play Mary Beale."

"I can't —"

"I know you're the director, but there are a lot of directors who act in the films they're

166

directing. Robert Redford, Clint Eastwood
—"

"How flattering to be mentioned in the same breath as such movie icons."

"Is it working?"

"No."

"Why not?"

"I already cast the role."

"Uncast it." In that declarative statement, she heard the strong leader in him, the one who would make a decisive director when he landed the department head job at the observatory. It would be a crying shame if Wes and the board of directors didn't hire Ranger. He deserved the position, and the observatory deserved someone like him at the helm.

Solidified in her aim, she said, "Sorry, no can do. The actress is very excited to play Mary Beale."

Ranger studied her with narrowed eyes. "Ember . . . whom did you cast?"

"Fiona."

He pursed his lips but did not seem put off. In fact, he smiled a little, which should have made her happy, but it did not. "Does Fiona have any acting creds?" he asked.

"More than you." She listed off Fiona's theater experience.

"Touché. Maybe you should get someone

else to play Beale."

"What about the endowment money?"

"Rats."

"You'll be fine. You did play the lead in *Our Town*."

"Yeah because I was trying to impress the science teacher who wouldn't let me into the summer intern program until I did something to prove I was well rounded."

"I see a theme emerging around you, Ranger Lockhart. You stick your head in the stars, people force you back to Earth, you stick your head in the stars, people —"

"This movie is going to suck so bad."

"It's not like it's a Hollywood production. It's basically just a long Chamber of Commerce tourism commercial. It'll be cute. Adorable. Forty years from now they'll still be playing it, and we'll watch it again and say, aww, look how young we were."

"Why do I feel like I've been sewn into a straitjacket?" Ranger mumbled.

Ember splayed a palm over her chest, pantomiming pledging allegiance to a flag. "Because you had a dream."

"I wished upon a star."

She'd so missed their bantering. "Be careful what you wish for, Professor. Dreams come with strings."

"A yarn store doesn't have this many

strings." He gulped his beer. "Going back to New Zealand seems easier. That job they offered is a sure thing, and they don't expect me to become a fund-raiser to keep it."

"You wouldn't really do that, would you?" she asked, trying to keep the alarm out of her voice. Ranger didn't need to know how much his moving back to New Zealand would kill her soul. The past year had been wretched enough without him.

"Are we being serious here?"

"As a heart attack."

Ranger leaned his head back on the couch, let loose a demoralized sigh. Which wasn't like him. Not at all. He was normally the opposite of demoralized. "If I don't get this position, what else can I do? It's not like jobs for double PhDs are falling from the sky."

"Overqualified. The bane of brilliant minds everywhere. You could just stay at the Silver Feather and be a gentleman rancher."

"The Silver Feather is Ridge's baby. Duke made that clear enough. Besides, I'd be bored out of my skull within a week. Ranching is monotonous as hell."

"A week? C'mon. You wouldn't make it two days."

"You see my dilemma."

169

"Suck it up, Lockhart. There are worse things than playing Edward Beale."

"It's not that. It's the whole fund-raiser thing."

"And now we're back to why you need a wife."

"Using a wife to further my career does not sit right with me."

"You're looking at this the wrong way. Marriage is a partnership. You do things for each other."

"The way you and Trey did?"

"Low blow."

"You're right. I'm sorry."

"Most men your age are married with families. It's normal."

"I'm not most men."

"For sure." It was one of the things she liked about Ranger. How he didn't fit inside any particular box, not even the genius nerd box. Yes, he was whip smart and lived inside his head, but he was also an earthy cowboy and a fiery poker player, and underneath it all, he had this gentle caring side honed by his own childhood misfortunes. He truly cared about people, even if he didn't always understand them.

She thought of all the times she'd seen his kindness in action — when he donated bone marrow to a local child with leukemia, the ten years he served in the Cupid volunteer fire department, the destitute family he let live in his guesthouse for free until they could get back on their feet. Altruism was a hallmark of his character. He hardly cared about money at all, which was why he was having trouble with the whole concept of fund-raising.

Ember figured this easy-come, easy-go attitude toward money stemmed from when he discovered that his mother, Sabrina, had accepted two million dollars from his father to walk away from the marriage and sign over her parental rights.

He'd come running to Ember one Christmas morning when they were eight, filled with percussive grief and betrayal. He'd opened a present from his mother to find a deck of playing cards and a Hoyle book on how to play poker, and a handwritten note telling him she was so sorry she couldn't be with him.

It was the first present he'd ever gotten from his mother, and initially he'd been ecstatic, but something about the letter niggled at him. The handwriting looked awfully familiar. He'd compared it to refrigerator notes written by his stepmother, Lucy. The "d" in Dear, looked an awful lot like the "d" in Dates on Lucy's grocery shopping list, and he'd confronted her with the evidence.

Kindhearted Lucy had only been trying to make Ranger feel better for lack of contact with his mother, and she hadn't expected the sharp kid to put two and two together. She'd admitted to writing the note and buying the presents, but when he'd asked her why she'd done it, Lucy had told him to ask his father.

Blunt Duke had popped out with the truth. "Yeah, your real mother left you and signed away all her parental rights for two million bucks. So what?"

That's when Ranger had come running to Ember.

Studying him now, his long legs stretched between the sofa and ottoman, his eyelids half-closed, his ruggedly handsome features softened in the dim light, Ember's heart melted like butter on a hot biscuit.

"Spend the night," she invited. "It's late and you've had beer."

"Throw me a blanket and pillow, and I'll stretch out right here on the couch."

"I've got a king-sized bed, Lockhart." It was the bedroom suite she'd inherited in the divorce; she'd gotten a new mattress, of course. "No need for the couch. Besides, that's where Samantha likes to sleep."

It wasn't the first time they'd slept in the same bed. They'd done it dozens of times as kids, and once, there was that time he'd come to visit her when she was in college and they'd been out to a wild party and got so wasted they passed out in the same bed.

Although, she remembered waking up in bed with him stunned, hungover, and thinking crazily, *I slept with Ranger Lockhart!*

It was the first time she ever really imagined them as a couple, but immediately she'd erased those thoughts. They were absolute best friends, and she wasn't going to let anything under the hot Trans-Pecos sun ruin that.

A strange expression slipped over his face, one she didn't recognize, and Ember thought she'd seen every one of Ranger's expressions there was to see.

"I'll be fine right here, Sparky. I don't mind sharing space with Samantha." His voice was low and suddenly weary, as if he'd trudged a hard mile straight up one of the Davis Mountains' peaks. He yawned and kicked off his boots, stretched out on the couch.

Her pulse pounded, skipping beats for no discernable reason. Ember went to the linen closet, found a blanket and spare pillow and brought them back to him. He'd taken off his belt and draped it over the coffee table and was sitting up.

She tossed the blanket and pillow to him from halfway across the room, wondering why she was wary about coming closer. Weird. Things had been slightly off balance between them since he'd come home, like a picture frame tilted on the wall after a minor earth tremor.

He smiled at her, that loopy, dopey smile that said he adored her as always. Nothing had changed. He looked content. Okay, maybe the picture frame hadn't tilted for him when he'd seen her again. Maybe it had only been that way for Ember.

When Ranger smiled the way he was smiling at her now, his eyes charged up like stars, twinkling and sparkling, enigmatic and unknowable. Distant, and unobtainable, but madly irresistible. She'd seen that smile bring grown women to their knees.

Ember thought she was immune to the effects of that particular brand of smile. But clearly she was not. Her knees were overcooked noodles, limp and soft. He had such interesting lips. Angular upper lip with well-defined peaks, and a full bottom lip that promised pillowy kisses.

Holy closing costs, why was she thinking about his lips? And how kissable they might be? She realized belatedly that she was staring, and blinked.

"Night," Ember chirped like some kind of small flightless bird. Which was not her. Not at all. If Ember had been a bird, she would be an eagle, fiery and free and fierce, unbound by rules and conventions.

And if Ranger were a bird, what would he be?

She cocked her head, contemplating as he switched off the lamp and settled into the cushions. An owl, she decided. One of the most intelligent birds in the animal kingdom. Wise and inquisitive. Shrouded in mystery, myth, and lore.

"You gonna stand there all night, Sparky?"

"No," she croaked, a bullfrog now, raspy and slow.

"G'night."

"G'night," she echoed. She scurried to her bed and didn't fall asleep until far into the wee hours of the morning, her turbulent mind burning with new and disturbing thoughts about her best friend.

One thing was certain, she had to get him fixed up with a partner and fast before she crossed a line that could not be uncrossed.

Ranger lay on the couch, as wide awake as Ember. His thoughts scattered, windblown.

Ember. Had she gotten prettier since he'd been in New Zealand, or was it his imagination?

Fiona. Was she a possible mate? She was attractive enough and unassuming, and hot dang she was a great poker player. *Ember.* He really should be mad that she'd finagled him into playing Edward Beale, and with camels? But hey, as with anything involving Ember, it wouldn't be boring.

He shifted on the couch, trying to get comfortable, heard a noise coming from Ember's bedroom. Smelled her intoxicating cinnamon-and-anise scent on the pillow. Imagined her in bed, sleeping in one of the oversized T-shirts she loved to wear instead of proper pajamas. Ranger smiled in the darkness. There was nothing proper about Ember. It was one of the things he loved most about his best friend. Her impropriety.

His imagination bloomed as he pictured her curled up in the bed, knees drawn to her chest, and he felt himself grow hard.

Think of something else, quick!

Andromeda, Aquila, Auriga, Boötes . . . okay, not Boötes . . . Boötes made him think of booty, which made him think of Ember's well-rounded booty and . . .

Stop! Just stop. Go to sleep.

What was happening to him? Sure, he'd

176

been physically attracted to Ember over the years. She was gorgeous, who wouldn't be? But they were best friends. They'd grown up together. These feelings — which were so damned strong since he'd come back from New Zealand — were completely inappropriate. If they were meant to be anything more than friends, wouldn't it have happened by now?

And obviously, she wasn't attracted to him the same way he was attracted to her. Why else was she throwing Fiona at him? Somehow, Ember must have sensed the change in his feelings for her and she was flinging up roadblocks.

Fine. He got the message, and honestly, she was right. Changing the paradigm of their relationship at this stage of their life was futile. But she had invited him to spend the night in her bed. What was that all about? His pulse chugged. Had it been a real invitation?

Nah. No. Nope.

He couldn't go there. Not even for a second. Because if he let himself hope, he'd be in that bedroom in a nanosecond, and what if that was not what she wanted at all?

CHAPTER 9

"Business, you know, may bring money, but friendship hardly ever does."
— Jane Austen, *Emma*

"Get up." Ember woke him the next morning. "We're going sailing."

"What? Huh?" He blinked at her, confused for a moment because he'd been dreaming of fast radio bursts and messages from outer space. More often than not, the breakthroughs in his research came to him in dreams, and he felt as if he'd been on the verge of discovery.

Ranger tried to hang on to the wisp of dream fragments and piece them together in a neat whole. He kept a dream log beside his bed at home for that purpose, but he couldn't drag back the fractured images.

Not with Ember standing over him in that oversized *Book of Mormon* T-shirt with a hem that hit her midthigh and a mug of steaming coffee in her hand. She wasn't particularly tall, but the woman was all legs.

He squinted against the morning sunlight tumbling in through the windows, tried not to notice how sexy she looked with her bed-tousled hair and come-hither grin.

Had he heard her correctly? Had she said "sailing"? There was nowhere to sail within two hundred miles of their desert home.

"Sailing? What? Where? Why?"

"Yes, sailing. Why? Because you need to get your mind off work and your head out of the clouds."

What he needed was for her to put on some pants before he started having very un-best-friend-like thoughts.

"You worry too much," she went on. "Time to get your body moving."

The way she said "body" wasn't the tiniest bit suggestive, but damn if it didn't have that effect on Ranger. His body tightened in all the wrong — or right, depending on how you looked at it — places.

"What makes you say that?"

"Well, you're always in your head, so there's that, but all night you were talking in your sleep about biosignatures and extremophiles and pyrolysis."

"How do you know?"

"I was going to the bathroom, and I heard

you mumbling and I came in here to check on you and stayed to take notes."

"Really? Do you have notes?"

She snorted. "As if! I have no idea what all that science-y gobbledygook means. But you were way into it. Thrashing around and smacking your pillow. Clearly, you've been under a lot of stress." She snapped her fingers. "So we're going sailing."

"Since when do you know how to sail?"

"I learn new tricks all the time, Professor. Keep up. You gotta start reading my texts more closely."

Ranger yawned and scratched his bare chest. "Where are we going to find a body of water to sail in?"

"Land sailing," she said.

"What's that?"

"Drink your coffee, get dressed, and you'll find out." She thrust the coffee mug at him, turned, and walked off, her fanny bouncing to the jaunty rhythm of her crisp steps.

An hour and a half later, they were at the entrance to the salt flats made from a shallow lake in the high desert that had dried up in the Pleistocene Epoch, strapped side by side in what resembled a kayak with three wheels and a wind sail.

"Helmets," Ember reminded him, and donned a pink helmet with a big white hibiscus flower on the side of it. "Oh, and sunscreen. Did you put on sunscreen?" She waggled a bottle of sunscreen at him, and she plied her skin with creamy liquid. "I'll share."

He could smell the coconut scent from where he sat in his rig just a few feet away from her. He wore a helmet with a visor, and he had a good suntan. There was a cool breeze this high up, and the sky was partly overcast. He'd be okay. To keep her from nagging, he said, "Once I get this helmet on."

"Don't forget." She put the sunscreen in his front pocket.

"Radios," said the land sail rental operator, and passed them walkie-talkies. Cell phones were useless this high in the desert unless you had a satellite phone. "Just in case."

"You sure this is safe?" Ranger asked Ember. "I've heard stories about people getting stranded out on the salt flats and dying of dehydration."

"One," Ember said, "I packed a gallon of water and a quart of Gatorade." She gestured to the picnic basket tucked into the back of what the land sail guy called the turbo pod. "And two, if there wasn't a bit of danger, it wouldn't be so thrilling, now, would it?"

She smiled as if she'd actually welcome getting stranded in the desert and having to find her way out. That was Ember, always up for a challenge.

"Maybe we should have a rain check," Ranger said, unnerved at the thought of breaking down in the salt flats. He'd gotten lost on the ranch once when he was thirteen, and had to spend the night alone in the desert listening to the coyotes all around him yip and howl. He'd been running away from home after a blowup with his father, and his horse had thrown him. Ember, of course, had been the one to find him the next morning, bloodied and bruised from his fall.

"No way," Ember said. "You're doing this. Wanna know why?"

"Why?" He couldn't resist asking.

"Because every time you take a risk and you come out on the other side, you feel stronger and more alive." She closed her eyes briefly, smiled as if she'd found nirvana and breathed. "What a rush."

"You're in good hands, dude," the operator said. "Em knows what she's doing." The guy winked at Ember and she winked back, and Ranger got this cold, lonesome feeling in the pit of his stomach like he had that long-ago night he'd gotten lost on the ranch.

"Have fun," the operator said, and went back to his wooden hut underneath a wide, colorful umbrella.

This time of the morning, on a weekday, they had the salt flats to themselves.

Ranger and Ember sat elbow to elbow, the sail's rigging stretched between them. For a moment, it was dead quiet. He liked these easy moments of belonging, when it felt like the two of them against the world. With Ember anything and everything seemed possible.

Ember did something with her hands on the rigging, raising the sail. The wind caught it and immediately, they were scooting along across the flats.

"Oh shit," Ranger mumbled, and held on tight to the sides as the craft picked up speed. "How did I let you talk me into this?"

"Same way I talked you into hang gliding. 'Member that? You can't resist my charms."

Hang gliding as a present from her for his eighteenth birthday. How could he forget? He'd been terrified of heights, but he'd gone anyway because it was Ember. He'd felt pretty damn powerful once they were back on the ground and they'd survived. Bonus, he'd also beaten his fear of heights.

The land sail zoomed along on the flat,

crunchy ground. The wind whipped his shirt around his shoulders as they picked up speed. Forty miles per hour. Fifty. Sixty. Soon they were clipping along at ninety miles per. The ground was a blur beneath their fast-moving wheels.

"How you doin', Professor?" she called, guiding the vehicle so it cornered fast on two wheels as she swiftly changed directions.

"Do you have to do that?"

"I don't *have* to do it, but if I don't turn we'll end up in the middle of the desert. Too far from rescue if the wind gives out on us."

"In that case, carry on. I'll try not to barf."

Ember laughed. "God, but I've missed you."

"Missed torturing me you mean."

"Don't be such a grouse. You know deep down you love having me push you out of your comfort zone, and you wouldn't have it any other way."

Cards on the table? She was right. His life was far richer because of her. See. That's really why he didn't want to get married. How could he build a life without his best friend in it?

Her face was a wreath of joy. This was the real Ember, joyous and free, not shutdown and nervous the way she'd been when she was married to Trey. This was what he loved about her most. How she thrived on madcap adventures, how her bright laughter lit up his stodgy world. If he could find a woman who possessed Ember's sterling qualities, he'd marry her in a heartbeat. She did something to make them go even faster, wind fully expanding the sail. The quick acceleration took Ranger completely by surprise.

"Good God, woman, can't you ever do anything *normal.*" He was teasing her, joking about her wild and untamed nature, but the light instantly dimmed in her eyes and she quickly glanced away, her smile vanishing.

Uh-oh. What had he done? Ranger felt a pang in his chest, physical, as if someone had punched him squarely in the heart.

"Ember?" he asked. "What's wrong?"

"Nothing." She was staring straight ahead, not meeting his gaze.

"Don't lie to me. I know when something's bothering you."

She slid a sidelong glance his way and in a bit, her lips curled into a new smile. "I can't hide anything from you."

"Ditto."

"I'm sorry I'm not normal enough for you."

"I didn't mean it the way it came out. I was startled. I enjoy the fact that you're not like other women. Please forgive me."

She shrugged, grinned again. "No biggie."

Maybe not, but the easiness between them was gone, and Ranger couldn't help feeling he deserved a swift kick in the ass.

They soared along for several more minutes, and then Ember put slack in the sail, slowing down.

"We're stopping already?" he asked.

"We're almost back at the start."

"So soon?"

"You want to keep going?"

"Well, we did come all the way out here."

Ember's nimble fingers worked the rigging and the land sail did a one-eighty.

His stomach lurched with the motion, but he'd asked for it. A helpless grin took over his face when she cornered on two wheels again, spinning them around in a complete circle. Once, twice, three times.

"Show-off," he accused good-naturedly.

She beamed. A right happy bit of sunshine. "Fun, isn't it?"

"No," he lied.

"That's a shame because I'm doing it again on the other side." She shifted, and they spun another two-wheeled circle on the other side.

"What am I going to do with you?"

"Nothing," she said, whispered almost inaudibly, "everything."

She winked at him, saucy and daring. He loved that wink. He *dreamed* about that wink. He let it wash over him like rainbows after a storm, luxuriating in the feeling, knowing if he permanently moved away to the opposite side of the world and could no longer see that wink every day, he would be poorer because of it.

Ranger didn't think she was normal either. That was her takeaway from their land sailing adventure.

They'd been having such fun, and then he'd gone and said something like that. Ranger, the one guy who she thought accepted her unconditionally. She was too much for him too, just like she'd been too much for Trey.

Why had she insisted they go land sailing?

Honestly? She'd wanted one last adventure with him before she started seriously trying to find him a wife. There weren't many more days like this in their future.

That made her sad.

Shake it off. Life moved on. Things

changed. People changed. They would still be friends even after she found him a *normal* woman.

Okay, that sounded a lot like self-pity, and Ember had no patience for self-pity, not even her own.

She glanced over at Ranger as he took off his helmet and handed it to the tour operator and oh, dear God. "You're toast."

"What?" He looked up at her, blinked, frowned, and twisted his mouth sideways.

"Burnt to a crisp."

He touched a hand to his face, to a cheek torched fiery red. "Ouch."

"I gave you sunscreen."

"I know. I'm an idiot." Looking chagrined, he took the bottle of sunscreen from his pocket and passed it to her.

"Not an idiot. Just forgetful." She dug in her oversized tote bag. "Hang on, I've got aloe gel."

Chewing on a licorice stick, the tour operator watched them with mild interest. "That bag is big enough to hold a dead body."

Ember ignored that, found the aloe, and surged toward Ranger, who was looking pretty sheepish in his scarlet sunburn. "Stand still."

She leaned in closer, her breasts accidentally grazing his shoulder. Instantly, a zing of electricity passed from him to her. Shocked at the intensity of sensation, she sucked in a deep breath, stepped back a few inches and tried to act like nothing had happened. But his masculine scent had gotten tangled up in her nose and she felt mildly dizzy.

"What are you doing?" Ranger asked, his voice coming out in gravelly clots.

"Um . . . um . . ." she said, not really sure how to respond. Her mind was still whirling from their unintentional contact. Her entire body tingling.

"She's trying to keep you from turning into a lobster, brother." The tour operator bit a chunk off his licorice stick. Chewed vigorously. Swallowed. "I'd do what she says."

"I'm not a kid," Ranger growled, and scowled at Ember. "Stop treating me as if I was one."

"Uh-huh," Ember murmured, dabbing his hot cheeks with aloe. The zinging tingle that had lit up her breasts when she brushed his shoulders now danced and pulsated in her fingertips.

"Quit rubbing on me."

"Stop grouching at her," the tour operator said.

"Shut it," Ranger told the guy.

"Just a second more." Ember massaged his chin, prickly with a day's growth of thick, dark beard, in a circular motion.

He reached out to manacle her wrist, stopping her in mid-daub. "Ember!" His tone was sharp, commanding. "Dammit woman, give me the gel. I can put it on myself."

There was something in the way he said "woman," all manly and in charge that sent her heart fluttering.

Jolted by his gruffness, she dropped the gel in his upstretched palm, her stomach whirling and diving, took another big step back. Felt sand shift over the side of her sneakers and into her half sock. Dropped her gaze. Saw Ranger had a partial erection.

Had she caused that?

Ranger smeared his face with a handful of gel and didn't meet her gaze, a guilty expression darkening his eyes.

Her best friend had gotten a boner over her touching him. Ember gulped. It was a lot to process.

"Babe," said the tour operator. "Don't bother with that guy. You can rub me with gel anytime."

"Shut it," Ranger and Ember hollered at him in unison.

"Well," said the tour operator, clearly

miffed. "If y'all are gonna be like that, I'm not offering you one of my licorice sticks like I was gonna."

"Thank God for that," Ranger said to him. To Ember he said, "Wanna get the hell out of here?"

"We need to talk about what happened back there," Ember said, driving her Infinity back to Cupid.

"Let's not."

"Denial is —"

"Nothing happened," he said, lacing his voice with steel. A voice that told her to drop the topic like a hot potato.

But Ember was notorious for ignoring commands. "You got a bo—"

"Ember," he warned. "Do not say anything more."

She clamped her lips together, a pulse at her temple throbbing visibly. "But —"

"Shh."

"I —"

"Hush."

"Did —"

"Don't even."

"Ranger, we —"

"Drop it," he snarled, and then added, "please."

"You have nothing to be ashamed of," she

191

forged ahead.

"I'm not ashamed."

"But you don't even want to talk about it."

Ranger groaned. "Look," he said. "Don't take it personally. I haven't had sex since Tonya. It doesn't mean anything." That wasn't true, but the last thing he wanted was to alienate her.

She pursed her lips, slipped a quick glance over at him. "I didn't think it did. Trust me. I get it. Long dry spell here too."

Whew. That was good. He guessed.

She was quiet for a moment, then added, "I was flattered."

Ranger smacked his forehead with the heel of his palm.

"What?" she said, sounding totally innocent, as if she had no idea how much she turned him on.

Maybe she didn't.

"We're best friends. We should be able to talk about this. We should be able to talk about anything."

Like the fact he wanted to ask her to pull over onto the shoulder of the road so he could take her in the back seat of her car, right here, right now. Yeah, that would go over like a lead balloon. He wasn't about to risk losing their friendship just because he'd gotten a boner when she'd put lotion on his face. Being in the friend zone was better than no zone.

"Ember," he said.

"Yes?" She turned her head, her blue eyes open and warm.

"For all that is holy, let us never speak of this again."

For the first time in thirty-two years, Ember seriously considered what it might be like to have sex with Ranger.

Oh sure, she'd had fleeting thoughts over the years, but the second they cropped up she'd immediately dismissed them. And she'd been pretty good at stamping them out.

Until he'd returned.

Something was different. About him. Between them. She didn't know what that something was, but she certainly didn't know how to navigate the current of sexual tension that had been building between them since she'd thrown herself into his arms at Susan and Bryant's wedding.

Now he was in her head, and all she could think about was having wild, crazy sex with him in all kinds of exotic and erotic places.

The boner was a big deal.

It meant he wanted her.

At least on a physiological level. But psychologically? There were a lot of land mines. More than she could count. Too many to take a chance on with this new sexual chemistry surging between them. If they tried to take their relationship to another level and one of those land mines detonated . . . goodbye best friend.

She really had only one choice. Get him hooked up with an appropriate woman ASAP. He needed somewhere to channel his sexual energy and she needed . . .

Well, what did she need?

She wanted Ranger to be happy, but at her own expense?

What was she saying? That she wanted more than friendship from Ranger?

Ember glanced over at her best friend. He was cocked back against the passenger seat, Stetson pulled down over his face, hands folded over his flat belly, booted feet stretched out. Mismatched boots.

Again.

She smiled at his absentmindedness, a tender tug at her heart, and she mentally erased the sexy thoughts bubbling in the back of her brain. Her best friend might be the hottest thing since Texas toast, but did she dare cross that line and make him her lover?

Ember was a line crosser from way back, but when it came to maintaining her friendship with Ranger, she respected the fact that this new, multi-faceted chemical reaction was like a downed power line.

Alive with electricity and dangerous as hell.

195

CHAPTER 10

"One half of the world cannot understand the pleasures of the other."
— Jane Austen, *Emma*

A week had gone by since the boner incident, and things had gone back to normal between Ranger and Ember.

At least on the surface.

They did the things they usually did. Texted or called each other at least once a day, met for Sunday brunch at the Sunshine Diner. Volunteered at the adult literacy center on Tuesday night, helping people learn to read. Played pool and shot darts at Chantilly's afterward with Rhett and his date, and nobody bothered to learn her name because they knew she wouldn't last. They spent Memorial Day weekend together, a party at the Silver Feather, riding horses in the desert, hanging out at Ridge and Kaia's house on Monday for a barbecue and spent the afternoon alternating between swimming in the pool and cuddling their goddaughter.

But underneath, something significant had shifted, something that they did not talk about or fully acknowledge even to themselves. Their easy camaraderie evaporated, and in its place was an odd alertness, an on-guard tension that had not existed before.

Occasionally, Ember would glance up and catch Ranger studying her with a watchful eye. Whenever they touched, instead of the casual brushing of their hands or knees or feet, suddenly everything felt weighted, important. It was as if even the simplest contact held new and mysterious meaning. A hidden context, deep and wary.

Ember was unhappy in this new reality, but she didn't know what to do about it, so she pretended it wasn't happening.

Ignorance was bliss, right?

Filming on *The Cupid Camel Corps* started Tuesday following Memorial Day, and the first scenes were being shot at Fort Davis. On that morning, the sun shone intensely bright, but there was a solid breeze coming down from the mountain, cooling things off.

Unfortunately, the wind was also kicking

up sand eddies and swirling bits of desert debris.

Ranger stood on the front steps of one of the old barracks, looking too damn handsome in his military costume, an enigmatic smile on his face. She knew how much he liked wind. He claimed it cleared out stagnant energy. He was the kind of man who shut off the AC and opened the windows whenever weather allowed.

Bullhorn in hand, Ember was in her element, telling people what to do. She might not be the most lovable person in town, but when she spoke, folks listened.

"Everyone gather 'round," she commanded.

Immediately, the film crew and actors ringed her.

She liked being in charge. It made her feel useful. Needed. Important. And after Trey, her ego could use the boost. Which honestly, wasn't that why she'd agreed when Luke approached her about directing the film?

Quickly, she introduced herself to those who did not know her well, welcoming everyone to the set, thanking them for being part of the team and launching into the housekeeping details — her expectations, rules and regulations, human resource issues, etcetera . . .

Her assistant, Chriss Anne, stood at Ember's elbow taking notes on her tablet computer. Ember hadn't forgotten Chriss Anne's request to find her a man. She'd just been busy with other things.

There were sixteen male crewmembers. Ten under the age of thirty. Six of those unmarried. Included among those six were Palmer and Zeke. Either one might work for Chriss Anne. But which was the right man?

On the one hand, you had flash and flair. On the other, you had true-blue, dependable, steady, but let's face it, a bit boring.

Maybe it was neither. Maybe Chriss Anne's best fit was someone else entirely.

Ember thought of the board game Mystery Date that she'd played with her sisters when they were kids. Open the door and find out if you got the prom date or the Nerd or somewhere in between. She'd always secretly been thrilled to get the Nerd, while everyone else sighed for the prom date. Face it, she was attracted to smart guys.

So why had she ended up with a go-getter frat boy type like Trey? Okay, he had been handsome as sin and built like a linebacker. Was she really that shallow?

Once everyone understood what was expected, Ember settled into the director's chair — metaphorically speaking. She wasn't the kind of director to sit and point. She was on her feet. Peering over Palmer's shoulder.

Palmer smelled really nice, she noted, and hoped Chriss Anne liked aftershave with undertones of balsam.

As for herself, Ember preferred Ranger's scent. A warm woody aroma, slightly sweet and papery — expensive leather, worn cloth, a hint of furniture polish. He smelled like a library, bookish and brainy. A magical bouquet as intoxicating to a reader as great wine was to a connoisseur — a literary version of vintner terroir. A fragrance of excitement, adventure, discovery, and knowledge.

Fiona, being bookish herself, should love Ranger's natural cologne too.

Everything was on track. So why did she feel a pang in the center of her stomach at the image of Fiona and Ranger lounging and reading together on a Sunday afternoon?

To kick-start something between Chriss Anne and Palmer, she positioned her assistant close to where Palmer was filming. Ember skipped ahead in the script, jumping to the scene where Edward — Ranger — and his new bride, Mary — Fiona — had first arrived at Fort Davis and poor Mary was dismayed with the harsh conditions she found in the arid desert land.

Skipping ahead in the script was a strategic move. The opening scene was set in Pennsylvania where Edward first kissed Mary and asked for her hand in marriage. From a directorial standpoint, she wanted Ranger and Fiona to be comfortable with each other when the big kiss finally came. And from a matchmaking standpoint, she didn't want to rush Ranger and Fiona's romance and throw them right into a kiss scene.

After all, a good courtship was well paced.

If everything played out the way Ember intended, by the end of the day, when filming wrapped, Ranger would take Fiona out to dinner and Palmer would be well on his way to asking out Chriss Anne. Even if Ember had to manipulate things a bit to make it happen.

But by noon things were not going according to plan.

Fiona and Ranger had zero chemistry on screen. They recited their lines by rote. No emotion, no verve, no joie de vivre.

Ember filmed take after take, nudging, cajoling, encouraging. "You can do this. C'mon, Ranger, remember Edward loves this woman. And Fiona, Mary was crazy enough about Edward to follow him to this

201

dangerous barren land. Let us see how devoted you are to him."

Fiona cleared her throat and raised a timid hand.

"You don't have to raise your hand," Ember said. "If you have a question, just ask it."

"Okay." Fiona bobbed her head like a prim little bird, a wren or something equally small and adorable.

Really, Ember? This was the life mate she'd chosen for Ranger? Upon reflection, this pair up wasn't the best idea. Ranger needed someone with more grit and fire.

Ember pushed that thought aside. She'd done a lot of work making over Fiona, and Ranger had seemed amenable to dating her. Fiona just needed to overcome her insecurities. Ember could help with that.

Fiona could be a good match because as a wife, Ember convinced herself, Fiona wouldn't get in the way of Ranger's work. When he needed to dive deeply into his research, Fiona was the kind of woman who would be easy to tune out — undemanding, accommodating, easygoing.

But was this matchup fair to Fiona? Didn't she deserve someone who was crazy for her?

And shouldn't Ranger have a woman who

captured his attention in every way? A woman for whom he would happily put a book down or step away from a telescope?

No.

Ranger's career was his reason for living. He wasn't like most men, given to whims of passion and the tumult of romantic relationships. He was controlled, observant, objective — practically tantric in his ability to clear his mind and steer his focus.

Idly, she wondered if he brought that same single-mindedness to sex. If so, Fiona was in for some serious fireworks.

A ping of jealousy hit the center of her chest like a sharp stone thrown from a long distance. Not because she was jealous of Fiona, but rather because she had never had incredible sex. At least not with a partner.

It was another reason that going through life solo seemed to be her fate. Nothing wrong with that. She'd tried marriage. It simply wasn't for her. She'd had to mold herself too much to fit. Had lost her individuality and independence, and it had taken her well over a year to get it back.

Besides, she was almost thirty-three. If there was such a thing as a soul mate, shouldn't she have unearthed him by now?

They broke filming for lunch and Ember sidled up to Palmer. "Good camera work."

Palmer flushed with pride and readjusted his collar. "Thanks."

"Could you spare a few moments to go over the filming schedule with my assistant, Chriss Anne, before we start again? I've changed some of the camera angles for the upcoming scene."

"Sure," Palmer said, staring across the cantina tent that had been set up by the caterers.

Ember followed his gaze to see what had captured his attention. Fiona stood talking to Ranger. He must have said something funny, that dry wit of his that not everyone got, and Fiona was laughing.

Good sign. Even though those two might not be dynamic on camera, they seemed to be cooking with gas on a personal level. She'd find a way to draw that out of them for the performance.

Ranger leaned in close and whispered something to Fiona, who laughed again.

That odd sting-ping nailed Ember's heart once more.

Palmer's eyes darkened. "Are Fiona and Ranger seeing each other?"

No, no, not Fiona. Palmer was supposed to be interested in Chriss Anne. "Yes, sorry." Ember shook her head, put a too-bad-for-you lilt to her voice. "They're going out. Sort of."

"Sort of?" Palmer raised an eyebrow.

"They're new as a couple."

"So there's a chance for me?" Hope sprang onto his face, like a kid jumping off a diving board on Memorial Day.

"I doubt it. Fiona's a one-man woman, and you've got something of a reputation, Palmer."

"The rumors are overblown." His gaze tracked Fiona as she left Ranger and headed for the buffet line. "I like to have fun, sure, but lately . . ."

"What?" Ember prompted.

"Um, could you excuse me?"

"Chriss Anne," she reminded him. "Get with her."

Palmer blinked, fish-eyed. "Get with her?"

"About the script," Ember amended, realizing she'd been a bit too forward. "She's a real sweetheart. You'll like her."

"Yeah, yeah." Palmer threw the words over his shoulder and beelined it over to Fiona as she turned from filling her plate at the cafeteria line and stood searching for a place to sit.

Palmer practically fell over himself pulling out a camp chair at the nearest table and dealing out that megawatt smile of his. Fiona smiled shyly back at him, ducked her head and sat down. Palmer dropped in the chair next to her.

Ember chuffed, irritated that her advice had been ignored, and located Chriss Anne, who had cornered Ranger by the drink station. Crap, why couldn't anyone do what they were supposed to be doing?

She hustled over and pulled Chriss Anne aside. "Sit next to Palmer and go over the flirting schedule."

Chriss Anne startled. "What?"

"The filming schedule. Go over it. With Palmer."

"You said flirting schedule."

"I didn't."

"You did," Ranger said, looking amused.

"Why would I say flirting schedule?" Ember sank her hands on her hips.

"That's the sixty-four-thousand-dollar question." Ranger took a sip of water, eyed her over the rim of his cup.

Ember turned her back to him, addressed Chriss Anne again. "Palmer, go to him."

"But he's with —"

"Go." Ember gave the girl a gentle shove.

"Playing matchmaker again, huh?" Ranger drawled. "Palmer and Chriss Anne, really?"

"Mind your own business."

"She's small town, and he's headed for the big city —"

"How many couples have you successfully matched?" She arched an eyebrow and sent him a parboiled look.

"None."

"I rest my case."

"Because I don't consider other people's love lives any of my business."

"Because you're not a matchmaker."

"Neither are you."

"Maybe not professionally, but I've successfully matched four sets of happy couples in the last two years."

"Some people might find it ironic that the matchmaker can't find a match of her own."

"Low blow, Lockhart."

"Irony. I'm a big fan."

Ember flicked a hand. "Then go over to Fiona and figure out why you two are so flat on camera together."

"Oh, I can tell you that."

"What is it then?"

He tilted his head to where Fiona and Palmer were eyeing each other. "She's got a thing for Palmer."

"No, she doesn't. She has a thing for you."

Amusement lit up his eyes. Ranger crossed his arms over his chest. "Okay."

"Okay what?" She scowled. When he backed off an argument, it meant he was stepping back to watch her stumble into a mess of her own making.

He raised his hands, palms up. "I'm staying out of this. You're the matchmaker. Have fun keeping Fiona and Palmer apart."

She raised her chin. "Go sit with Fiona."

"It's good to see you back in rare form, Sparky. I was afraid Trey had stomped the spice out of you." His face was animated and he stepped closer.

"Fiona." She pointed and snapped her fingers.

"Only if you come sit beside me."

"I'm the director. I have to keep myself apart from the actors and crew."

"And why is that?"

"It's lonely at the top."

"Top of the bullshit heap?"

"Are you going to do this or not?" Ember sank her hands on her hips.

"Or not." He turned and walked away.

Ember hurried to catch up with him. Talk about self-sabotage. Didn't he want that job at the observatory? "Why not?"

"Because Fiona and I have a date tonight."

"Well, all right." Ember bobbed her head, but her chest was strung so tight she was having trouble breathing. "Why didn't you say so. That's good. Good for you."

"Ahh . . ." He started and then just let the sound hang there in the tent, unattached to anything.

"Ahh what?"

"I was just wondering."

"Wondering?"

"Is it good for you?"

"Is what good for me?" Okay, she was starting to sound waspish. She heard it in her voice, softened her tone and her stance.

He smiled, the enigmatic Dr. Sphinx, PhD.

"Stop doing that," she said.

"Doing what?"

God, the man could drive her up the wall. "Acting like you know every thought that goes through my head."

"I never said a word."

"You didn't have to. You had *that* look on your face."

"What look is that?"

"Smug. Superior. The way Ricky Ricardo looked at Lucy when she did something he thought was goofy."

"Well, you are a redhead, and you do come up with some daffy-assed schemes." His smile widened and his eyes were full of tenderness, letting Ember know he approved of both traits.

"You forget," she said, grinning right back.

"Forget what?"

"By hook or by crook, one way or the

other, no matter how goofy, Lucy always won," Ember said.

"But then she would jump into another scheme that Ricky would have to fish her out of, and start the whole cycle all over again."

"If Ricky hadn't always been trying to make her toe his chauvinist line, Lucy wouldn't have had to plot and scheme."

"Ricky was a product of his time."

"And so are we."

"Meaning?"

Before Ember could figure out what the hell she was talking about, the makeshift tent door flopped open and a long-legged, platinum-blonde goddess strolled in.

The gazelle goddess paused, sunlight streaming in from behind her, lighting her up like rare treasure. Her golden tresses flowed down her slender shoulders, a waterfall of gorgeous hair. She glanced right, then left, finally spied Ranger and broke into a beatific smile.

Damn if Ranger didn't smile twice as big, his entire face basking in the heat of her ethereal glow.

"Dawn!" he exclaimed.

"Ranger!" the goddess said with a New Zealand accent, flew across the room, flung herself into his arms, and hugged him as if they were fated.

And Ranger, majestic in his Edward Beale historically accurate costume, hugged her right back.

CHAPTER 11

"Badly done, Emma, badly done."
> — Jane Austen, *Emma*

"One big question for you, Ranger." The goddess pronounced his name Ran*ja*.

"What's that?" he asked.

"Why are you dressed like a wanker?"

Ranger's face flushed, and he plucked at the collar of his period piece uniform. "I got wrangled into the lead role for a Chamber of Commerce film."

"You?" The goddess hooted as if it was the funniest thing she'd ever heard. "An actor?"

"Ridiculous, isn't it." Ranger's grin was lopsided and adorable, like a puppy tripping over his own too-long ears.

Ember cleared her throat, making a solid aren't-you-going-to-introduce-me-to-the-mystery-woman-in-your-arms noise.

Ranger jerked his head around, slung his

arm over Dawn's shoulder, and scooted her closer to Ember. "Hey, there's someone I want you to meet."

For a second there, Ember didn't know if he was talking to her or Dawn, but then he followed up with, "Dawn, this is my best friend in the whole world, Ember Alzate."

Dawn, the sunbeam of a woman, pumped her hand as if Ember were a slot machine and would spit out money if she just kept priming her. "It's so good to finally meet you." Dawn glanced back to Ranger. "She's as sweet as . . ."

Ember waited for her to finish the simile, but Dawn did not. Sweet as what? Sugar? Vinegar? Turpentine?

Ranger's eyes were trained on Dawn, and Ember's stomach was in her throat. Fiona and Chriss Anne looked as surprised as she felt, while the tongue of every male in the place was practically hanging out over Dawn.

The old Four Seasons's song "Dawn" rolled through her head. *Dawn, please go away.*

But old Dawn was as sweet as honey. Yes, Ember was going to finish the simile rather lamely. Her smile was genuine, her enthusiasm contagious, and the woman was a walking centerfold. Ember wanted to hate her,

213

oh yes she did, but she just couldn't.

"Ember, this is Dawn Reid, my research partner from New Zealand."

"Oh." Ember stared, shocked but trying not to show it. "I thought your research partner was named Don."

"No, it's Dawn. Like the morn." Dawn giggled as if the mistake in gender was the most hilarious thing she'd ever heard. "You thought I was a dude."

Ember cast her mind back to all the phone conversations she'd had with Ranger over the past year since he'd been gone. When he spoke of her or texted her about his research partner he'd called her Dr. Reid or just plain Reid. She couldn't ever recall him using a pronoun in reference to Dawn. Using instead, "we" or "us" or "our." Had that been intentional?

A drop box of disappointment opened up inside Ember. Had Ranger been keeping secrets from her? Did his relationship with Dawn extend far beyond research partners?

It certainly seemed that way.

Dawn and Ranger were grinning at each other like . . . well . . . like *she* and Ranger usually grinned at each other. As if they were in on a cosmic joke the rest of the world knew nothing about.

"Don't take this the wrong way, but —"

Ranger began.

"Why am I here early?" Dawn asked, finishing his sentence.

"Exactly. I thought you weren't coming until September."

"Change of plans. You're not happy to see me?" Dawn tickled him in the ribs the same way Ember did when they were horsing around.

"Thrilled." Ranger beamed. "Why didn't you tell me?"

"I wanted to surprise you."

"We're all surprised." To say the least. Ember sandwiched herself firmly between Dawn and Ranger. "Why *are* you here?"

Dawn blinked those soft doe eyes at Ranger, looked all innocent and sweet, but she didn't fool Ember, not for a second. "You didn't tell her?"

"Tell me what?" A lump of fear skidded into Ember's throat. Were Dawn and Ranger dating? Engaged? Secretly married? Her stomach slumped to her shoes. She felt like a passenger jumping onto the caboose as the train was pulling back into the station. She hated being the last to know something.

"I got a fellowship at the observatory. I'll be living in Fort Davis for the next year," Dawn said to Ember. Several men ringed around them mumbled happy noises at that news. To Ranger she said, "Why didn't you tell your friend about me?"

Ranger splayed a hand on his nape. "Um . . . it sort of slipped my mind."

Dawn, with her damned musical laugh, punched him lightly on his shoulder. "Trust you to forget me, my absentminded professor."

Ember gritted her teeth.

"We should have you meet everybody." Ranger slipped his arm around Dawn's waist. "I'll introduce you around."

Chriss Anne eyed Ranger and Dawn's cozy stance, and jammed her hands in her skirt pockets.

Fiona watched the pair and chewed her bottom lip. Ember caught Fiona's eyes and touched her own lip, mouthed, *nervous habit.*

Picking up on her cues, Fiona stopped gnawing.

Clearly, Ember wasn't the only one distressed by Dawn's unexpected appearance.

Ranger guided Dawn over to where Zeke and Palmer were standing slack-jawed. A whole queue of men lined up behind them, eager to shake Dawn's hand.

Ember leaned in toward Fiona, whispered, "You okay?"

"Are you?" Fiona whispered back.

"Why wouldn't I be?"

"Because Ranger has a 'down under' Ember."

"Why should I care?" Ember shrugged like it was no skin off her nose, but she cared. Oh boy, did she care.

"Umm . . . maybe because you're wrong about Ranger being the man for me." Fiona traced a finger over her chin and slid a glance over at Palmer.

"Trust me," Ember said, more because she wanted to break up this thing between Ranger and Dawn than because she thought Fiona and Ranger were a perfect match. "Dawn is *not* a threat."

Bad matchmaker. Bad, bad.

Who was she trying to convince? Fiona? Or herself?

Honestly, she was flabbergasted to discover that Dr. Don Reid was Dr. *Dawn* Reid, and she still couldn't figure out if Ranger had allowed her to assume Dawn's gender was male.

Ranger and Dawn were gabbing like it was old home week, talking about their adventures in New Zealand over the past year. A year that Ember knew little about.

She had to do something to break up this chummy tête-à-tête, or her plans to hook him up with Fiona were kaput. Fiona was already staring at Palmer with knight-in-shining-armor eyes.

Dammit. When had things started unraveling?

"We should go out for a beer later," Ranger told Dawn. "Celebrate your arrival in Cupid."

Jealousy was a jumping jack, bouncing around inside Ember. Oh no, no, no. Ember could not let those two get alone for beers and giggles.

Ember grasped Fiona by the arm and thrust the poor girl in front of Ranger. "Aren't you forgetting your date with Fiona?"

Ranger smiled at Fiona, a kind, gentle smile that did *not* say *I find you hot and sexy.* "You wouldn't mind if everyone joined us on our night out."

He said it as a statement, not a question, and dear, sweet, mousy Fiona simply nodded, the lovely Mary Beale bun pinned to the top of her head bobbing along with the rhythm.

"Whoever wants to join us," Ranger announced to the populated tent at large. "We're headed over to Chantilly's after we finish filming today. See you there."

Then he looked straight at Ember and winked as if to say, *checkmate.*

■ ■ ■ ■

"So *Dawn,* huh?" Ember pinned Ranger down just like he hoped she would after everyone had dispersed to various places before filming resumed at one o'clock, leaving just the two of them, and the caterers cleaning up, in the cantina tent.

"Uh-huh," he said smoothly, loving how flustered she looked.

When Dawn had called him three days ago to tell him she was on her way to Texas earlier than expected, he'd enlisted her help to make Ember jealous. He kept his fingers crossed, praying his plan would work.

After that day they went land sailing, Ranger knew something monumental had shifted between him and Ember, but he also knew the woman was as stubborn as the day was long, and it would take something big for her to admit her changing feelings for him. When she got an idea in her head and set out on a course to achieve her objective, it was almost impossible to derail her.

But derail her he must, if he hoped for them to have a happy ending. A lot was riding on this scheme. The very fabric of their relationship. He could only pray she would forgive him once she found out what he was up to.

From the irritated expression on his best friend's face, his ploy to make her jealous was working far better than he imagined. Good start.

The tables have turned, Sparky. She wasn't the only one who enjoyed matchmaking machinations.

"Do you think that was fair to Fiona?" Ember sank her hands on her hips and tilted her head in that listen-to-me way of hers.

"What?" he asked, playing dumb.

"Inviting the entire cast and crew on your date."

"In case you haven't noticed, Palmer and Fiona have taken a liking to each other."

Ember pooched out her bottom lip in an exaggerated pout. "It wasn't supposed to work out this way. I was prepping Fiona for you."

"Fiona's not a pawn, Ember. She's a real person with feelings. You don't have to keep throwing her at me. I like her, but that's all. We're not a love match, and Fiona feels the same about me."

"I know." Ember chuffed, and her shoulders sagged, defeated. "I thought I had this whole matchmaking thing worked out."

"You can't control fate," he said tenderly, caressing her with his eyes, mentally sending her, *I'm your fate* messages, but she wasn't picking up on it. He wanted to just come out and tell her what he was feeling, but he was terrified she'd blow him off. Or worse, tell him she did not feel the same way. Suddenly, he was filled with doubt about this whole make-Ember-jealous game he'd enlisted Dawn to play.

"It was supposed to work." Ember tucked a curl of that beautiful bouncy red hair behind one ear and looked perplexed. "Why didn't it work?"

"People are fickle and unpredictable and often can't see what's right in front of them." He stared at her pointedly, willing her to get his meaning.

It soared right over her head. She knotted her chin and her fists. "Okay, I messed up with Fiona, but I'm on it. I *will* find the right woman for you."

"Why do you even bother to match people up? What's in it for you?"

"Because I want to see my friends happy."

"And they have to be in a relationship to be happy?"

"Everyone is happier when they have a soft place to land," she murmured.

"Friends can't be that soft place?"

"Of course." She cocked her head at him. "But everyone needs a little passion in their lives too."

"You can have passion without having a relationship, and you can have a relationship without passion."

"Ah, but can you truly be happy with just passionate sex?"

When it came to Ember? No. But he wasn't happy with just friendship anymore either, and Ranger knew if he ever made love to Ember, he could never be satisfied with just a sexual relationship. He wanted it all. Their entire future was on the line.

"About Fiona—"

"She likes Palmer," he said firmly.

"Palmer is for Chriss Anne."

"Palmer likes Fiona back."

"Palmer just doesn't know he likes Chriss Anne. He hasn't given her a chance."

"And you know what Palmer likes better than he does?"

"I'm trying to keep him from making a mess of his love life."

"Like you made of yours?" Ranger asked, and the second the words were out of his mouth, he regretted them. "I'm sorry. That wasn't fair."

"Back to Fiona," she said brusquely, hiding her wounds with a razor-thin smile. "I can bring her around to you again. She liked you before Palmer."

"Leave Fiona be," he said. "I have someone else in mind as girlfriend material."

"You do?" Ember gulped visibly. She was worried.

Ranger suppressed a grin; he had her on the ropes. "Yes."

"Making your own matches now, huh?"

"Yep."

"Who is she?" Her eyes widened and her lips parted, and she stopped breathing.

So did he.

Emphatically, Ranger drilled Ember with his eyes, praying she would finally get the hint, and fall into his arms and he could forget this whole charade, but his dear, sweet, stubborn Sparky missed the point.

Again.

"It's Dawn, isn't it?" Her voice was as clipped as a putting green.

He did not confirm that, because it wasn't true, but he let the silence stretch out leaving a long blank space, which she readily filled in with her own assumption.

"Of course it's Dawn. Why wouldn't it be Dawn? She's gorgeous. What I can't figure out is why you allowed me to believe your research partner was a man."

"That was your interpretation," he said, keeping his tone as mild as Ivory soap.

"Which you allowed me to perpetuate."

He said nothing, adding more blank space. He really didn't know why he hadn't been clear that Don was Dawn. Maybe it was because for a couple of months when he first arrived in New Zealand he'd thought maybe he and Dawn would hook up. They'd even kissed once, but the whole time his thoughts had been on Ember.

Here was the truth.

Ranger had not been with a woman since Ember divorced Trey. Their timing had been off all their lives. One of them was single when the other was in a relationship, then vice versa. In the back of his mind, had he been thinking that if he stayed out of any romantic entanglement, he'd finally be free at the same time Ember was?

And then he'd taken off for a year.

Why?

Who knew? That was one for the psychologists.

"I thought we told each other everything." Her voice dipped and softened. She was hurt.

Ranger put a hand to his mouth, camouflaging a wince. He hated hurting her, but a small amount of pain was necessary to his endgame. Happily-ever-after with Ember. "You didn't tell me how bad things had gotten with Trey."

"That's different," she said. "I was ashamed."

"Maybe I'm ashamed too."

"Of Dawn?"

No, of not being there for you when you needed me most. Of not knowing your marriage was shit. For not saving you.

He should have known Ember's marriage was rocky. That she was barely keeping her head above water. He should have been more attuned to her needs. But they'd drifted apart in the three months she'd been married to Trey. Mainly because of Trey. The man had resented their friendship, so Ember had backed off to appease her husband. But that was no excuse. Ember was his best friend. Had been his best friend for as long as he could remember. He should have known she was in trouble. Should have whisked her away from the jerk.

As if Ember would have allowed that. She was tough and independent and she hated to appear weak and she loved being in charge and he admired all those things about her.

"Well?"

"Huh?"

She knocked lightly on the side of his head with her small fist. "Where did you go, Professor?"

"Just thinking."

"About Dawn and why you're ashamed of your relationship with her?"

"I'm not ashamed of her."

"Then why didn't you tell me something was going on?"

"Nothing's going on."

"Not yet," Ember said.

Again, he did not reply, kept drawing those blanks, so she could fill them in. He *wanted* her to get jealous. To want him. To fight for him.

"Oh gosh!" she exclaimed. "Is it really 1:05?"

"Yeah," Ranger said, not even looking at his watch because he was too busy staring at Ember. Her gorgeous red hair was mussed, windblown from her time outside. She wore a green visor pulled down low, a matching green V-neck T-shirt that clung nicely to her breasts, and a snug pair of stretchy skinny jeans. He wanted to wrap his arms around her so badly he had to clench his hands to prevent himself from doing just that.

"That's crazy. It was just fifteen till."

Time flies when you're with the one you love, he wanted to say, but didn't. If he tipped his hand too soon, this whole thing could blow up on him. He had one shot at convincing Ember they were meant to be together, and he couldn't risk blowing it. He might be a gambler, but he was shrewd, and if things didn't feel right, he'd walk away from the table and come back another day.

She tapped the face of her watch as if that would alter facts. "We're late."

"You're the director. I'm the lead actor. They won't start without us."

"Let's go." She took hold of his hand.

Ranger steeled himself against the impact of her touch. How could she not know how much she affected him? Couldn't she feel it in his body? The tension, his yearning.

"C'mon. You know how I hate to be late."

Opposites attract, he thought. Time could slip away from him like a catfish off a poorly cast rod and reel.

Ember towed him from the cantina tent, across the desert, past cactus and sunning lizards back to the bunkhouse salted with cameras, cast, and crew. Ranger let her pull, savoring the moment of her hand locked around his wrist.

Would he ever get to manacle her in a totally different scenario — say naked in his bed with a safe word of her choosing?

Hold the course, man. Play the game. You'll get there, you'll get there.

But would he? Would Ember ever let herself see him as anything more than her best friend? Was this scheme with Dawn over-the-top? What would he do if she didn't get jealous? If she just wished him well and told him to have a happy life?

Doubt cut into him for the first time.

What if in the end, she simply did not feel for him the same deep-rooted feelings he felt for her. What then?

The thought was unacceptable, so Ranger did what he always did when emotions got too thick. He stepped onto the bunkhouse steps, became Edward Beale, camel commander, and got lost in a dreamworld.

CHAPTER 12

"It is not every man's fate to marry the
woman who loves him best."
— Jane Austen, *Emma*

It was five forty-five, and most everyone
from the set was packed into the back room
at Chantilly's, rapid-fire ordering drinks
before happy hour ended at six.

Ember considered the day a success,
despite the many takes. They'd finally managed to film the scene to her satisfaction.
She'd stayed behind to wrap things up, and
she was one of the last to arrive.

The line at the bar was so long she figured
she'd never make it to the counter before
happy hour was over and instead went to
look for a place to sit. She'd almost skipped
out on what was fast becoming a party in
honor of Dawn's arrival, but she didn't
because she knew Ranger would text her
and ask her where she was, and she had a

matchmaking mess to untangle.

Her to-do list went like this: 1) Get Palmer next to Chriss Anne; 2) Get Zeke away from Chriss Anne, who was buzzing around her like a fly; 3) Get Fiona next to Ranger; 4) and most important of all, get Dawn out of the picture completely.

She wasn't quite sure how to maneuver that last part, but she was working on the other three. Getting rid of Dawn might take some time, seeing as how she had a fellowship at the observatory, and Ranger seemed glued to the woman.

Pensively, Ember glanced around the room, looking for someone to hook up Dawn with. It really didn't matter who it was. She wasn't trying to make a love match for the woman, she just wanted to clear the way for Fiona.

"Em!" Dawn called gaily, rose on her gazelle legs and gestured wildly like she was trying to signal a landing plane. "Over here."

The ballsy Kiwi was taking liberties with her name. Ember gritted her teeth. She put up with being called Em only by her family and Ranger, and now, apparently Dawn, as well.

She picked her way through the crowd, found Ranger and Dawn sitting at a long table. Zeke was next to Dawn, but the spot beside Ranger was empty, except for a frosty mug of beer.

Dawn waved her toward the empty chair. "The beer's for you, love."

Dammit, why did the woman have to be so likable?

Ember glanced around for Fiona, Palmer, and Chriss Anne. She found Chriss Anne and Palmer pitching darts. Ahh, at least someone was cooperating with the match she had in mind. Now to find Fiona.

"Where's Fiona?" she asked, linking the strap of her purse around the back of the chair and easing in beside Ranger. Her foot accidently bumped against his, but he didn't move away. Neither did she.

Instead, he smiled on just one side of his mouth, all Humphrey Bogart, and said, " 'Of all the gin joints in all the towns in all the world, she walks into mine.' "

Ember felt her cheeks heat. She wasn't a blusher. There wasn't a coy bone in her body, but damn if she wasn't feeling all hot and flustered underneath her skin. They were both Humphrey Bogart buffs, had watched together every movie he'd ever made.

" 'Play it!' " she quipped.

Dawn, that impossible thing, started humming "As Time Goes By."

"I debated ordering you a margarita," Ranger told Ember. "Since my acting inabilities put you through your paces."

It wasn't his acting abilities, or lack thereof, that had slowed filming, rather it was the zero on-screen chemistry between him and his costar. Whenever they acted together, Ranger and Fiona came off flat and unbelievable as a couple. Ember had finally settled on a rather lukewarm take, knowing it was the best she was going to get out of them, and crossed her fingers that things would improve as they settled into their roles.

"You have that margarita look in your eyes," Ranger said, flagging down a server. "I should have listened to my gut and gone with the margarita."

"The beer is fine." She shook her head at the server who popped over. She didn't even really want the beer. "I'm good."

"You sure?" Ranger studied Ember with narrowed eyes as if trying to read her mind.

"Thank you for thinking of me." Ember took a big gulp of beer to show her appreciation, but she was feeling out of sorts and small and she couldn't really pinpoint why.

Dawn laid a hand on Ranger's shoulder and *zing,* she pinpointed why.

"Ranger is always —" Ranger nudged her with his elbow, cutting Dawn off. Probably to keep her from telling Ember some quaint story of his time with Dawn in New Zealand. She didn't ask the other woman what he was always doing with her because Ember really did not want to know. What happened in New Zealand needed to stay in New Zealand.

"Where's Fiona?" she asked again.

"In the ladies'," Dawn said.

All rightee. Fiona was in the restroom. Chriss Anne and Palmer were together. That only left Dawn to pair off with someone besides Ranger. Get rid of Dawn and she could plead Fiona's case with Ranger.

She spied Rhett in the corner chatting up some girl Ember had never seen before. Her mental cogs whirled. Aha. Ranger's little brother would do nicely for Dawn.

"Excuse me," she mumbled to Ranger, slipped out of her seat and sidled over to Rhett, who was leaning with one arm against the jukebox exaggerating one of his rodeo stories to the wide-eyed brunette.

The sound of Jimmy Buffett's "Why Don't We Get Drunk and Screw" staggered out of the jukebox and had half the bar singing along.

Seriously, Rhett? The guy was twenty-seven, not seventeen. Would the boy ever grow up?

Rhett whirled around as if Ember had said that out loud, which she hadn't, had she? Sometimes she had a hard time holding in her opinion. Rhett held his arms in the air like he was being robbed at gunpoint. "I didn't play it!"

"I did." The brunette looked sly. Aha, not as wide-eyed and innocent as Ember had thought. Maybe she should play match-maker for these two.

Um, you're supposed to be using Rhett to distract Dawn away from Ranger so he can see what a catch Fiona is.

"You don't say." Rhett leaned in closer to the brunette. Many people thought whiskey-haired, hazel-eyed Rhett was the handsomest Lockhart. Ember did not agree. He was the shortest of the brothers at five-eleven, and was a tad bow-legged from all that bull riding, and Rhett had a cockiness about him that turned Ember off, but it seemed to be a magnet for the wrong kind of woman.

"Come with me." Ember took Rhett by the collar the way she used to do when they were kids, and Rhett pulled Aria's braids just to hear her scream, and dragged him away from the brunette.

"Hey, hey!" He wrestled away from her.

234

"Lemme go."

"You'll thank me for this later."

"What?" He gave a squirrelly little shake of his shoulders the way he did after a snorting bull had thrown him.

"The brunette, she's not right for you."

"Gawddammit, Ember, any girl who plays 'Why Don't We Get Drunk and Screw' on the jukebox where everyone can hear is the right girl for me."

"How is it that you and Ranger are brothers?"

"Half brothers," Rhett reminded her.

"Oh yeah."

Clearly, Rhett had inherited more of Duke Lockhart's DNA than his older brother had. Ember had to remind herself Rhett still had time to grow up and become a man when the swagger of his prize-winning rodeo days was over. Which, from his current injury that had knocked him out of this year's running for the PBR finals, seemed to be coming up sooner rather than later.

"Now that you've so rudely interrupted my conquest in progress, whaddya want?" Rhett tipped his straw Stetson back on his head at a rakish tilt and looped his thumbs through his belt buckle.

"See the willowy blonde with Ranger?"

Rhett squinted across the room. "You

mean Dawn?"

"You know her?"

"Honey, I know every pretty girl that blows into this town."

"Ply your wiles on her."

"Why? I've already got one woman half in my bed." He inclined his head at the brunette.

"Dawn's new in town and —"

"She's with Ranger."

"She's his research partner. They're not an item."

Rhett gave her a you-poor-dumb-deluded-ninny look.

"They *are* together?" A heavy, hot feeling burned the bottom of her stomach.

"Define 'together.' "

Don't panic. She had no reason to panic. Rhett saw the entire world through the lens of conquest, whether bedding women or riding bulls. She wasn't going to let his limited worldview of *Life's a rodeo; ride it hard* affect her.

"So there's no chance you could lure her away from Ranger?" she said, issuing the one thing she knew Rhett couldn't resist — a challenge.

Rhett narrowed his green-brown eyes and flashed Ember a grin that had caused many a young lass to drop her panties and accused, "You're *jealous.*"

"Don't be silly." Ember lifted her nose, her shoulders, and her dignity. "Ranger is my best friend in the entire world. I just want to see him happy, and Dawn isn't the woman who can do that."

"How do you know?"

It was a reasonable enough question, and Ember didn't have a reasonable answer, so she scrambled for the first thing that popped into her head. "Dawn will only be in Texas for a year, then she's back to New Zealand."

"What's wrong with that?"

"Some people need long-term relationships to be happy, Rhett, although I'm sure you don't understand that concept."

"Maybe Ranger isn't one of those people either. Maybe he and Dawn are just fine with a year-long ride."

"Trust me, he's not, although he might not know it yet." Ember gazed over at Ranger, who had his arm around the back of Dawn's chair. The hairs on her arms lifted and a cold chill passed through her.

"Are you?" Rhett asked.

"Am I what?" Ember frowned as Ranger leaned his head so close to Dawn they were practically touching. Ranger whispered. Dawn giggled. Ember stewed.

"One of those people?"

"Look," she said, "would you at least go ask Dawn to dance?"

"What's in it for me?"

"I'll give you twenty bucks."

Rhett snorted. "Twenty bucks? Seriously? Keep your money, Miss Big Spender. I'll do it just to mess with Ranger."

Ember pressed her palms together in front of her heart. "Thank you."

"But . . ."

"But what?"

"There's one question that you just gotta ask yourself." Rhett readjusted his Stetson again, and for a split second looked so wise it surprised Ember.

"What's that?"

"Why do you care so much about who Ranger hooks up with? I mean if you're just best friends?" With that parting shot, Rhett sauntered off to ask Dawn to dance. Thankfully, not to "Why Don't We Get Drunk and Screw." The song on the jukebox had shifted to "Until You Came Along."

Ember smiled into her hand.

Perfect.

She rubbed her palms together, building up some heat. Now, to get Fiona in front of Ranger and fast-track their romance.

"You're trying to fix up Rhett? Seriously?"

Ranger hooted when Ember settled into her seat beside him. It was funny as hell to watch her mess with his plan to mess with her.

"Says who?" Ember blinked, trying to act all who-me innocent.

"Woman," Ranger said, "you're not as devious as you think you are."

She tipped her head in that bulldozer tilt she pulled out when she was trying to convince people that her way was the only way. "I merely asked Rhett to dance with Dawn."

"You've got your work cut out for you with that one." Ranger nodded as his little brother dipped Dawn low on the dance floor. Dawn let loose with a happy laugh. He would have to warn his research partner about encouraging his brother. Remind her of what he was trying to accomplish with Ember. He couldn't make Ember jealous if she didn't view Dawn as a threat.

"Maybe you underestimate your little brother."

"Rhett's not the type to settle down."

"Funny" — Ember cut her eyes at him — "he said the same thing about you."

"What do you think about that?" he asked.

Ember lowered her lashes, allowed her beautiful springy red curls to fall over her

239

face as she reached for her beer mug, hiding her expression from him. Which wasn't like her. Normally, she was quite bold and didn't blink an eye when matching someone's stare.

Ranger noticed the tension in her shoulders, and he wanted to reach out and brush back her hair so he could get a good look at her face and see what was going on inside her. But she downed the beer like she could find the answer to his question at the bottom of the glass.

"Sparky." He softened his voice, felt a heaviness sag to the bottom of his gut. "You all right?"

She tossed her head. A no in answer to his question? Or was there something weighty on her mind that she was trying to shake off? They knew each other so well. He could sense when something was troubling her. She reached for the pitcher of beer in the middle of the table, but he moved it out of her reach.

"Em?"

Her long lashes swept upward as she finally made eye contact, her blue-eyed stare hitting him with a hard one-two punch. The pulse at the hollow of her throat throbbed, moving as swift as a flood-swollen river.

Ranger felt his pulse jump and sprint, felt

his muscles tighten. "What is it?"

She shook her head again, but did not blink or look away. *That* was his brave Ember.

"Let me guess, you're afraid you've lost your matchmaking mojo," he said, trying to lighten things up.

That got the reaction he was going for. She grinned and sent him a sliding-door look, open and accessible. Letting down her guard for him, letting him in. "Not a chance. One way or another, I'm gonna find you the perfect wife."

"Ember . . ."

There were a million things he wanted to say to her. How much he admired and respected her. How much he wanted to deepen their relationship, go to the next level. How he prayed she felt the same way.

But it was too soon. She wasn't ready to hear it. He could tell because she was still frantically trying to match make him with all the wrong people, avoiding what was so blatantly clear to him.

They belonged together.

She had to get there of her own accord. In her own time. He couldn't rush her. Until then, Ranger could wait. Good thing he was a patient man. Months of being bedridden could do that to a fella.

"Yes?" Her voice went up on a hopeful note.

"I —"

Dawn plunked down in the chair to his left, breathless and glowing. "Your brother is an amazing dancer."

"Not too shabby yourself." Rhett sauntered over to the table.

Dawn giggled, her face aglow.

"So . . ." Rhett pulled up a chair from a nearby table and squeezed in between Ranger and Dawn. "Tell me all about yourself."

Ember leaned back in her chair to whisper something to Rhett behind Ranger's back. He didn't have to see what she was doing to guess that she gave Rhett a secret thumbs-up. He knew his Sparky.

Egged on by Ember, Rhett slung his arm around Dawn's shoulder and signaled a nearby server. "Could we get another pitcher and an extra mug over here? I've found my spot for the evening."

"Should we order food?" Chriss Anne asked as she and Palmer came back to the table and sat down across from them.

Dawn patted her flat belly. "Let's have a feed."

"Nachos," Rhett told the server.

"Artichoke dip," Fiona said, settling into

her chair between Palmer and Chriss Anne.

"Potato skins," Zeke added from the far side of Dawn.

"Fish tacos," Dawn said.

"What do you want?" Ranger asked Ember.

"Do you really have to ask?"

"Two orders of hot wings." Ranger grinned, ordering for them both. "Extra spicy."

"Who's paying for all this?" asked the server. "Or is it separate checks?"

"I am," said Rhett, the show-off. There was a reason his little brother was always broke despite the money he made bull riding. He loved grand gestures.

There was a chorus of, "Thank you, Rhett."

Rhett preened, puffing out his chest and passing his credit card to the server. "Start a tab."

Dawn leaned forward to catch Ranger's eye. "You weren't kidding when you told me Cupid is the wop-wops."

"Huh?" said everyone.

Ranger grinned at the confused faces at the table. "Wop-wops is Kiwi for the middle of nowhere."

"We call it the sticks," Fiona said.

"Boondocks," Palmer supplied.

243

"Tulies," Chriss Anne added.

Zeke started with, "Bumfu—"

"Be nice," Ranger interrupted.

Zeke finished with, "Bumfuzzle, Egypt."

"I could listen to you talk all night." Chriss Anne sighed to Dawn. "I love the way you basically ignore the vowel 'e.' "

"Me too," Palmer said. "Killer accent."

"I don't have an accent." Dawn laughed. "You do."

"Honey," Zeke drawled, "you're the foreigner. *You* have the accent."

Dawn met Ranger's gaze. "Your friends are choice."

"Choice?" Fiona seemed completely lost.

"It means 'awesome' in Kiwi," Ranger translated.

Fiona's face unfolded in a bright smile. "Why, you're pretty choice yourself, Dawn."

Rhett leaned in closer to Dawn. "More like USDA prime, if you ask me."

Dawn beamed.

Dammit. His little brother was messing with his plan to use Dawn to make Ember jealous. He needed to get her away from Rhett.

Ranger pushed back his chair and held his hand out to Dawn. "Would you like to dance?"

"My!" Dawn exclaimed, pressing a palm

244

to her chest. "I feel like the belle of the ball."

She sank her hand into Ranger's, and he led her out on the dance floor. He tried to be cool, but he couldn't help casting a surreptitious glance over his shoulder to see if Ember was watching.

But no. She was huddled with Fiona, leaning across the table, engrossed in conversation, paying absolutely no attention to him and Dawn.

Leaving Ranger surprised, and wondering if his best friend did not harbor deeper feelings for him, as he did for her.

CHAPTER 13

"Time did not compose her."

— Jane Austen, *Emma*

Mumbling a lame excuse about having to get up early to greet the camels when they arrived the next day, Ember left the party early.

Ranger didn't even talk her out of it, except to point out she hadn't eaten a thing. How could she eat hot wings when a rock the size of the famed Cupid stalagmite in the local caverns sat in her stomach? She could take watching Ranger and Dawn dance and coo and laugh it up for only so long.

Her instinct had been to cut in and claim her friend, but she'd managed to quell her boldness. How petty would that have been?

Dawn was so disgustingly perky. Everything she said came with an exclamation mark. Really, seriously, who was that animated?

Aimlessly, Ember drove out to Lake Cupid, which was really not much more than a pond. She parked in the gravel lot and walked out across the sand and down to the water. A local fisherman who worked at the feed store was gathering up his rod and reel and string of sun perch. "Evenin'," he greeted her with a friendly nod.

Ember was so caught up in her ruminations about Ranger and Dawn, she barely nodded back, and it was only after the fisherman climbed into his pickup she realized how rude she must have seemed.

She clambered onto the concrete picnic table overlooking the water. She and Ranger used to come to swim when they were teenagers and itching to get away from their families. They'd bicycle the sixteen miles from the ranch, swim, share a picnic lunch, and cycle back. They'd talk for hours about everything and nothing. Gabbing, then lapsing into comfortable silences, then bursting forth with fresh conversation.

Sitting cross-legged on the table, she took her cell phone from her pocket, looked to see if Ranger had texted her.

He had not.

But why would he? He was at Chantilly's

having fun.

With Dawn.

If she could have dredged up one flicker of kindness, a single sweet word of kinship for the golden goddess from New Zealand, it might have salvaged Ember's sinking opinion of herself. Ashamed of her petty jealousy, and pissed off for her inability to change her way of thinking, Ember sat glumly watching the sun kiss the horizon, staring at the mossy green water.

In two months she would be thirty-three, and yet she felt as inept and clueless about life as she had at twelve and sitting on a bench outside the principal's office in trouble for starting a food fight in the school cafeteria.

She'd gotten the same message then as she'd gotten from Trey. *Be a good girl, toe the line, don't be yourself, and you'll be loved.*

And if not?

She would end up sitting on a picnic table by herself disappointed because she had no idea how to turn herself into the person everyone wanted her to be.

Well, everyone except Ranger.

She smiled softly as the sky drew darker. He'd always egged her on to be more of who she was, not less. He'd been in on that food fight too, which Ember had started to distract him from the news that his step-mother's cancer had returned, and she wasn't going to beat it this time.

But now Ranger was with Dawn.

Dammit.

She should be happy for him. She wanted to be happy for him. What was wrong with her?

Ember gave herself a strong shake. *Wake up. Get over yourself.* Be the kind of friend to him that he was to her. Even if she had to fake her way through it, she wouldn't let Ranger know how upset she was about Dawn.

As far as Ranger knew, she loved, loved, loved Dawn.

Fake it till you make it, right.

Who knew? Maybe one day she'd actually believe it herself.

Convinced that she would be able to keep her selfishness under control, Ember switched on her key-ring flashlight and wandered back to her car.

Just as she buckled her seat belt, her cell phone rang, playing her special ringtone for Ranger. A snippet of Queen's "You're My Best Friend."

Grinning, Ember hit Accept, breathed, "Hey there, good-looking."

Only to hear Dawn say, "You do realize

Ranger's birthday is coming up in a couple of weeks. You and I need to get together to plan his party."

The following morning, after her conversation with Dawn about what to do for Ranger's birthday, Ember was the first to arrive on the film set.

She had intended that it would be just the two of them for his birthday celebration as it usually was — maybe a trip to San Antonio to his favorite Mexican food restaurant and a stroll along the River Walk. Although last year she had thrown him a small party as his send-off to New Zealand.

But Dawn had blown a hole in her plans, and now Ember had to scramble to help Dawn host some big shindig. Ranger hated a big deal being made over his birthday, but Ember couldn't convince Dawn she was right and a subdued celebration was what he wanted.

The day was sunny and moderate, the small mountains rising up from the desert floor cast cooling shadows. The sky's interplay of orange, purple, yellow, and blue accentuated the barren beauty.

She paused in the silence of that moment, took a deep breath, smiled wistfully.

Growing up, she hadn't much appreciated

the quiet solitude of the desert, but after almost a decade in San Antonio, and passing her thirtieth birthday, she had begun to see the appeal.

Ember loved living in Marfa, and she loved being a real estate agent. Matching people with their perfect-for-them homes. She loved matchmaking too for the same reason. She *liked* finding those diamonds in the rough, polishing them up and helping others discover the connections they'd missed.

Happiness rushed over her warm as the late spring morning breeze. She was so glad to be back home. Although part of her kept whispering she needed to return to the city where the action was. This past year away from San Antonio was starting to feel like a permanent shift, and it surprised her.

And if she couldn't have her own happily-ever-after, maybe at least she could help others find theirs. Ranger in particular.

If only he would cooperate and be more open with the women she threw in his path.

He's open with Dawn.

Ember swatted her hand beside her ear as if waving away an annoying fly, chasing off that thought. Dawn wasn't right for him. Those two were too much alike with their heads in the stars. Ranger needed someone who could bring him down to earth and keep him grounded. Someone like Fiona.

But was Fiona too boring for Ranger? Too placid? Perhaps he needed someone fierier. Someone passionate and proactive.

Someone like you?

No.

Why not?

Why not? There was the whole best friend thing. That's why not. She couldn't think about him in any other context.

Why not?

"Shut up, Ember," she scolded herself out loud and took a sip from her coffee thermos. Made a face. One thing she missed about city living, a Starbucks on every corner. Her coffee-making skills left a lot to be desired.

On top of the mountain in front of her, a one-ton pickup truck appeared, hauling a long black trailer behind it down the steep road.

Oh goodie, the camels were here!

She'd been around camels before when Duke kept them at the Silver Feather, but she didn't know how easy it was going to be to film with them. While mostly even-tempered, camels could kick and spit when they were agitated. Being dragged across Texas in the confines of a small trailer in the desert heat could easily constitute as being agitated.

The windshield of the truck caught the eastern sun and glinted light back into her eyes. Ember squinted, pulled her sunglasses from her purse, and put them on, watched the truck progress toward the fort.

Some of the crew drove up to her from around the other side of the mountain, arriving from Cupid — Zeke Tremont among them.

Zeke got out of his weathered old Ford pickup and sauntered over, his gaze following Ember's, and sank his broad hands on his hips. "We're in for some fun."

"Are you being facetious?" she asked.

"Huh?" Zeke lifted his cowboy hat to scratch his head.

"Never mind."

"You know almost as many big words as Ranger." Zeke grinned, good-natured and self-effacing. He was such a nice guy.

"Where do you think I learned the big words?" Her voice came out deep and respectful, which surprised her a bit. But it was true. Ranger had stretched her vocabulary far more than college had.

"Can I ask you a question?" Zeke drawled.

Ember tensed. Was he going to ask about her relationship with Ranger? "I guess it depends on how personal it is."

"It's not personal at all. At least not about you. It's about Chriss Anne."

"What about her?"

"Is she seeing anyone?"

Ember bit back a groan. What was it with people? Why did they always want what they shouldn't have? *I dunno, Ember, why do they?*

"I think maybe Palmer likes her."

"No," Zeke replied. "He likes Fiona."

Good gravy. How was she ever going to sort this out?

"Do you think Chriss Anne would go out with me if I asked her?" Zeke's face was shiny in the sun.

"She's stuck on Palmer," Ember said firmly.

"Are you sure? 'Cause I could swear that she was playing footsie with me under the table last night."

Ugh. TMI. Then again, was anything TMI for a matchmaker when it came to affairs of the heart?

More people were driving up. Everyone getting out of vehicles and coming over to watch the trailer full of camels bumping up and down over the sand in an ambling manner as the vehicle came toward them, surrounded by a dust cloud.

No time to sort out Zeke and Chriss Anne; she had a film to direct.

"I really like camels." Zeke readjusted his Stetson to keep the windshield glint out of his eyes. "They're witty, smart, and very sturdy, much like Chriss Anne."

"Word to the wise, Zeke, *do not* tell Chriss Anne that she reminds you of a camel," Ember whispered as Chriss Anne drove up in her Ford Fiesta.

Wearing red and white canvas platform espadrilles, Chriss Anne minced over to where Ember and Zeke were standing, tablet computer tucked underneath her arm. She looked cute as a candy cane in a red cap-sleeved top and white denim skirt, and quite inappropriately dressed for a day of filming camels in the desert. Was she trying to impress Palmer?

Ember cast a glance at the suave cameraman who had his lens trained on the incoming camels. He hadn't once glanced Chriss Anne's way.

Zeke, however, was eyeing her up one side and down the other like he was picking out a specialty cheesecake on his birthday at The Cheesecake Factory.

The trailer full of camels halted right in front of them. The odor was immediate and deeply pungent.

"Eew. Someone forgot to take a shower." Chriss Anne gagged.

"Oh, it's not us," Zeke said. "It's the camels."

Ember murmured, "She's joking."

Zeke looked chagrined. "I knew that."

Chriss Anne rolled her eyes. "Camels smell disgusting."

Zeke's face lit up. "Camels may be stinky, but they are lovely creatures, and you'll get used to the smell."

"Ain't gonna happen." Chriss Anne pinched her nose.

The drivers got out of the truck, and Zeke surged toward them as if meeting a long-lost relative.

"He really likes camels, huh?" Chriss Anne said.

"Apparently." Ember took care to breathe through her mouth.

Chriss Anne's gaze dropped to Zeke's butt encased in well-worn Wranglers, and she mumbled, "He does have a nice ass, but he's going to smell like camels."

"No doubt we're all going to smell like camels before the day is done," Ember said, willing herself not to gag along with Chriss Anne as the truck drivers let the trailer gate down.

"The smell will get better," Zeke promised cheerily. "Once they are out in the open."

"He's an optimistic sort, isn't he?" Fiona

256

said, coming up on Ember's right.

"You do have to admire someone with so much zeal for camels," Ember said.

"And they called it camel love," Palmer sang to the tune of "Puppy Love" and wriggled his eyebrows suggestively.

Chriss Anne giggled.

Fiona scolded, "Don't be a perv. Zeke is a nice guy."

Zeke was busy helping the drivers unload the eight camels and hopefully didn't hear any of Palmer's camel love nonsense.

Ember glanced around and counted heads. Everyone from the cast and crew was there except Ranger. She pulled out her phone. No text. She texted him. Where R U????

She waited a bit, watched the camels unloading. Despite Zeke's obvious adoration for the animals, they stunk to high heaven, groaned thunderously, and rolled their eyes frequently. It had been fourteen years since there were camels at the Silver Feather, and Ember had forgotten about the reality of what they were like up close and personal.

All eight camels were led out of the trailer, and the truck drivers helped Zeke tie them together, caravan style.

No text from Ranger.

Should she text again? It had been only five minutes. Give him some space. But not too much space. The drivers would be leaving soon, and eight camels were too much for Zeke to handle on his own.

"Camels' feet expand when bearing weight to keep them from sinking in the sand," Zeke announced to the group at large, for no reason in particular it seemed, but he zeroed in on Chriss Anne, stepped closer to her.

Chriss Anne waved away buzzing flies. "Good for them."

"Camels are one of the few mammals who make love sitting down," Zeke went on as if he was Camel-wikipedia.

"Huh? How does that work?" Chriss Anne asked.

From behind his camera, Palmer sang again, "And they called it camel love."

"Has anyone seen Ranger this morning?" Ember asked.

"Yeah," said one of the grips. "I saw him and Dawn going into La Hacienda Grill when I was driving over this morning."

Oh really? Ember whipped out her phone again, took her sunglasses off. Texted: Put down the rancheros huevos and come to the set. Camels R here.

Immediately her phone dinged, and she

smiled. She had his attention at last.

Right behind U.

She turned and there he was. Grinning. Ember grinned back and then she saw . . .

. . . Dawn.

Looking even blonder, taller, and more goddessy than ever, her arm linked around Ranger's elbow, the sun glinting off her golden cheekbones.

Ember gritted her teeth, forced the corners of her mouth upward, and hoped she didn't look like a shark. Quickly, she shot a glance at Fiona to see how she was taking this unfolding situation with Dawn, but Fiona was whispering in Palmer's ear.

Fudge rockets. Nothing was going according to plan.

Time to gain control. Ember clapped her hands. "People, people, may I have your attention?"

Every eye in the desert swung her way, including the camels'. One of them spit a stream of yuck that landed just short of Chriss Anne's espadrilles.

"Eew, eew! He spit a loogie at me!"

"Actually," Zeke said, "he's a she and it's not really a loogie. A loogie is phlegm coughed up from the lungs. Camels are ruminants. It's basically vomit."

"Gross! Gross!" Chriss Anne trotted far away from the camels.

"All in all, vomit is not any worse than phlegm." Dawn shrugged pragmatically. "They both wash off."

"That's a Kiwi for you," Ranger said proudly. "Sensible as the day is long."

Oh yes, New Zealand was heaven and all those who lived there, saints.

"Are you aware," Fiona whispered in Ember's ear, "that you're grinding your teeth?"

"Bullhorn." Ember snapped her fingers at Chriss Anne, who hurried to her car as quickly as she could in the desert-inappropriate footwear to retrieve the bull-horn. Zeke watched her go with a smitten look on his face.

Ranger and Dawn were talking about fellowships and the McDonald Observatory and the fast radio bursts. Palmer had swung his camera around to Fiona and was filming her instead of the camels.

Ember sighed. It was shaping up to be a very long day.

And it only went downhill from there.

The scene required eight of the actors to ride camels. Only Zeke, who wasn't acting in the film, Ranger, and Ember had ridden camels before. Although Ember's experience was limited. She'd ridden twice, many moons ago, when there had been camels at the Silver Feather — and both times, she'd gone tandem in the saddle with Ranger.

History — and the script — called for Mary Beale, a.k.a. Fiona, to learn to ride a camel under the tutelage of her husband, Edward.

Fiona, however, folded her arms over her chest, hardening her chin, as stubborn as a camel, shook her head and declared, "I am not riding that *thing.*"

No amount of wheedling could change her mind.

"I'll do it," Dawn said gamely. "I'll be Fiona's body double. I can wear a wig, and you can film me mostly from behind and at a distance."

Hey, hey! Who was the director here? Ember smiled like a razor blade. "Don't you have a job at the observatory to get to?"

"Pah." Dawn waved a slender, beautiful hand. "Doesn't start until next week. I'm game for camel riding."

Smile. Smile. Ember wasn't going to let anyone know she was anything less than thrilled with Dawn's suggestion. "Thank you for your generous offer, Dawn, but you are far too tall. You're what? Six foot?"

"Five-ten," Dawn supplied.

"Mary Beale was only five foot four, like Fiona and me."

"Does it really have to be *that* historically accurate?" Dawn asked.

It was all Ember could do to lock down her temper and stay civil to Ranger's research partner.

"I'm sorry to be such a bother," Fiona apologized. "But I'm just not a camel person."

"Who is?" Palmer asked, sidling over to Fiona. "No one is blaming you. Face it, you could get hurt climbing on one of those smelly things, and that would be terrible."

Fiona slid him a sunbeam smile and he inched closer.

"You could play Mary Beale, Em," Ranger said, looking snappy in his military period costume. "Wear a brunette wig. Be Fiona's body double."

"I'm directing."

"You can do both. Palmer can handle setting up the shot." Ranger was giving her a look that sent an inappropriate thrill through her.

Was it her imagination, or was he feeling the heat too?

She just about had herself convinced there was something different in his eyes when he watched her, but then he slipped his arm around Dawn's waist and planted a kiss at her temple and whispered something in her ear.

Dawn giggled. "Right," she said to Ranger. To Ember she said, "I challenge you to a camel race. First one to reach that billboard . . ." She waved toward a large billboard, a quarter of a mile away, depicting a cowboy roping a giant armadillo and advertising a local western wear shop. "If you win, you're Fiona's stand-in. But if I win" — Dawn lowered her voice, all hot and whispery — "I play Ranger's lover."

She should have said no. Should have pulled rank and ordered Dawn off her set. But the impulsive part of her, the competitive part of her, hell, the *jealous* part of her, said, "You're on, Blondie."

And before anyone could protest, Ember threw herself atop one of the seated camels Zeke had just saddled and took off.

CHAPTER 14

"Full many a flower is born to blush un-
seen, and waste its fragrance on the
desert air."
— Jane Austen, *Emma*

Or at least that was her intention.

The camel, who had been jostling in a
trailer for days, crowded in close with her
fellow dromedaries, was in no mood for an
impromptu race.

Quite out of sorts, the camel refused
Ember's bidding.

Ember nudged the animal with her heels
as if she were a horse, urging her to her feet,
but the mulish creature turned her head and
spit a stream of yuck that came perilously
close to landing on Ember's shoulder.

"Watch out!" Chriss Anne cried and par-
roted Zeke. "Remember, camels have sex
while sitting down."

"And they called it camel love," Palmer

crooned.

"Shut up!" Ember yelled at him. Fudge rockets. The wheels were coming off the cart, and she was losing her cool. Not good.

Palmer grinned, unoffended. He knew he was being obnoxious.

"See you at the finish line, loser," Dawn, who'd climbed aboard a camel of her own, called over her shoulder.

"Zeke," Ember commanded. "How do I get this old girl on her feet?"

"Stop trying to control her," Zeke instructed, rushing over to help.

"Eat my dust!" Dawn said, and quite literally kicked dust over Zeke, Ember, and her lackadaisical beast of burden.

Dammit! Ember hated to lose. Especially to the golden goddess.

Sputtering against the gritty sand on her lips, Ember glowered at Dawn's departing back.

Suddenly, the camel decided she was going to get into the game, and she lurched up on her back legs.

"Lean back in the saddle, lean back in the saddle!" Zeke hollered.

The camel rocked forward as she rose to her front legs. It felt as if the entire world was shaking. Clutching the creature around the neck, Ember sucked in wind and slammed her eyes closed.

"Lean forward, lean forward!" Zeke said.

"Make up your mind!" Ember wailed.

Ranger, the unhelpful sod, stood on the sidelines laughing his ass off.

She blew a raspberry at him.

The camel seemed to think the rude salute was intended for her. She let out a fierce noise, snorted, and shot across the sand like a jackrabbit.

Ember shrieked.

Zeke grabbed the bullhorn and started running after her, calling out technical instructions. "Adjust yourself so you're sitting in the middle of the saddle. Try to cross your legs in front. It'll distribute your weight more evenly."

Yeah, that was so not happening. It was all she could do to hang on. The camel seemed jet-propelled, clearly on a mission to kill Ember.

Zeke was still following her but starting to lag. "Place one hand on the wooden handle in front of you. Put the other hand on the handle behind your seat."

What wooden handle? She didn't see any wooden handle.

Um, it would help, Alzate, if you opened your eyes. She tried it. Regretted the move when she saw the ground flying away beneath the crazy camel's churning legs.

Shit, shit, shit. She was going to fall. She was going to die. Okay, she was going to try not to land on her head and break her fool neck. This was what she got for being impulsive and competitive and jealous and stupid . . .

"Sit comfortably and glide with the movements, don't resist the sway . . . just relax," Zeke broadcast over the bullhorn.

Oh, she wanted to take that bullhorn and his advice and show him what he could do with it. Every muscle in her body tensed. Yep. Today was going to be the day someone died. Possibly Zeke for his ridiculous instructions. Could be Ranger for laughing at her. More likely it would be her for her moronic tendency to assume she could figure things out as she went.

And oh look. She was *gaining* on Dawn.

How had that happened?

Her camel, once ignited, flamed like the sun, streaming along, not the least bit troubled by Ember screaming a terrified, "Ahheee" that rang out across the desert.

Dawn whipped her head around, looked utterly surprised to see Ember pulling up beside her. The cowboy-roping-an-armadillo billboard was mere yards away. She could beat the Kiwi. She could win.

"You!" Dawn exclaimed.

"Me," Ember confirmed through clenched teeth. *Don't mess with a determined redhead, Blondie.*

Ember's camel flew past Dawn, but once she reached the billboard — winning, by the way — her camel just kept going.

"Whoa, whoa," she said, pulling back on the reins.

The camel bulleting along at a healthy clip, suddenly plunged all four feet into the sand, coming to a complete, teeth-slamming stop.

Sending Ember flying over her head and onto the hard desert earth. She ended up spread-eagle on her back in a patch of thorny vegetation, gasping like a landed guppy and staring blurrily at a drooling dromedary.

"Ember! Ember!" Ranger knelt at her side.

Her empty lungs could not respond.

Eyes shooting wide open, face draining of color, Ranger grappled for her wrist, pressed two fingers to her pulse.

Yes, dear friend, I'm alive. I have not died.

"Em? Can you hear me?" He dragged her into his arms. Strong, safe, harbor-in-a-storm arms and gathered her close to his chest.

If she could breathe, it would feel nice —
really nice — resting here with her head
cradled against his elbow.

"Em?" His eyes searched her face.

Okay, I'm okay. She nodded.

"If I wasn't so worried about you, I'd swat
your fanny for that stunt," he said, his voice
heavy with kindness. He was the only
person on the face of the earth who could
get away with saying something like that to
her.

Her breath slowly came back to her and
she turned her head to say something, but
felt a prickling sting shoot down her back.
Something was poking her in the neck.

She groaned, winced.

"Medic! Do we have a medic on-site?"
Ranger yelled, uncharacteristic panic in his
voice.

He was the least panicky person she knew.
She wanted to tell him she was perfectly
fine if he'd just pluck the thorn out of her
neck, but she couldn't draw in air past the
lung spasms.

"Th . . . thor . . ." She wheezed, trying to
reach around to pluck the thorn from her
neck.

"Don't thrash, you could have a neck
injury."

She did. A damn thorn. "Thor . . .

thor . . ."

Ranger held the back of her head in his palms, immobilizing her. "Thor? It felt like Thor struck you with a lightning bolt?"

Sometimes it was annoying to have a friend who was too well-read. Who the hell else would think she was talking about Thor, the Norse god of thunder and lightning?

Ranger moved this thumb, accidentally driving the thick thorn deeper into her flesh.

Ember yelped. Good news, her lungs were working again.

"What is it?" Alarm deepened his voice.

She squirmed, struggling to move from his strong grip.

"Oh shit, Sparky, you have a huge thorn in your neck."

"Well, duh, Professor. Get it out."

Gently, he turned her head to one side, cupping her cheek in his palm. She was still lying in the dirt, her back supported by his thighs where he knelt.

"It's in there deep, babe."

Babe?

Not once in their lives had Ranger ever called her "babe." Why was he doing so now?

Ember was having a hard time catching her breath again, and this time it had nothing to do with hitting the ground after catapulting over a camel's head.

"It's a mesquite thorn, babe." There it was again. "This is probably going to hurt . . ."

"It already hurts."

He made a hissing sound.

Ember was vaguely aware that the cast and crew had strolled over to ring a circle around them, gawking at the proceedings. But what captivated her was Ranger's lap. He shifted as he examined the best way to get at the thorn, sliding into a cross-legged position, his butt planted firmly on the earth. Her head level with his crotch.

She thought of the day they went land sailing and her face flushed hot.

Despite the crowd, it felt too damn intimate. If her knees hadn't been rubber, she would have jumped right up, yanked the thorn out on her own, and gone right back to work.

But Ranger was doing this strange thing, tenderly stroking her temple and breathing so slowly and deeply she found herself helplessly matching his rhythm. He was murmuring something about the cosmos, a run-on, stream-of-conscious kind of thing, hypnotic and lulling.

"A comet," he said as if he were reading it straight from a textbook, "isn't as glorious as it sounds. It's basically just a dirty snowball made of space ice and rock debris."

She laughed softly, felt the sound vibrate through the stiff denim of his jeans, and that made her think of land sailing again, and she froze.

Holy amortization, what was wrong with her? Why this immense and undeniable sexual attraction to her best friend? It was wrong. It should be taboo, and yet, and yet . . . God, how she wanted him in every way possible.

"There you go, sweetheart," Ranger said.

Sweetheart? First *babe,* now *sweetheart*? What did this mean? she thought miserably. Weren't he and Dawn an item? Argh, she was so confused.

He held an open palm in front of her face. "All out."

She stared at the half-inch-long gray thorn, the tip of it tinged with her blood. She'd been so lulled by his mesmerizing voice and gentle touch she hadn't felt him extract the thorn.

"We need to clean that wound, so it doesn't get infected."

"I've got the first-aid kit," Chriss Anne said helpfully, and passed the white box with a red cross on it to Ranger.

Ember couldn't say why she didn't get up

at this point. She should have gotten up. She hated appearing weak and helpless in front of people. But there was something happening here between them. Not sure what, but something. Something more than their regular friendship and affable bond.

Something that felt rare and divine.

Unless she was just fooling herself.

But he'd called her *babe* and *sweetheart.*

So she just sat there while he cleaned the puncture site with alcohol and dabbed on antibiotic ointment and finished off with a Band-Aid.

Ranger got up, reached down, offering her his hand.

She touched his palm, felt a bolt of energy course between them so fierce it belonged in a fairy tale. She stared into his eyes and he stared back, and suddenly he was so much more than her best friend, Ranger. He was every dream she'd never dared dream for fear of ruining their closeness.

She sucked in a deep breath.

So did he.

"I'm sorry you got hurt," he said. "But you did beat Dawn. You get to be Fiona's stand-in." He looked inordinately happy at that turn of events, but maybe she was projecting.

Ember's legs were currently so shaky she

couldn't even answer.

"A win is a win," Dawn said. "I'm not afraid to admit when I've been bested. Good on you, Ember."

"Enough entertainment for one morning," Ember barked, back in director mode, and dusted off her clothes. "Back to work everyone."

"Um." Fiona was lacing and unlacing her fingers; her face was screwed up into a wellspring of guilt. "Could I talk to you a minute, Ember?"

"You don't need to feel badly about skipping out on this scene. Camels can be hard to handle." Ember brushed her palms down her fanny, dispersing sand.

"I'm really sorry."

"No biggie. I can deal."

Fiona cleared her throat, but didn't quite meet Ember's eyes. "I'm not just begging off from this scene."

Ember stopped dusting herself, straightened, and tilted her head. There was a tone of finality in Fiona's voice. "What's wrong?"

"I . . . the scene where Edward kisses Mary . . . I don't feel comfortable doing it. Could you possibly . . ."

Yes, cried Ember's heart. *Yes!* But her mouth said, "I know kiss scenes are difficult, but it doesn't mean anything. Look at it like a job."

"You're doing the camel scene for me. I was just hoping you could step in on this one too."

"It can work for me to be your body double on a camel, but it's not going to work for close-ups. The kiss scene has to be shot close up."

"Ember." Fiona's voice went up an octave, high and stringy, pleading for understanding. "I don't *want* to play this scene with Ranger. I don't want to kiss him. I'm saving my kisses for one person . . ." Fiona slipped a glance over at Palmer.

"You and Palmer are together?"

Fiona shrugged, grinned coyly. "Last night, after everyone left Chantilly's Palmer and I . . . well, let's just say I'm no longer the least bit interested in Ranger."

"Okay, that's fine. No harm, no foul, but you can still do the film with Ranger."

"That's the thing. I kind of want out of the film."

"But you love acting," Ember said. "That's what you told me when I cast you for the role."

"Not as much as I want to explore this thing with Palmer." Fiona giggled.

"Oh." Ember blinked. "That was fast."

"I told you I was ready for a man in my life."

"What can I say?" Ember was steamed, but trying not to show it. She couldn't force Fiona to stay on the film.

"I appreciate everything you did for me," Fiona said. "Truly."

"You're totally walking away?"

"I know that means you'll have to reshoot my scenes."

"I could ask Luke if he could pay you a little something, if you stay. But —"

"It's unfair to everyone else," Fiona finished for her. "It's not about the money. Truly, it's about Palmer and me."

It took everything Ember had in her to smile. "You're free as a bird." She sounded cool, oh yes she did, but inside she was scrambling for a solution. She was the one who'd hired Fiona, and she'd have to tell Luke she'd made a mistake in casting the church secretary. She hated when she was wrong.

Fiona kept knotting her fingers. "I'm so sorry —"

Ember made a stop sign with her palm. "Think nothing of it. You do what's right for you. I mean that." And she did. Life was too short to feel guilty. She would figure out this new curveball later. "Have fun with

Palmer."

Fiona slapped her palms together like she was saying a prayer. "Thank you, thank you! You're the most awesome person."

"I'll do it," a voice said from behind Ember.

Ember turned to see Dawn looming behind her, and stifled a groan. "Do what?"

"I'll play Mary Beale. I can't *wait* to kiss Ranger."

Jealousy was a runaway freight train whizzing right through Ember. "We already discussed this. You're too tall," she said brusquely.

"Palmer could adjust the camera angle to make me look shorter." Dawn's face was gold, glistening in the morning light. "I already talked to him about it."

"Fellowship. Observatory." Ember was so freaked at the idea of watching Dawn kiss Ranger that she couldn't form complete sentences.

"Next week," Dawn reminded her.

"Filming for three weeks."

"You could film all my scenes with Ranger first."

Damn the woman for being so helpful. "Appreciate the offer," Ember lied like a shag rug at Graceland. She did *not* appreciate the offer. Not one little bit.

The worst part of Ember's personality wanted to say, *He called me "babe" and "sweetheart." Put that in your pipe and smoke it, Kiwi goddess.* But her better side won out — dammit — and she simply smiled.

"What's up?" Ranger asked, strolling over.

"Fiona's quitting the film," Dawn said.

"Aww, too bad." His tone was sympathetic, but he didn't look the least bit unhappy.

"Dawn was generous enough to volunteer to take her place." Ember had to force her jaw to unclench.

"But Ember's going to do it." Dawn sounded unexpectedly giddy and gleeful.

Ember whipped her head around in time to see Dawn and Ranger exchange a weighted glance. A meaningful glance that made her sick to the very pit of her stomach.

"Hmm," Ranger said, then turned and walked away without another word.

Holy second mortgage. Was he upset? About Fiona? Or the fact she was going to play Mary Beale? Ember raced to catch up to him. She *had* to see his face.

"Range?"

He stopped, peered over at her, his expression mild and noncommittal. Oh she knew that look, had seen it across a poker table many times.

It was the face of a man in possession of a killer hand.

Only, she had no idea what game they were playing.

He was going to kiss Ember.

The thought burrowed deep into his brain, and Ranger literally could not think of anything else. After almost thirty-three years of knowing her, and loving her a dozen different ways, this new dimension of love hit him like a winter tornado, shocking, surprising, twisting him inside out.

He was about to kiss his best friend.

Granted, it was not the optimal way to share a first kiss. It would be for a film, in front of cast and crew, but it didn't matter. At long last, he was going to kiss her.

And because it was for the film, if things turned sour and she didn't reciprocate his feelings, then no harm, no foul. They could go right back to how things were before.

Safe. He was completely safe. He couldn't miss.

Or so he told himself.

He stared at Ember's lips, so ripe and pink and lush, and he almost kissed her right then and there, the film be damned. So many years he'd looked at those lips, and yet until this moment he'd never quite seen them.

Not in the way he was seeing them now — soft, succulent, sensual, celestial. Incredible instruments of love.

"Are you all right?" Ember asked.

"Yeah, sure," he grunted, putting on his poker face. Hell no, he was not okay. He was madly in love with his best friend, and he was about to kiss her in front of all these people, and he was scared to the core of his bones that she was not going to love him back in the same way he loved her. "Why wouldn't I be?"

"Because Fiona doesn't want to kiss you —"

"I wasn't the least bit invested in Fiona. *You* were the one who thought we'd make a good match. She and Palmer are much better suited."

"I can see that now."

"So are you going to stop matchmaking people?"

"Well —"

"Em*ber.*" He put emphasis on the last syllable of her name the way he did when he meant business.

"Chriss Anne asked for my help . . ."

He raised an index finger. "Stay out of it."

"This feels like another Lucy and Ricky

Ricardo moment."

"Which means if I want you to stop matching people up, then I can't tell you to stop or you'll charge in guns blazing."

Her mischievous smile lit a fire inside him. "Now you're catching on. Strip."

"Huh?" Ranger blinked. "What are you talking about?"

"Strip off your shirt. Haven't you read the script? In this scene, Edward is bare chested."

He'd memorized his lines, but he hadn't paid much attention to the stage directions in the script. "You gotta be kidding me."

"Don't worry, we'll slather you with sunscreen."

He remembered the last time she'd slathered him with lotion. Hell, he was already lathered up, and it had nothing to do with sun exposure. Unless you considered Ember the sun, which come to think of it, was a pretty accurate metaphor for his best friend — bright, hot, intense. The sun was essential, but it could burn you up if you didn't respect its power.

And every single day, scientists feared the loss of the sun.

Without the sun, there was no life.

Without Ember, *he* had no life.

A chill went through him. An ice block of

terror. Without the sun, without the sun, without the sun . . .

Frozen.

A wasteland.

"Strip," Ember repeated, grinning like it was her birthday.

And he was already starting to sweat. Both hot and cold. Time seemed to warp, feverish and dreamlike. A desert mirage. How long had he felt this way? Was it a good thing or a bad thing that he loved, desired, and feared his best friend?

Feared her because if anything happened to her, to their relationship . . . if he lost her, oh if he lost her . . . life was an empty black hole. A vacuum of nothingness.

If he was stronger, bolder, braver, he would take that chance and just tell her what he was feeling. But that fear, the icy bite of it, still held him in its teeth from the day he'd stood beside her at the altar as her man of honor and watched her marry Trey.

Her eyes were latched on to his, and they stood in the heat. Staring and breathing.

A challenge of some kind.

A dare he didn't know if he should take. Her blue eyes mysterious as quarks, lustrous and shimmering with energy. In the face of so much heat, he glanced away. Terrified he'd go blind if he did not.

There was that fear again.

His knees were stiff with it. His heart swollen and sluggish. What human being hadn't felt fear in the face of such great love? The sheer force of letting go, of trusting another, of being fully and completely vulnerable.

And yet, there was the hope that behind the fear lay an oasis of joy.

He met her eyes once more. *Go ahead. Stare at the sun. Be bold. Stick with the plan. It will work.*

Finally, he wrenched his gaze from Ember's, smiled over at Dawn as if *she* were his sun, and said, "Could you help me get naked?"

CHAPTER 15

"How often is happiness destroyed by preparation, foolish preparation!"
— Jane Austen, *Emma*

They were standing on the front porch of what had at one time been Edward and Mary Beale's home when Edward was stationed at Fort Davis in 1857.

Ranger was in front of Ember, naked from the waist up, the sun glistening off his tanned body. Droplets of sweat pearled at the hollow of his throat. His dark hair curled around the top of his ears. He exuded masculine power and panther-like grace.

Ember stared at her best friend, who looked so incredibly different to her now. Peering through the flimsy gauze of the past, through memory and dreams. Seeing him, fully seeing him for the first time.

It was as if she'd been blind for thirty-two years and undergone a miraculous new surgery to restore her sight, and with the removal of surgical bandages, every detail was sharply vivid and brand-new.

She noticed everything. The sensual curve of his mouth, the small bump at the bridge of his nose, the silvered scar tracking down the middle of his chest, the flex of his honed muscles, the bob of his Adam's apple as he swallowed.

Fascinated. Captivated. She was stunned by the freshness of her sight, overwhelmed by the blooming catalog of his spectacular attributes.

Palmer brought the main camera in for the close-up. The boom mike dangling over their heads. The crew and cast members stood watching, Fiona peeping over Palmer's shoulder. Everyone was about to watch her kiss Ranger for the very first time.

No big deal. It was just a kiss for a film. It didn't mean a thing.

Short. Sweet. A touching of their lips. No open mouths. Chaste. Innocent. A family-friendly film.

Except Ember's pulse was racing and her breath came out fast and shallow, and all she could taste was the strong, cool-hot tang of the peppermint she'd popped into her mouth. What if they didn't get it right on the first take? What if they had to kiss again and again and again?

She pushed up the sleeves of her Mary Beale costume and took a step closer to Ranger.

"Ready?" she whispered.

"Ready." His tone was airy, but his eyes, oh those deep brown eyes, were heavy, full of mystery and danger.

Dangerous. This was very dangerous. She was treading on unstable ground. How had she ever believed she knew him?

Silently, she shifted to director mode and counted down on her fingers, arm at her side, signaling Palmer when to start filming.

Ranger stepped closer, until mere inches separated them. He dipped his head. Sighed softly. "Mary."

Oh shit, oh shit! Stop. Cut. Cut. Cut. Bail out. Bail out. Once she did this, there was no undoing it.

Ember didn't know where she found her voice or the courage, but she managed to stay stock-still and murmur her one-word line with heart and heat. "Edward."

His bare chest was a wall, striated with well-honed muscles, the old scar, and a whorl of dark hair. His body was a heater, radiant and hot, blasting straight into her.

Perspiration slid between her breasts, and it was all she could do to remain rooted to the wooden floorboards.

She had a purpose. An intention. Film this scene. Make this picture. As if she knew what she was doing. As if she had the slightest clue.

Her pulse was a hammer, hard and resilient, thundering out a message — *kiss him, kiss him, kiss him.*

Ranger looked down at her, his dark brown eyes unfathomable, revealing nothing. The gambler playing his cards close to his vest.

Just do it. Just kiss him. Don't think about it.

Ignoring her trembling legs, and her quivering belly, Ember slipped her arms around Ranger's neck, paused a moment and shot a glance at Palmer. "Are you getting this?"

The cameraman gave her a thumbs-up.

Ranger made a low sound that only she could hear, a soft chuckle. "God," he murmured, "you are amazing."

If she really was amazing, wouldn't she be handling this much better? Wouldn't she just breeze on through and get it done, rather than tying herself into knots over the idea that she was about to kiss her best friend, and no matter how she tried to trivialize it, nothing would ever be the same again.

It would haunt her dreams. She would know exactly what he tasted like. How his lips felt against hers. How —

Gak!

Ranger settled his hands at Ember's waist as was called for in the script. Script or not, it felt good to be held like this.

Too good. She was getting distracted. She was supposed to be performing a role, not enjoying herself.

His gaze locked on her and his smile widened, and she thought, *This is real, this is happening.* The urge to flee was overwhelming. She *would* have fled if she could have moved.

Her knees quaked and chills ran up and down her spine, excitement playing her like a glockenspiel. She was aware that every eye on the set was locked on them, and it seemed as if the entire crew held a collective breath.

Or maybe that was just all in her head.

Ember tightened her grip around his neck and peered into his eyes and forgot everything that wasn't Ranger. No more cast. No more crew. No more cameras. Delete, delete, delete. Vanished. Gone. Nothing but the two of them.

He pulled her closer, snuggled her against him.

Panic flooded her bloodstream. He was going to do it. He was going to kiss her. Yes, he was!

Her legs were boiled spaghetti. Her insides marshmallow, soft and sticky. How was it that she was not a puddle of melted goo glued to the floorboards at his feet?

Crazy, insane thoughts pinged around her brain. *I belong with you. You belong with me.*

Match made. Call Father Dubanowski. Book the wedding chapel. Send out the invitations. Shop for wedding gowns.

It was as if her brain was filled with Red Bull. A whole freaking case of the stuff. Hyped. Hyper. High.

High on Ranger's nearness. The smell of him, his touch. So familiar and yet so different. It was as if she'd been walking on a trail she walked every day, knew every stone and plant along the way, and one day, the earth shrugged with a tremor, shook, cracked open like an egg and she fell through to a whole new dimension.

A beautiful, magical world she had not even known existed.

He pulled her closer.

She gasped. Was she losing her mind?

"Ember," he whispered, not *Mary* as he should have.

She should have yelled "cut," stepped

away, gone for a walk, and taken a breather. Used any excuse to get away from him and clear her head.

But she was too far gone to care.

Their gazes were linked as if by a glittering gold chain. The moment was upon them. They couldn't get any closer.

The sun beat down, turning up the heat. Somewhere a camel belched.

Loudly.

Ember giggled.

Ranger laughed.

She was about to yell "cut," but she couldn't.

Because Ranger was kissing her.

Instantly, her body responded. Leaning into him. Clinging to his shoulders. Pushing against him as if she could push herself all the way *into* him. The urge to merge was immediate, overwhelming.

This man. Mine. Now.

Fiery tingles flashed from his lips to hers and back again, completing the electrical circuit. Lighting them up. Pulsating. Vibrating. Humming like a power plant.

Humming.

So much damn humming.

It was a deafening chorus of humming. A million honeybees dancing. The high, hot licks of bonfire flames. The wild, colorful

290

whirling of a spindle top.

Goose bumps spread over her arms. Her nerve endings seemed to split, divide, shatter, and then reassemble until she was glowing, shimmering, buzzing.

Dizzy, dazed, she staggered against him, realized his knees had buckled just as surely as hers, and they were holding each other up.

How vast this was! How delicious the extent of his mouth and teeth and tongue. There was not a single sentient soul on earth, and all the other planets, galaxies, and universes in the endless expanse of the cosmos, that wouldn't kill, bare-handed, for this feeling.

Alive.

Electric.

Plugged in.

Through his kiss, she felt plugged into all that is, all that had been, and all that ever would be. Connected. Filled with love and light. Open. Raw. Shocked and delighted by the sheer power of her awakening.

It was as if she wore new skin, heard with new ears. A brand-new soul. Alive for the first time. Drawing her first breath.

She yearned for him with a longing so deep and wide it could never be filled. His mouth ravaged hers as if he were tasting some sweet nourishing fruit. A fruit that if he just ate enough of it, would heal all wounds, past, present, and future.

And that humming! On and on it went. A symphony, a chorus, an opera.

That indescribably beautiful sound. Harp-plucking angels could not play so pleasingly.

All along, all along, Granny Blue had been right.

"Ranger?" Ember whispered, the word coming out of her mouth stunned and stumbling.

"Uh-huh?" His eyes were half-lidded, his voice molasses.

"Do you hear that?" She'd ruined the scene take, but she was past caring. The bottom had dropped out of her world in a wonderful, glorious way.

"What? The camels?"

The humming was fading like the volume slowly being turned down. She had to test it. Had to find out if she could start it back up.

She kissed him again.

Boom!

There it was. The humming. Coming at her in acoustical waves. An ocean of sound. Rolling over her. Through her. Inside her. Singing the song of the women in Granny Blue's ancestry, a steady repeating hum of

This One!

Ranger.

It had been Ranger all this time. Of all those frogs she'd kissed. The frog she'd married. The right one had been under her nose from the beginning.

Ranger was The One!

Her best friend was her true love. Her childhood playmate was her grown-up soul mate. Her destiny. Tears filled her eyes, and no matter how hard she tried not to cry, no matter how tough she pretended to be, Ember could not stop the tears from spilling down her cheeks in a blustery rain of joy.

"You're crying." Ranger pulled back, alarmed at her tears. "Are you okay? Have I hurt you?"

"Not me," she said, because she could not yet tell him what was in her heart and in her head. Not now. Not here. Not in front of all these people. She needed time to recover. "Mary. Mary is weeping to be reunited with her husband again after his long trek across the desert."

"You're acting." He sounded both disappointed and relieved.

"Yes," she agreed, because she was coming unhinged like old doors on a fixer-upper and because she had no idea what to do about it. What was he thinking? Was he as bowled over as she was? Or had it been uneventful for him? Could this humming thing be one-sided? She had so many questions and no clear-cut answers. An uncomfortable state of being for a woman who liked being in charge.

The humming was slipping away, and she could not bear to hear it go.

"Kiss me again," she said.

"What?"

"We need another take. We flubbed the other one. This time, shh. No talking. Just kissing."

"Got it," he said, and kissed her with gleeful intent.

The rush hit her like water from a fire hose, just as potent as before. Maybe even more so. Sound filled her head. Amplified. Exalted. A humprint, she decided, of his lips branding hers. Endless and intoxicating.

Her hands were shaking. It seemed too easy. So perfect. The rightness of them overwhelmingly simple. One kiss and her happy fate sealed.

But in the back of her mind, something niggled. A forgotten thought. A feather tickle in her stomach, gathering clouds in her chest; she was on the brink of a precipice, terrified that she should, but could not, jump.

Simultaneously, as if he picked up on her doubt, they broke the kiss. Sprang apart.

"Holy camel shit!" Zeke hooted. "I don't know about y'all, but I ain't never seen two best friends kiss like that."

Ranger was not the kind of man who believed in magical thinking. He was a scientist after all. Facts. Concrete details. Mathematics revealed how the world worked in provable equations. Those were the tools of his trade.

Then again, there was Einstein and his quandary with quantum mechanics. The "spooky actions at a distance" of particle entanglement. There *were* mysteries in the universe that science, as yet, could not fully explain.

The complexity of the human brain being one of them, and its relationship to emotion and the human heart.

As an astrobiologist, he believed in probability of life elsewhere in the universe; why not believe that there was such a thing as a predestination? Just because he couldn't prove it didn't mean it wasn't possible.

What could it hurt? This overwhelming belief that he and Ember were meant to be together. That their names had been written on some cosmic slate before they were born. An entanglement theory to top all entanglement theories.

Yep. Magical thinking. All the way.

And yet, he reveled in it. Embraced it. Breathed it in. Breathed *her* in. Wanted her more than he had ever wanted anything in his life. Wanted her with a craving far beyond physical need.

So what to do about it?

Come clean? Tell her how he felt? Own up to his undying love for her?

And risk ruining their friendship?

She'd cried during the kiss, and he'd thought, *Yes, yes, she feels it too.* This power. Their connection.

He'd never seen her cry when she was not in physical pain. When it came to feelings, Ember had a tough outer core. She let very few people see her emotional wounds. But when he'd asked her about the tears, she'd tossed off a smile and said she was acting, and all the stars had fallen from the sky because in his heart, in his head, *he* had forgotten all about the film.

Ranger had been fully invested in that magical moment. Fully kissing her, tasting her, living the experience of her. He hadn't been pretending to be Edward Beale kissing his wife, Mary, after coming home from a long journey. He'd been Ranger Lockhart, kissing his best friend. The friend he'd been aching to kiss since the time she'd come to visit him when he was in college and they'd gotten drunk at a party and ended up in bed together.

They had just fallen asleep, of course, no touching, nothing untoward or suggestive, but he'd awoken wanting so much more from her. It had taken monumental restraint not to seduce her.

At the time, he'd had a girlfriend and she'd had a boyfriend. She'd made him scrambled eggs in the morning, and they had drunk chocolate milk and laughed over their hangovers and taken aspirin and that had been that.

A missed opportunity? Or had it been part of a divine design, everything slowly leading to this moment?

What to do? Did he announce he was in love with her? Or did he play it cool? Wait? Let her make the first move? Or sweep her off her feet?

Ranger was good at waiting. Spending much of his childhood as an invalid had honed his patience. Sharpened the idea that good things came to those who waited.

Ember was a good thing. A great thing.

The best damn thing in his entire universe. He'd waited almost thirty-three years for her. He could wait a few weeks more if that's what it took.

But what if, oh what if, she hadn't felt the earth crack open as he had? What if, as he'd feared all along, she saw him as nothing more than a dear friend? What if he kept waiting and she never made the first move?

Because, reality slap here, if she'd had deeper feelings for him, would she really have married Trey in the first place?

Whatifwhatifwhatif?

He thought of a story Ember's Granny Blue had once told them as children around the campfire at her cabin in the mountains. A cautionary tale about letting your fears get the best of you. He remembered it now with vivid clarity, a fable about how Rabbit was once a great warrior, but because he feared the magic of the unknown to such an extent, he betrayed his friend and his true nature. Crying his fears so loudly he called Eagle to him, and that was the end of Rabbit.

The moral of the story being if you fed the fear, then fear was what you would bring into your life. Granny Blue had looked into the face of each child circled around the campfire and said, "If a rabbit has hopped into your life, it is a sign to stop talking about the horrible things that could happen and scrub *what if* out of your vocabulary. *Stop it now!*" The elderly woman's voice was in his head, as loudly as if she'd been standing beside him.

Had he, with his head in the stars, unwittingly become a rabbit? Letting fear rule his life?

Blinking, Ranger glanced around and realized he'd been so caught up in his thoughts that he hadn't heard a thing people had been saying to him, and now, everyone was staring.

"Was the take good?" he asked, his lips still pulsing with the pleasure of kissing Ember.

"Best film kiss ever," Palmer said. "You two have sizzling on-screen chemistry."

"That's because we've been friends forever." Ember efficiently brushed her hands together. Her countenance was the same. Brisk, in charge. Nothing had changed. At least not for her. "Now that we have that scene in the can, we can break for an early lunch."

Without saying a word to him, she pivoted and walked off the porch.

CHAPTER 16

"Mr. Knightley, if I have not spoken, it is because I am afraid I will awaken myself from this dream."
— Jane Austen, *Emma*

The minute that filming was finished for the day, and after turning down an invitation to head over to Chantilly's with the cast and crew, Ember practically flew her Infinity to the Silver Feather to see her younger sister.

She found Kaia sitting nursing baby Ingrid under a shaded pergola beside the shimmering pool, in a lavish outdoor space that Ridge had built for his wife who loved water. A pitcher of tea and two glasses filled with fresh ice sat on the table in front of her.

Ember looked at the two glasses. "Were you expecting someone?"

"You." Kaia gave her that heavenly Madonna smile that she'd picked up since she'd married Ridge and given birth to her daughter. As if she knew the secrets to the universe.

It could be really annoying.

"How did you know I was coming over? And don't give me any of that Granny Blue, a crow flew north at noon, baloney."

"No crow flew north at noon to the best of my knowledge." Kaia chuckled and shifted Ingrid to her shoulder, patted her back for a burp. "Ridge texted me when he saw you blow past the mansion. He's over helping Duke hang drywall for the new nursery."

Yes, Duke's third wife, Vivi, was pregnant — with twins — the four Lockhart brothers would have two new half brothers in four months. Making young Ingrid older than her uncles. Duke would be a father again at sixty-one. Here was hoping he'd do a much better job this time around.

"Have a seat." Kaia kicked out the leg of the chair across from her with her foot. "You look off balance."

Ember sat down, although a part of her wanted to run far away. She was the big sister. She should be the one doling out advice, not the other way around. But Kaia was the only one who had experienced the humming, other than Granny Blue, and she wasn't in the mood to get a wise, I-told-you-so nod from her grandmother.

"How's the filming going?" Kaia poured tea over the two glasses of ice, pushed one toward Ember.

"Great, fine, listen . . ." Ember brushed back a lock of hair that had fallen from her ponytail.

"All ears, sis. What's up?"

"Um . . ." How to start? *Just shoot from the lips. It's what you do.* "I heard it."

Kaia cocked her head, a whimsical smile lighting up her eyes. "And what did you hear?"

"You know." Ember bobbed her head, wriggled her eyebrows, trying to get her point across without having to come out and say the words. *"It."*

"I'm not sure what *it* is."

"You're enjoying this," Ember accused.

"Enjoying having tea with my big sister? Yes, I am." Kaia winked.

"Good gravy, Kaia, you know what I mean."

"Do I?"

"I heard the humming, okay? Is that what you want to hear? Hum, hum, hum. There, I said it. I heard the freaking hum."

Rather than tease her as she expected,

302

Kaia's face took on the same rapturous hue it did whenever she looked at her husband or Ingrid. Her voice became soft as baby duck fuzz. "Oh Ember, I am so happy for you."

Kaia got up and settled Ingrid into her infant carrier, came over, knelt beside Ember, and wrapped her in the most loving, accepting hug Ember had ever gotten.

Ember's heart melted, and the tears she'd cried on that front porch at Fort Davis and pretended it was just acting pressed against the back of her eyelids again. Fudge rockets! Did the humming turn you into a sap?

"That's wonderful." Kaia rocked back on her heels.

Unable to speak, Ember merely shook her head no.

"It's not wonderful?"

"It . . . I . . ." Words escaped her. Her lips were empty. She had nothing to shoot with. How could she begin to put into words the magnitude of what had happened to her?

"It's Ranger, isn't it?" Kaia guessed.

Ember nodded, this time managing not to cry, but Kaia saw the shine in her eyes and handed her a tissue.

"Well, that's the best news ever. You already love him."

"This is . . . different."

303

Kaia took both of Ember's hands into hers, gazed into her eyes. "Yes, yes, it is. What you are feeling is so much more than you possibly know right now."

Those damn tears were at her again. She pressed the tissue to her eyes, held her breath, willed herself not to cry.

"Aww, see? You *are* moved. Not much moves you to tears, but having your best friend also be your soul mate? Sweetie, *everyone* wants that. You are one of the rare few who've found it."

"I don't even believe in that soul mate stuff," Ember protested.

Kaia's eyes were kind and nonjudgmental. "I didn't either in the beginning, but now I *know* that it is so. This new love you feel for Ranger is on a whole other plane. You'll see, you'll see."

"How can I know he feels the same?"

"Trust the humming. I know it sounds silly, and I know you hate letting go of control." Kaia laughed. "I know it's hard turning the reins over to the" — Kaia cupped her hands over her ears, smiled wider, and rolled her eyes heavenward — "hum. But it is so worth it."

"Listen to us. We're talking like this is —"

"Real?"

Ember nodded.

"It is. Love *is* real."

"But this humming —"

"Don't get caught up in the sound," Kaia said. "Although I do know how difficult it is to ignore the hum when it vibrates through-out your entire body. The energy . . . well, I don't have to explain it to you. You know."

"What do you mean? The sound is how I *know*. Know what?"

"No." Kaia rested a hand on Ember's knee and peered up into her eyes. "The sound just confirms what you already know deep in your heart. Ranger is meant for you and you for him."

"He didn't act interested. He just stood there, poker-faced, as if he felt nothing."

"Ranger is a scientist. If you think this humming thing is tough for you, imagine how he's trying to explain it to himself."

"He heard the humming too? Does Ridge hear it?"

"As far as I know, only we Alzate women are lucky enough to hear the humming. But our men? They feel it. They know, even when they're afraid to know."

"But Ranger is interested in Dawn," Ember said glumly.

"His Kiwi research partner?"

"Yes. You should see the two of them together. They are like peas in a pod."

Kaia scoffed. "She's got nothing on you."

"Have you seen her? She's a golden goddess with legs that won't quit."

"And you're a redheaded sprite with enough fire to ignite the whole Trans-Pecos."

"Goddess trumps sprite."

"Thirty plus years of friendship trumps the hell out of research partner."

Ember wrung her hands, frustrated with this new indecisive part of herself. "What should I do?"

"Tell Ranger about the humming." Kaia shrugged as if that was the easiest thing in the world.

"What if he . . . what if he just wants to be friends?"

"What if frogs had wings? They wouldn't bump their butts when they hop. *What ifs* come from fear, and you know what Granny Blue says about fear."

"I'm scared, Ki." Ember could barely hear her own whisper. Ingrid whimpered in her sleep, a low, soft baby sound. "I know you are used to me being the brave, bold one, but it's all an act. Deep down, I'm scared as everyone else."

"What are you so afraid of?"

"That this is going to change everything. I don't know that I'm ready to change."

"There's nothing to be afraid of." Kaia matched her whisper and took Ember's hands in hers. Her palms were cool and dry. "Close your eyes and think about all the memories you've shared with Ranger."

The dominant, go-getter part of Ember's personality wanted to resist. This was foreign and scary and she didn't like being vulnerable. She snorted and shifted and muttered, "Fuck this," but then she did as her sister asked. She closed her eyes and squeezed Kaia's hand . . .

Called up a memory of her and Ranger at four years old, making mud pies from sand and water in the backyard of the foreman's house where she'd grown up. That image morphed into the two of them riding bikes down the country lane the year after he'd had heart surgery; her in a pink gingham blouse and cutoff blue jeans; Ranger in blue-and-red swim trunks, a gap in his smile where he was missing a front tooth, the scar at his chest fresh and dark pink. He challenged her to a race, and his face had bloomed into a proud smile when she'd bested him. She saw him propped up in bed on a pillow, his chest swathed in bandages, his face deathly pale in the recovery room after surgery. They played Parcheesi, and he called her on it when she let him win. She smelled the watermelon they'd eaten on the picnic table numerous times every summer and heard bottle rockets exploding on the Fourth of July, the smell of sulfur and gunpowder on their hands from lighting a match to the fireworks. She saw him at his stepmother Lucy's funeral in a blue suit that was too small for him, the orange clip-on tie hanging askew. She heard "Wherever You Will Go" one of the biggest songs on the radio their junior year in high school and danced with him at the prom and went swimming with him at midnight at Balmorhea State Park instead of going with their classmates to an after-prom party. They'd held hands as they jumped feet-first into the water. They were sixteen in his first vehicle, a beat-up blue Ford ranch truck with two hundred thousand miles on the broken odometer. They were five and at her brother Archer's sixth birthday party, blind-folded and playing pin the tail on the donkey. They were thirty at Ember's wedding to Trey, Ranger as her man of honor, looking like a movie star in an ebony tuxedo, and his sad, I'm-losing-you smile.

The images flittered through her head, moving like an elongated video of their lives, and now she was sitting with her baby sister by the cool pool in the desert where they'd grown up, talking about a brain hum that could tell you who you were destined to love.

And in that moment Ember knew exactly what she had to do. She leaped up from her chair, mumbled, "I gotta go," and went to find Ranger.

Ember sped to the earthship house on the north side of the ranch as fast as she could drive without taking out a cow or some other random critter, her heart pounding like a Native American drum calling up rain.

Fear was chalk in her mouth, but joy was a counterbalance, and she swung back and forth on the seesaw of doubt and certainty.

Her pulse tapped out panicked beats, jumping around like a sugar monkey. What a risk! But what rewards! Treasures untold.

If he reciprocated.

OhmyGodohmyGodohmyGod.

She pulled up in front of his endearingly oddball house. When he'd told her he was going to build a solar sustainable house, she thought him nuts. The design looked like a lump-monster pushing up from the earth, humped and skulking, lying in wait to devour unsuspecting visitors. As a real estate agent, she warned him against limiting his options for potential buyers to the few with his esthetics and ecological ideology.

He reminded her that he couldn't sell the house without his family's permission anyway, and the earthship house really pissed off his father, and there was something satisfying about that. During the building of the earthship, Ember had tried her best to be encouraging because Ranger was her friend. Biting her tongue over the concrete floor and unattractive solar panels and walls made of ram-packed earth encased in recycled steel-belted radial rubber. But then as she'd watched the house change, spent days and weeks helping him design, build, and decorate; working side by side to create a unique and earth-nurturing structure, something unexpected occurred.

She began to like the place. It charmed her like a hobbit house, small and colorful. Ranger had taken trash and turned it into treasure. The house embraced the sun and the wind. And wasn't that just like Ranger and her? She, the hot fire. He, the intelligent stir of air. They installed a solar cook box and a wind-powered generator. And with the long, glass windows that lined the front of the house, an indoor garden could be grown year-round. It was a slow lure, this labor of love, and by the time the house was finished, it no longer looked like a lump-monster to her, but the entrance into an enchanted world.

This evening, the house was dark and silent. Ranger's truck was not in the driveway.

He wasn't home.

Of course not. The realization was a whack to her head. He was still at Chantilly's.

She pulled out her cell phone to text him, but she had no idea what to say. Stuffed the phone back into her purse. Did she go find him at Chantilly's, surrounded by their gang? Or wait until later?

No, she couldn't wait. She'd drive herself crazy if she waited. She had to see him tonight. Impulsive yes, but Ranger was the one person who embraced her spontaneity. He wouldn't mind. She fingered her lips, put the Infinity in gear, and drove the sixteen miles back to Cupid. It was seven-thirty when she rolled up to the bar and grill. Still plenty of daylight left.

But Ranger's truck was not there.

If he'd been headed home, she would have passed him on the road, and she had not. Where was he? She wanted to jump out of the car and pace like first-time homebuyers waiting to hear if their offer had been accepted, desperate for any scrap of news.

Zeke came strolling out of Chantilly's, spied her sitting in her car, engine running, and wandered over. She rolled down the window.

"You looking for Ranger?" he asked.

"Why would you think that?"

Zeke's shrug was barely a hitch upward. "Why else would you be sitting out here with your engine running?"

"I could be waiting for anyone."

"Are you?"

Ember sighed. "Do you know where he is?"

"He and Dawn headed up to the observatory over an hour ago. She wanted to show him her new office." The way Zeke said "office" made it sound like that was *not* what Dawn intended on showing Ranger.

"Thanks," she said, put up her window, and took off, leaving Zeke standing in the parking lot shaking his head in the orange glow of encroaching twilight.

Did she look as dazed and lost as she felt?

It was almost dark by the time she got up the mountain to the McDonald Observatory. A stargazing party was in progress, and vehicles crammed the parking lot. Sure enough, Ranger's truck was in the employee lot, parked next to Dawn's lease car.

She'd been to the observatory hundreds

312

of times with Ranger, and most of the employees knew her. She skirted the tourists in line for the star party and went straight to the building where the faculty offices were located.

One of the security guards, Heath Lumley — who, as it just so happened, she'd gotten a great deal on a house in Fort Davis for him and his wife the previous month — let her in without a visitor's badge. They chatted a few minutes about how much he and his wife loved their new property.

"It sure was nice of you, helping us get a second lien instead of having to buy private mortgage insurance. We know you didn't have to go out of your way like you did," Heath said. "The wife and me, we were new to house buying. Babes in the woods, but you didn't let us get taken advantage of."

Well, of course not. She treated her clients as if they were family members, but right now, it was all she could do not to push Heath aside and go running down the hallway yelling out Ranger's name.

"Michele has started an herb garden in that little atrium in the center of the house and . . ." Heath went on and on, but truthfully, Ember stopped hearing him. It took all her restraint not to tap her foot and yell,

Out of my way, dude. I have undying love to profess.

Ember tilted her head, met Heath's eyes, and tried to look interested. He was a nice man, earnest and genuine. He deserved her full attention, but she just didn't have it to give right now. *Slow your roll, child,* she heard her mother's voice in her head. *Patience is a virtue.*

Yeah, yeah, whatever.

"The basil is growing wild, but we must be doing something wrong with the cilantro." Heath tapped his chest with an index finger. "It's just not thriving."

Uh-huh, uh-huh.

Impatience. Another of her qualities that Trey disapproved of even though he was ten times more impatient than she. Growing snappy and temperamental at the slightest obstacle.

She knew better than to allow her impulsiveness to get the better of her, but she just couldn't help it. She had to talk to Ranger *now.* She couldn't wait one second longer. Not knowing if he felt the same way was uncomfortable. Like wearing too-tight clothes and getting soaked in the rain.

It felt as if something . . . no wait, as if *everything* . . . needed to be peeled off and thrown away.

314

"Excuse me, Heath, I would love to hear more about Michele's garden, but I need to speak to Ranger about something important."

"Sure, sure." Heath's warm, forgiving smile made her feel like an asshole for cutting him off. "He's in the lab at the end of the hall."

"Thank you, thank you." Ember waved a grateful hand and exhaled forcefully.

Heath went outside, off on his rounds, happily whistling "Our House."

Ember forced herself not to run. She was only yards away from Ranger now and the fieriest declaration of her life. *I love you, my best friend.*

But how best to say it? Blurting, while definitely her style, seemed too sudden. How did one work around to such a monumental statement?

I love you!

Each step brought a fresh rush of blood to her head until her temple was pounding, pounding, pounding with pressure, exquisite in a painful way. The pulsing told her she was alive and the world was filled with exciting potential.

The door to the laboratory was partially glass, and the rest shiny chrome. She went up on the balls of her feet to peek inside the windowed door, hesitant to simply rush in if he was in the middle of something important.

She had, in all honesty, completely forgotten about Dawn.

Until she saw Ranger and Dawn huddled together over an electron microscope, their heads almost touching. Probably studying a meteorite, she guessed. Ember had done that with him, in this very room, dozens of times.

As she watched, Ranger slipped his arm around Dawn's waist and guided her down onto a tall stool. Dawn tilted her face up to him. Ranger took off her safety glasses, set them on the counter and then settled his hands on the other woman's shoulders. Pushed his own safety glasses up on his head.

And then he stared deeply into Dawn's eyes.

Ember stopped breathing.

Ranger lowered his head, closing in on Dawn's face. The look in his eyes was faraway, unfocused. He cupped his palm at Dawn's cheek, angled her head farther back.

Dear Lord, no! Her beloved was about to kiss someone else!

Ember could not watch.

Sickened, her stomach bulleted into her

throat, and she let out a little squeak, stumbled backward. Fell over her feet.

Hit the floor.

Immediately, she hopped up and sprinted for the exit as fast as she could run with a broken heart.

CHAPTER 17

"I certainly will not persuade myself to feel more than I do. I am quite enough in love. I should be sorry to be more."
— Jane Austen, *Emma*

"What was that?" Dawn asked as Ranger plucked a loose eyelash from her eye.

"I don't know." He frowned and moved to peer out the door's glass window. Saw a flash of red hair just as the exterior door at the end of the corridor slammed closed. Smelled cinnamon-and-anise perfume lingering in the air.

Uh-oh.

He put two and two together. Ember had been here, had peeked through the window, and had seen him bent over Dawn intent on retrieving the lash from her eye. Ember must have mistaken the gesture for intimacy. He knew it as surely as he knew his name was Ranger Thomas Lockhart.

318

Dammit.

It felt as if he was in a starship, far above earth, standing unsuspectingly on a trap-door that had just unhinged and dropped him weightlessly into the abyss of deep space.

"I think it was Ember," he said.

Dawn straightened on the stool. "Oh."

Should he go after Ember, track her down, explain what had been going on with Dawn? Should he come clean about everything and tell Ember exactly how much the kiss they'd shared on set today had rocked his world?

Why was it so damn hard for him to express his feelings? Why had he shut down after the shoot? Withdrawn instead of taking Ember aside and confessing what that kiss had done to him? Why was he feeling crowded and quite honestly terrified of the thing he wanted most?

Romantic love with his best friend.

Maybe it was because his mother had taken off on him and his father hadn't been very loving. Maybe it was because emotions scared the shit out of him. Or maybe it was just because he was a guy, and the feelings were so big he didn't fully understand them.

How could he express what he didn't understand?

What should he do? How should he play

this? Should he go after her and risk making things worse? Or leave her be and act like he hadn't known she'd been there?

"Leave her be," Dawn said, eerily reading his thoughts. "You wanted to make her jealous. Believe me, she's jealous now or she has zero romantic feelings for you."

"Yes, but now it seems cruel. Before it was just a tease. This feels . . . wrong." He paused. He knew Ember so well. She was proud. She would never let on how badly she was hurting, but if she'd seen him leaning over Dawn, it would have been so easy to misinterpret what had been going on. Was Ember having feelings for him? His heart leapt, full of hope.

"Maybe I could just text her, see how she is."

"No," Dawn said. "If you want her to realize how much you mean to her, she needs to feel the jealousy."

"The last thing on earth I want is for Ember to get hurt." He shook his head. "I have to talk to her."

"And you will, but let it arise naturally. If you go to her now, she'll be embarrassed and probably deny what she's feeling."

Dawn was right about that.

"Don't make a big thing of it," Dawn coached. "You'll see her tomorrow. Feel things out then. Who knows? Maybe it wasn't even her at the door."

"It was Ember." He was certain of that. No one else smelled like his best friend, so spicy and delicious. "I don't want to be the cause of her pain. It's cruel."

Dawn stood up, rested her hands on his shoulders, stared him squarely in the eyes. "Sometimes, darlin'," she drawled, affecting a Texas accent. "Here's the bottom line. Sometimes, you gotta be cruel to be kind."

Regroup! Regroup!

Ember pounded her forehead with the palm of her hand. Stupid. Stupid. Stupid.

She had started down the mountain road, headed home to Marfa, but her hands had been shaking so hard, she'd pulled over on a scenic turnout to collect herself. The sun had disappeared down the horizon, but she could still see the ghosts of orange and purple light fingering the sky.

Her chest was tight, achy; her heart ragged and bruised. Her pride in tatters.

Dammit, she was mad.

Not at Ranger. He was doing what she'd pushed him to do. Find someone who was marriage-worthy to boost his career. How could she blame him? He had no idea how she felt. No idea she'd heard the humming.

And when he'd asked about her tears after the kiss, she'd told him she was acting. What was he supposed to think?

No, not mad at Ranger.

She was pissed off with Kaia and Granny Blue and the whole damn humming thing for getting her hopes up. She felt deceived, betrayed.

But mostly, she was angry with herself. She'd jumped the gun, jumped the shark, jumped every last bit of common sense and impulsively crawled out on a limb. If she'd stayed home, she wouldn't have seen him lean in to kiss Dawn.

And she'd still be having pipe dreams about happily-ever-after.

Truthfully, setting her jealousy aside, Dawn was good for Ranger. They were both tall and tanned and gorgeous. Both scientists. Dawn knew his world. Had great social skills. She would be an asset to any man trying to climb the academic ladder.

She should have recognized this right off the bat.

For God's sake, Ember, you are not a match-maker. She had gotten lucky with four couples. Most likely they would have ended up together without her meddling.

Face it. She was clueless.

She didn't know anything about making a

long-term romantic relationship work. Who was she to tell anyone anything?

You got that right, Trey's voice echoed in her brain. *How many times do you have to get hit upside the head before you learn?*

Apparently, a lot.

Which left the big gaping hole of a question: What did she do about the humming?

Did she tell Ranger how she felt when it was clear that he and Dawn were already pairing up and things were going well for them? Or did she suck it up, ignore the humming, and keep her feelings to herself?

Her heart begged her to run to Ranger and spill her guts. Tell him everything. But the part of her that wanted him to be happy above all else, whispered, *Shh, shh, shh.*

What if after she told him everything she was feeling she learned Ranger did not feel the same way? Her heart cracked at the thought. No, no, she didn't think she could bear the weight of his rejection.

If he didn't love her the way she loved him, she'd have to leave the Trans-Pecos. There would be nothing for her here but heartache.

But what if he does feel the same way? What then, her soul murmured.

For that, Ember didn't have an answer.

To get through the rest of the filming of *The Cupid Camel Corps,* Ember donned her emotional armor and girded her feelings. She was strong and capable. She could do this. Her old boss had called her the Cutthroat Redheaded Real Estate Warrior.

Warrior.

She liked that. She was in warrior mode. Yes, okay, sometimes that meant she had to bark orders. So be it. It kept people at a distance. But not Ranger. He wanted to know what was wrong. She told him she had to focus on film production to keep the cost down. He asked how he could help. She told him the best way was for him to stay out of her hair. He invited her to hang out with the cast and crew after filming. She growled that if she mingled with the help they wouldn't take her as seriously. He'd grinned and said, "It's lonely at the top, huh?"

She nodded sharply and replied, "Shoo."

The hurt look on his face had taken a slice out of her heart, but she erected a stony wall and refused to let herself feel.

Okay, that was a lie. She still felt the pain; she just sucked it up like any good warrior.

At times, she would catch him watching her moodily across whatever room they were in for family gatherings, or the film set, and just when she'd convinced herself that her keep-away strategy was the wrong one, Dawn would swoop in, link her arm through Ranger's, and carry him off.

In the wee hours of the morning, an impulse to text him would come over her, and she'd pick up her phone only to stare at his picture on her speed dial, get choked up, and put the phone away.

But what stung most was that he'd stopped texting her too.

Stupid. Yes, she knew that. She'd *wanted* him to curtail contact, but she hadn't truly expected him to do it. He must seriously be into Dawn.

Good. Fine. Great. Perfect.

On the day they finished filming the final scene, two days before Ranger's birthday party, Dawn slipped her arm through Ranger's and pulled him aside for a cloistered conversation, and Ember realized something monumental. The very thing she'd feared would happen if she told Ranger she loved him was already happening.

Their friendship was dissolving.

She was losing her best friend.

Ember felt as if her guts were being pulled out through her belly button. Ruptured. Eviscerated.

You caused this.

Yes, yes, she knew that, but if Ranger had feelings for Dawn, she needed to come to terms with it and get out of their way.

The longer she and Ranger didn't hang out together, the harder it was to bridge that widening gap, and the louder the self-doubt monster roared in her head. Which wasn't her. Not at all. Usually, when she made a decision, she stuck with it. No second-guessing. That was the way of the warrior, after all.

But with Ranger? She couldn't seem to move past the choice she'd made to let him go.

It was as if they were walking a single tightrope across the Grand Canyon, coming from opposite directions, and if they met in the middle one — or both of them — were going to fall off.

So they both stood trembling on the wire, afraid to make a move.

On this last day of filming, no one invited her to come out with them when they wrapped. She couldn't have gone anyway, but that didn't stop her from feeling left out. It wasn't an unusual feeling. Most of her life she'd felt out of step, even with her own family. The only person she could always truly be herself with was Ranger.

Until now.

That's what hurt. Losing the one person who not only accepted her, but also celebrated her differences.

Ember went over to Luke's house to review their work.

With her experience in advertising and production, Luke's wife, Melody, had already been editing the film dailies, revising and making filming notes for Ember. Tonight would be her first time seeing the short film in its entirety.

She was anxious.

They sat in Luke and Melody's theater room, complete with popcorn and soft drinks, and the first image on the screen, after the opening segment, was of Ranger in his commanding officer uniform standing on the porch of the Fort Davis house. At the sight of his dear face, Ember's heart fluttered.

Wildly.

In her estimation, Ranger Lockhart was the most handsome man on the face of the earth. She sat in the dark room feeling swept away and more than a little weepy. But she did not cry. Not in front of the Nielsons.

It wasn't easy, watching him on-screen, longing for him, missing him, unable to fix what she'd broken.

The film wasn't perfect. Far from it. The production value was clearly on the . . . um . . . affordable side. But the overall acting wasn't bad. Not Hollywood by any stretch of the imagination, but for a local Chamber of Commerce tourism film, it got the job done. The camels were a hoot and even the snafus were amusing, which they kept as outtakes.

She started bracing for the on-screen kiss before it arrived. Telling herself to chill out, but her coaching did no good. She gripped the arms of her chair and held her breath, and when the camera panned from the camels and desert to Ember wearing a brunette wig as Mary Beale, standing on the porch beside Ranger, her heart took off like a jackrabbit running from a coyote.

When he kissed her on-screen, it was like experiencing the kiss all over again. As his lips touched hers, a steady hum began at the base of Ember's brain and spread out until her entire head tingled with the vibration and one solitary thought pounded.

The One. The One. The One.

A lump lodged in her throat as she watched tears of joy flow down her face.

Felt corresponding tears of loss pushing at her now. She blinked her eyes and gritted her teeth, overcome, overwhelmed.

Do not cry in front of Luke and Melody. Do not do it. You are the Cutthroat Redheaded Real Estate Warrior. Crying is for wimps.

What she saw next hit her like a jagged lightning bolt splitting an aged oak tree.

The expression on Ranger's face after the kiss. He was gazing at her with such rapt attention, his eyes a bit dazed as if he was in shock. The way he was looking at her was the exact way she felt when he'd kissed her. Stunned by a stunningly divine epiphany.

And she wasn't the only one who noticed.

"Oh my gosh, Ember," Melody whispered. "Did you have any idea that Ranger was crazy in love with you?"

"I can't do this anymore," Ranger told Dawn as they sat at the bar at Chantilly's. He had a beer in front of him, but had barely taken a sip. He didn't want it. Didn't want to be here. Dawn was fine company, but not being with Ember was killing him.

"You do love her so much, don't you?"

He nodded. "I can't wait any longer. I have to tell her what I figured out in New Zealand. I love her with everything I have in me."

"Tread lightly," Dawn warned. "Remember, you were doing this for Ember to slowly realize she's in love with you. Jump the gun and you could lose her forever. You've had a year to figure out that you were in love with her. If you go barreling in, professing your undying love before she's ready to hear it . . ." Dawn shrugged. "Look how she's already backed away from you. Give her time and space. Let her come to you."

Ranger kneaded his brow with two fingers. Dawn's argument sounded convincing, but his heart just wasn't buying it. He knew Ember better than he knew anyone else in the world, and he wasn't so sure that her pride would ever let her be the one to say it first.

Expecting Ember to be something she wasn't was like saddling a camel and calling it a horse. He didn't want her to be anything other than who she was. He didn't want to change her or alter her in any way. He loved her just as she was, faults and all, because God knew he had plenty of faults of his own. And she made allowances for him.

"I gotta go." Ranger got up off the barstool.

Dawn laid a hand on his palm. "Go see her if you must, but for God's sake, don't throw the L word around. Not yet."

"I appreciate the advice," Ranger said. "You've been a good friend."

"Apparently, not as good as Ember. She loves you so much she's willing to let you be with me if she thinks it's best for you. If you were my man, I'd scratch the eyes out of any woman who came within ten feet of you." Dawn paused, screwed her mouth up in a pensive gesture. "Unless of course, Ember really doesn't love you the way you love her."

Dammit. Why did Dawn have to throw a doubt blanket over him?

Maybe she was right and he should keep the L word off the table for the time being, but that didn't mean he couldn't go see Ember.

He settled his Stetson on his head, told Dawn good-night, and went to find his best friend.

Ember left Luke and Melody's house — located halfway between Marfa and Cupid — bathed in a cold sweat. She was headed back to Chantilly's to find Ranger. She'd thought about texting him, but didn't know what to say. This conversation required a face-to-face meeting.

It was almost dark, but she didn't have to get up early in the morning and neither did

Ranger, as far as she knew. Their talk couldn't wait.

The road was empty, a straight desert stretch of highway. The horizon flowing endless miles into the distance. The Davis Mountains lay to her right; the twinkle of Cupid's lights were directly ahead.

Every muscle in her body was tight and her mind whirled dizzily. If Ranger was as in love with her as it looked like on film, why had he been kissing Dawn?

Well, she had told him she was just acting when he asked about her tears. What was the guy supposed to do? Pine for her forever?

Okay, okay, she was not going to think or question or second-guess anything. She was just going to find him and ask him point-blank.

A few miles away, coming from Cupid and headed for Marfa were the headlights of an oncoming vehicle. She didn't pay much attention to the car. Thoughts of Ranger swamped her mind. All she could think about was finding him and telling him she'd been wrong to try to find him a proper wife because *she* wanted the role.

Unfortunately, Ember was not very proper.

Not in the least.

She was a bit too passionate, a bit too loud, a bit too bossy by half, but she didn't know any other way to be. Fortunately, Ranger seemed not to be put off by her personality, but rather, awed by it.

Such a man was a rare and precious find. And he could be hers if she was brave enough to tell him.

What if she found him with Dawn again? What if they were in bed together?

Oh lalalala, shut up, shut up.

The other vehicle — a pickup from the level of the headlights — seemed to be driving as urgently as she. Someone else on an impulsive mission? The truck, on the opposite side of the road, bulleted past her.

Wait! Holy Cupid, it was Ranger's truck.

Ember tromped the brakes, the tires of her Infinity screeching in protest. She heard a corresponding squeal of tires behind her. She spun the wheel, U-turned into the opposite lane, saw that Ranger had done the same thing.

Laughing, she drove happily toward him.

They stopped when they were abreast. The only two cars on the long, lonely desert road. Simultaneously, they rolled their windows down.

Her heart somersaulted at the sight of him, his Stetson off, his hair rakishly mussed.

The electricity vibrating between them was high-voltage, hot and impossible to ignore, striking like dry lightning on a cold desert night.

"Hey," he said.

"Hey yourself, cowboy."

"I was coming to find you," Ranger said, resting his arm outside the window, studying her with hungry eyes.

"Same here."

"Why?" he asked.

"We need to talk."

"I know."

"A *long* talk."

"The Silver Feather?"

"Too many prying eyes. Marfa? My place?"

"I'll meet you there."

She headed toward Marfa, her fingers drumming on the steering wheel. She turned on the radio, fiddled around for a song, stumbled across Jewel singing "You Were Meant for Me." Belted it out as loudly as she could. Joy spreading her mouth as wide as it would go.

And she decided this was going to be the very best night of her life.

CHAPTER 18

"If things are going untowardly one month,
they are sure to mend the next."
— Jane Austen, *Emma*

Ranger's heart felt like a fledging eagle leaving the nest to fly free for the first time, the sky unfurling endlessly before him. It was as if a great weight had dropped from his shoulders, and he found himself darting down the highway headed toward his favorite place.

And his favorite person.

They were one and the same.

Ember.

Excitement pulsed through him and goose bumps spiked his skin. His hands trembled. *Dammit, Lockhart, get hold of yourself.*

But he could not. All he could think of was getting Ember alone.

He kept flicking his gaze to the rearview mirror, making sure she was still behind him, both concerned for her safety and still not quite believing she was there and they were going to her house for a *long* talk. He prayed "talk" was a euphemism for something else, but even if it wasn't, he didn't care.

All he wanted was to be with her.

A year away in New Zealand had brought that into sharp focus, and he couldn't deny it any longer.

He didn't realize he was driving a good ten miles over the speed limit, until the wail of a siren and red-and-blue swirling lights appeared from the other side of the Prada Marfa art sculpture.

Aww crap. He knew better than to speed past the faux shoe store. The wacky work of art was Deputy Sheriff Calvin Greenwood's speed trap of choice, especially on Friday nights.

Grunting, Ranger pulled over.

The patrol car parked behind him.

A few seconds later, Ember drove by, tooting her horn as she passed. Ranger was still grinning when Calvin rapped his knuckles against the driver's window and shone his flashlight into the pickup.

Ranger rolled his window down. "Evening, Calvin."

"Deputy Greenwood," Calvin corrected,

even though they'd gone through school together. "Where's the fire?"

In my pants, Ranger thought, the snickered reply of fifteen-year-olds the world over. Lord, it had been too long since he'd had sex if that's the best his addled brain could come up with.

"Just heading over to Ember's," he said.

"Ahh, so that's where the fire is."

Huh? What? How did Calvin know about his feelings for Ember? Belatedly, it dawned on him that Calvin was making a pun. Fire. Ember. Haha.

"Real Code Red, huh?" Calvin chortled at his own joke. Code Red, Ember the redhead. Hardee-har-har.

"Barn burner." C'mon, why didn't Calvin just give him the damn ticket already?

"There's always a five-alarm blaze with that one," Calvin said, nodding in the direction of Ember's swiftly disappearing taillights. "You never know what she's up to."

"What are you suggesting?" Ranger tensed, tightening his grip on the steering wheel, and felt his neck muscles knot up.

"You know," Calvin went on, clearly not picking up on the undercurrent of anger pushing through Ranger. He didn't care that Calvin was law enforcement, nobody, but nobody dissed *his* woman. "She's outrageous and outspoken and . . . just plain out there. Remember the summer before she started high school when she —"

"*I'm* out there too," Ranger growled, the sound coming out low and deliberate, heading Calvin off at the pass before he started talking about that time when they were all fourteen and attending summer camp together.

A group of campers had snuck out of their cabins at midnight. In retrospect, Ember had been the instigator, organizing the girls to meet the boys down by the small mountain lake. A dozen of them had gathered on the dock and Ember had yelled, "Last one in is a rotten egg," stripped down to her skivvies, and dove into the water.

Ranger must have sounded pretty threatening, because Calvin instinctively settled his hand on the butt of his duty weapon nestled in the holster at his hip, and in a clip, curt tone announced, "License and registration."

"Hey, I didn't mean to get testy." Ranger handed over his driver's license and truck registration. "Knee-jerk reaction. Ember's my best friend."

"I know you're as protective of Ember as if she were your sister." Calvin dropped his hand from his gun and looked a bit sheepish. "I didn't mean anything by that 'out there' comment. Ember can be a handful, but she keeps things lively around here."

"That she does."

"I'm letting you off with a warning." Calvin scribbled out the ticket. "But do us all a favor and slow yourself down."

"Got it." He jiggled his leg, waiting until Calvin went back to his patrol car before he pulled back onto the two-lane road.

By the time he arrived at Ember's house, he was itchy with anticipation.

She sat on the porch swing, her creamy complexion aglow in the light of the rising moon. "Hey."

"Hey." He stepped onto the porch, the boards creaking underneath his cowboy boots.

"Ranger got caught speeding," she said in a singsong voice, moving over to make room.

"That's right." He dropped down on the swing beside her. His pulse was a tiger, roaring through his veins, ravaging the jungle of his heart. "Speed Racer, I couldn't wait to be alone with you."

"Mmm." Her cute nose tipped up, playing hard to get, but she was happy to see him and trying hard not to smile. "Why the sudden need?"

"Missed you."

"I missed you too," she whispered.

"I was going to bring flowers," he said. "But nothing florally stays open late around here."

"Nothing florally? You have two PhDs and that's the best description you can come up with? And why would you bring me flowers?"

"I owe you an apology."

She pulled her knees to her chest, hugged herself, rocking the porch swing, rocking him. "What for?"

"Ghosting you."

"Did you do that?" Her tone was as mild as her smile, but he knew this woman inside and out. She was suppressing, and fibbing. "I've been too busy to notice."

Normally, he was not the kind of guy who rattled cages. More the type to give people their space and clear out, but here, now, tonight, too damn much was at stake not to do some cage rattling.

He grasped the back of the porch swing with his right hand, used it as a lever as he planted his right foot on the floor and in one smooth move, he pushed up and pivoted his body over hers. Smacked his palm down on the other side of the swing, sandwiching her between his hands planted parallel to her shoulders.

He leaned in.

Her eyes widened in surprise and she drew her knees tighter into her chest.

"Bullshit," he said succinctly.

Ember swallowed hard, her throat muscles jumping with the movement.

"You ghosted me first," he accused. They were almost nose-to-nose over her drawn up knees, and he could smell her lovely cinnamon-and-anise scent.

She moistened her lips. "When did you pick up this macho alpha man crap?"

Operating on drive and instinct, and praying he wasn't going too far, he growled and lowered his head. Another inch more and their lips would be touching.

Ranger stared into her eyes and held his breath. "You like it?"

"Hell, yes," she said.

He breathed.

She sighed.

They both laughed.

And immediately they quieted; desert sounds suddenly loud in the silence — hoots, chirps, howls.

Their gazes were chained together. Locked shut. He couldn't have looked away if someone had put a gun to his head. Still acting on instinct, hands holding the back of the porch swing on either side of her, Ranger opened his mouth and spoke his truth.

"I want you."

Ember's face blanched.

Ranger's gut wrenched. Oh shit. Had he ruined things already? Her hands were trembling. Hell, his were trembling too. What did he do now? What did he say?

"Say that again," she whispered.

Did he dare?

No risk, no reward, right? Ranger gulped. In for a penny, he might as well go for the gold. He'd been pussyfooting around for far too long. "I want *you*."

Ember cocked her head and studied him so intently it stole his breath. What did she see in front of her? Her longtime friend or the lover he ached to be?

"Do you mean you *want me*, want me?" Her voice was strong, but he heard the faint quaver of fear that anyone else would have missed.

"What else does it mean when a man tells a woman he wants her?" He growled again, deeper, longer, trying to get his point across. *Baby, it's you.*

"I dunno. It could be anything."

"Anything?"

"Yes, for instance, it could be I want you

to come hold the stepladder while I screw in a lightbulb."

"Sparky," he murmured, and lowered his eyelids. "I'm not the least bit interested in screwing lightbulbs."

"Oh, my."

"Yeah. Oh *you.*"

"You want to have sex?" She put a hand to her chest. "With me?"

"I do." He also wanted to tell her that he was in love with her and not just as her best friend, but he remembered Dawn's caution and he held back his rush to say the L word.

"I've wanted to make lo . . . have sex with you for a very long time," he said.

"Really?" she squeaked.

"You know how I always said Harry in *When Harry Met Sally* was wrong?"

"Yes."

"I lied," he confessed. "Harry was right."

"How long have you wanted to jump my bones?"

"Since the summer we turned fourteen." He pressed his forehead to hers, stared at her until his eyes crossed. "When you stripped down to your bra and panties and jumped into the lake. I still remember your bra was pink and your panties were turquoise. They didn't match and you didn't give a damn."

"I didn't even know they were supposed to match," she said, her eyes crossing too.

He backed off so he could see her, gauge her reaction. "I thought it was hot. I thought you were hot, and I wanted to smash in the other boys' faces for staring at you."

"I got kicked out of camp for that stunt."

"I know. I left in protest."

"Why are you just now getting around to telling me this?" she asked, arms folded tightly across her chest, accidentally pushing up her creamy breasts, showcased in the moonlight.

His mouth watered. "What can I say? I'm a late bloomer and a cautious man . . . most of the time. You, however, bring out the Speed Racer in me."

"I had no idea." She pressed a palm to her chest, and he could tell from the awe in her eyes that she meant it.

"Question is, do *you* want to have sex with me?" He searched her face; his gut wired and tangled.

She hauled in a deep breath, her gaze latched tight to his, and slowly nodded.

Ranger felt as if he'd been plugged into a light socket, indigo blue and shocking, thought of a Walt Whitman poem "I Sing the Body Electric."

"If we do this . . . what does this mean for

us?" she asked, and the thin high note in her voice yanked his heart into his throat.

His spunky, scrappy best friend — the same one who'd pushed down a bully on the playground for taunting Ranger about his mother running out on him the day he'd returned to school after being out for several months — was scared.

Rarely had he heard her sound rattled.

Good.

She needed to think this through. He needed to think it through. Once they had sex, they could never undo it. Personally, he didn't *want* to undo it, but if going to bed together killed their friendship, he would never forgive himself.

"Do you want to know what's in my mind?"

Ember gave him a look that said she wanted to roll her eyes but was restraining herself. "No, I want to know what's in Einstein's mind."

He grinned at her, his sharp-witted friend. He wanted to tell her that in his mind he saw sex and marriage and more sex and babies and more sex and love, love, love. But what if she wasn't feeling the same way? Yes, she'd acknowledged she wanted to have sex with him, but that didn't mean she wanted to be anything more than friends with benefits.

"In my mind," he said, weighing his words, "we're going to have a hell of a good time."

Her smile faded a bit, and her eyes turned stormy, but she quickly patched up her defenses and said, "Then what are we still doing on the front porch?"

Sex.

She was about to have sex with Ranger. Her womanly parts were very happy about that, but her heart, well, that was another story. While most everything below her waist sizzled and tingled, everything above her neck moped and sighed.

Sex was great, fabulous, sweet, sick, awesome, whatever superlative you wanted to tack onto it. But Ember, well . . . it's just that she'd been hankering for more.

Did she push him to define the perimeters of their evolving relationship, or did she just go with the flow and see where things went? She wasn't by nature an overthinker. She left that to Ranger. Normally, Ember jumped in with both feet.

So when he held out his hand, she took it, the very air rippling between them as Ranger led her into the house.

Don't look down. Just make that leap.

The moment, loaded with meaning and promise, would have been dead sexy, except Samantha met them at the door, mewling loudly, wanting to know why her dinner was late.

"Sorry," Ember apologized, dropped his hand and headed to the ceramic cookie jar where she stored the cat food. "It'll just take a sec."

"Take your time," he said, going over to open the drawer of her hutch and pulling out some scented tea candles. "I'll set the mood."

Pros of sleeping with your best friend? He knows where the candles are kept. Ranger carried the candles and lighter to the bedroom.

Cons of sleeping with your best friend? He makes himself right at home.

Not that she minded that, not really. It's just that now that this long-dreamed of moment was about to happen, she needed reassurance that their friendship was not going to implode. The last several days of avoiding each other had been weird indeed. She couldn't handle more of that.

"Range?" she asked, leaving Samantha munching away in the kitchen and trailing down the hallway after him.

"Uh-huh?" he mumbled as he set the

vanilla-scented tea candles along her dresser and lit them one by one.

"We need to set some boundaries." Boundaries? Why had she said that word? That's not what she meant. Boundaries sounded so distant as if she didn't want him coming close when, in fact, she wanted the exact opposite. Wanted him so close there wasn't a millimeter of space between them.

His eyebrows shot up and a crafty smile played at the corners of his mouth. "You mean like a safe word?"

"Good Lord, man, we're best friends. Do we really need a safe word?"

"Point taken. If we had a safe word it would be . . ." In one simultaneous breath, they said, "Pocketknife."

Laughed.

Pros of sleeping with your best friend? He's familiar with all the skeletons in your closet.

"There's just one tiny thing I need cleared up before we . . ." She inclined her head toward the bed, felt her pulse skip a beat. "Do this."

He straightened, sauntered toward her. "And what is that, Sparky?"

Just staring at his lips started her head humming.

Cons of sleeping with your best friend?

He makes a terrible racket in your head. Or maybe that was a pro. It was a really soothing sound, but it was heavy with significance.

"I need clarification on your status with Dawn. I can't . . . we can't do this if you and Dawn are hooking up. I'm sorry. Call me a serial monogamist. I'm just not wired for dual ongoing relationships."

"Dawn and I are just friends," he said easily.

"The way you and I are just friends?"

He stepped closer, his eyes sultry and half-lidded. "No, Ember, not even close."

Her pulse did that skipping thing again, and she swallowed back her fear. "I have something to confess."

"What's that?"

She sank a hand on her hip, tried to look in control, figured she failed because he launched himself onto her mattress, landing butt first, and stretched out. Turning onto his side and propping himself up on one elbow like a *Playgirl* centerfold and grinned at her.

"All ears," he said.

A lump lodged in her throat, and it took her a minute to gulp it down. "I . . . I went up to the observatory to surprise you the other night and I . . . I . . ."

"Yes?"

Shoot from the lips, Alzate. Just say it. "I saw you kiss Dawn."

"Did you?" His voice dropped to that deep scholarly tone he took on when he was about to tell you why you were wrong about something.

"Yes, Professor," she said, trying to keep it light. "I did."

"Are you sure about what you saw?"

Was he going to lie to her? A cold chill splashed down her spine. "I peeked in through the laboratory door. You two were bent over a microscope —"

"Looking at meteorite dust," he finished for her.

"So you're not going to deny it?"

"Nothing to deny. We were definitely looking at meteorite dust."

"And then you took her goggles off her face and set her down on a stool and leaned in to kiss her —"

"Did you actually see my lips touch hers?"

Ember shook her head, unable to speak; the humming was growing louder and louder. If it was this potent just looking at his lips, not even kissing him yet, what was going to happen when they made love?

She shivered. Not make love. He never said that. Sex. They were going to have sex.

It might lead somewhere, or it might not. She would not put any expectations on tonight. If indeed, they even got as far as sex.

Who knew? Either one of them could bail out at the last moment. Hit the eject button, pull the rip cord.

"If you'd stuck around, you would have seen that Dawn had something in her eye and I was getting it out for her."

"Oh." Ember's hopes chugged up to the top of the roller coaster. Really? "That's all it was?"

"That's all it was."

"So you and Dawn —"

"Never kissed."

"But you were so chummy. Touching each other, hanging out . . ."

He grabbed a pillow, bunched it up underneath his head. "I've got a confession."

Down with the roller coaster of her stomach. Up with her fear. That sounded ominous. "What is it?" she whispered, standing as far away from the bed as she could get.

"I asked Dawn to pretend to be interested in me."

Her chin wobbled. "Why?" she asked, hearing cloudy bewilderment in her voice.

"To teach you a lesson."

"A lesson?" Irritation flared inside her.

"Who are you to teach me a lesson?"

"The man who knows you the best. I wanted you to knock off the matchmaking. You kept trying to stick me with Fiona when she wanted Palmer, and you tried to hook Palmer with Chriss Anne when Zeke wanted her. You were sticking your nose in where it didn't belong because you got the crazy idea you're unlucky in love, and the only way you can experience romance is by living vicariously through the matches you made."

"I never matched people up for that reason!" She glowered.

"Are you sure?" he challenged.

Was she?

Her ego certainly got stroked when people told her what a good matchmaker she was. Had matching up others helped her ease the sting of her own marital mistake? Was she sticking her nose in where it didn't belong? But no, all she'd ever wanted to do was help.

"I'm not saying this to hurt you." Ranger's tone was gentle. "Just pointing out that for some crazy reason, you've closed yourself off to lo . . . romance."

"So you're not in any way shape or form interested in Dawn?" she ventured, her hopes on tiptoes, ready to twirl.

"Only as a friend and colleague."

"Okay, well, that clears that up." She rubbed her palms together, gave him an oopsy smile, and all the misery she'd suffered over the past several days rolled away. Ranger was not interested in Dawn.

Whew!

"Anything else you want to discuss?" he drawled, and toed off his cowboy boots. They hit the floor, *plunk, plunk.* He rolled over onto his spine and interlaced his fingers, and cradled the back of his head in his palms, crossed his legs at the ankle.

He'd brought it up. This was her opening. Bull by the horns time.

"Is this going to be a one-time thing?" She just came right out and said it. Shot from those lips of hers. Prayed her bluntness didn't stop things dead.

"Is that what you want?" He narrowed his eyes and sent her an indolent gaze.

"What do you want?" she asked, backing up until her butt hit the dresser and the impact sent the tea candles flickering wildly. *Fudge rockets, Ember,* said the irrepressible part of her. *Kiss the man.*

He sat up, all Mr. Poker Face. "I want what you want."

"So . . . ?"

They watched each other like two cage fighters, circling, assessing, and weighing their choices . . . and their chances of coming out of this unscathed.

"Ember, I can only tell you one thing," he said.

"What's that?"

"I want you. With every beat of my damn heart. With every freaking fiber of my being. Now get the hell over here before I come after you."

It wasn't settled. She shouldn't go for sex until things were settled, but she wanted him more than she wanted to breathe. Ranger wanted her, and she wanted him, what could be wrong with that?

There had already been way too much talking.

In the space of a heartbeat she was across the room and in his arms. Jumping in with both feet.

Crazy, impulsive, not looking where she leaped. Not caring what people thought. It was what she did best.

Just ask Trey.

But here, tonight? She did not care.

CHAPTER 19

"No! Thank you for thinking I am thoughtful."

— Jane Austen, *Emma*

"We're really doing this?" she whispered, searching that dear face, probing the unfathomable depths of his dark eyes.

"I sure as hell hope so."

"Um, how do we start?"

"A nice bubble bath," he said.

"I'm more of a shower person."

"Not tonight you're not. Tonight, we're doing it my way. Slow and easy."

Tonight, we're doing it my way. He said it as if there would be other nights, and other ways they might do this.

Her heart — and other parts far south — did a happy dance. *Do not get ahead of yourself.*

"Be right back," he said, leaving her on the bed alone and disappearing into the bathroom. She heard the sound of running water and he popped back into the bedroom for the tea candles, and disappeared again.

She sat up to watch his gorgeous butt walking away, realized she'd soon be seeing him completely naked. Heat swamped her, and she covered her face with a pillow, barely able to believe this was happening.

He returned for her, took the pillow away, picked up her hand. Led her into the bathroom where the tea candles were lined up on the edge of the clawfoot tub, reflecting soft white light into the mirror. It was the only illumination in the room.

They didn't speak.

He crouched to slip off her shoes and set them aside. She touched the top of his head to balance herself, felt energy pulse from his scalp into her fingers, travel up her arm to her shoulder, neck, head, where it set up a steady vibrating hum.

It was jolting. It was exciting. It felt both familiar and weird.

She didn't tell him about the humming. Did not want that to influence him in any way. But the humming stirred within her, this supreme energy. Made her think about her lineage. The long line of women who'd known when they'd found their soul mates.

Before she had kissed him, she didn't

believe any such lore was possible, but now that it pulsed within her, she knew the truth of it. They *were* connected. Always had been and always would be, no matter what happened.

There was a safety in knowing that. A level of trust and intimacy she'd not thought existed.

Ranger stood up, and her hands slid from his head to his shoulders. He wrapped his arms around her waist and peered into her eyes. Slowly, he reached for the top button on her blouse and unbuttoned it, his knuckles grazing her bare skin.

The humming in her head quickened, a nice steady buzz, whispering, *You are alive, you are alive, you are alive.*

She fixed her attention on his mouth, the shape of his lips, the sweet crook of his smile. Blissful, she shivered.

"Mmm." His eyelids lowered, long dark lashes brushing down as he reached for the second button, then the third. His fingers were warm and capable. He might be a scientist, but he was a cowboy too, and years of ranch work had left even the small muscles in his fingers strong and delineated.

A sexy five o'clock shadow had sprouted across his jaw, and her hands twitched to caress the scratchy patch of stubble.

His fingers loosened the last button, and her blouse fell open. He looked at her, and his voice tumbled out husky and rough. "You still with me on this, Sparky?"

This was her way out. She could check her impulsiveness. *Back up. Think for once.*

But she didn't want to back out. The last thing she wanted was to think. All she wanted was to feel — his kiss, his touch, his body inside of hers.

"Em?"

She met his laser beam eyes, whispered, "Still with you."

His smile was a rainbow after a flood, beautiful and filled with promise, and the hot look in his eyes lit a spark low in her abdomen, caught fire, spread flames up to her stomach, her breasts, her lips.

He slipped his palms around her bare waist, his touch a sweet blister, melting any last obstacles. They stared into each other, and with magical movements he slipped her blouse off her shoulders. It floated to the floor.

The air was cool on her skin, a sharp contrast to the fire inside her. Her knees were trembling. Oh hell, who was she kidding? She was trembling all over.

He kissed her. Their second kiss. Not in front of an audience this time.

The humming in her head was the music of love and belonging. Song of the Soul Mates, Granny Blue called it and Kaia confirmed it.

She thought of those many frogs she'd kissed when her Prince Charming had been on the Silver Feather all along.

She leaned into him, boneless and wiped out.

"How was that?" he murmured.

"You have to ask?" She gifted him with a smug smile, a woman impressed by a man.

"Did you . . . hear anything?"

She didn't want to lie to him, but neither was she ready to admit she heard the humming. She knew he was her soul mate, but she didn't want to put pressure on him. She loved him too much to burden him with her vulnerability. Not yet. Not now. They were best friends, and she didn't want that to change.

If she admitted the humming it would change everything.

Too late, sweet cheeks. Everything had already changed.

Instead of answering him, she wrapped her arms around his neck and tugged his head down to meet hers, and this time, she was the one who kissed him. Taking charge and not a bit ashamed of it.

The humming was their love song.

"Hear anything?" she teased.

"The wild beating of my heart."

"Ranger," she whispered.

"Ember." His fingers moved to the snap of her jeans. "Your bath is getting cold."

She reached over and twisted on the hot water faucet. "Our bath," she corrected. "I'm not getting in there by myself."

"No?"

"We can't have me clean and you dirty."

"Aww, why not?" he teased.

She grabbed the front of his Western shirt and tugged hard, and grinned as the snaps popped open.

"That wasn't slow and easy." He groaned.

"You go at your pace, Professor, I'll go at mine."

"How in the world is that going to work out? You fast, me slow?"

"I wasn't the one who got a speeding ticket tonight," she said.

"A warning," he said. "It was only a warning. Calvin told me to slow myself down."

She chuckled. "That explains that. You always were a rule follower, Lockhart."

"Not always. Not whenever I was with you."

"True." She stroked his cheek. "I've led you astray so many times."

"I went willingly. You were the sunbeam of my life, Ember." His tone turned serious. "I hope you know how special you are."

He was just as special, but this was getting mushy when it was supposed to be getting sexy. She twisted off the hot water, straightened, steam rising between them.

His warm, agile hands went to her hips and he peeled off her jeans, taking his time, pausing to plant hot kisses on her thighs as he went, sinking to his knees. Leaving her standing in her bra and panties, her heart pounding so hard she could see it beating beneath her skin.

He planted one long kiss at the apex between her legs, his hot breath searing through the thin material of her white cotton panties, unraveling her in a dozen different ways.

When it was her turn to take his pants off, she shucked him like an ear of corn, and he threw his head back and laughed so loudly it touched a soft place deep inside her. And she kissed him boldly between his legs. Felt his shaft harden and rise inside his black boxer briefs.

"Ooh-la-la," she said.

"By God you are fun!" he declared, pulling his breath in through his teeth in a hissing sound and dragging her back to her feet.

"Funny and smart and outrageous."

He meant it to be a compliment, she knew that, but the word "outrageous" was a personal trigger. Trey had thrown it at her every time she did something to step out of what he considered the lines of propriety. Which, in his view, consisted of being too boisterous, too outgoing, too happy.

Forget Trey. That's over. You're here with Ranger.

"I'm getting in the tub," she mumbled past the lump in her throat, and without waiting to see how he would respond, she pinned her hair to the top of her head with a barrette from the counter, undid her bra and let it drop. She wriggled out of her panties and without looking back, slipped into the water.

Closing her eyes, she sank in the claw-footed porcelain tub until her chin touched the bubbles. She heard him walk toward her, but she did not peek.

He climbed in on the other side, the water sloshing and displacing as he eased down. His legs spread out and she clamped her knees together so he could surround her. His feet were at her hips. Her feet . . . well . . . her feet were perilously close to the most masculine part of him.

Ember kept her eyes closed. Savoring the

moment. Understood the sublime truth. She was in the bath with her best friend who was about to become her lover. The lover, who according to the humming in her head, was her soul mate, her destiny.

The logical part of Ember had trouble believing this, fumbled to find an excuse for the humming, most of it dire — tinnitus, going deaf, a brain tumor. But another part of her firmly believed in the magic. She had not heard the humming *until* he'd kissed her.

Wish fulfillment, argued her logic.

Cosmic energy, said her magical brain.

Does it really matter? whispered her heart. *Trust what you feel.*

She could feel Ranger studying her, and she smiled faintly. Delighted with this man. *Her* man. Listened to him breathing, audibly. Long. Slow. Deep. Calming and peaceful. His soothing tempo and sound. A steady man, reliable and patient.

Ranger took hold of her big toe, wriggled it. "This little piggy went to market . . ."

She opened her eyes. His head was cocked to one side, and he looked both inquisitive and rakish. His muscles were toned and taut as any athlete's. Once he'd recovered from his childhood illnesses, he'd always made fitness a priority. A sexy professor. A red-hot scientist. A rugged cowboy. Mmm. What a combo.

"You okay, Sparky?" he murmured, massaging her big toe between his fingers.

"I'm way more than okay. I'm over the moon."

"Me too." He moved onto the next toe. "And we just got started."

She moaned softly. His touch felt so good.

"That's what I like to hear," he said. "Your pleasure."

He bathed her gently, tenderly, caressing her with a soft washcloth and lavender-oatmeal soap. It had been a long time since anyone had taken such care with her.

And when he was finished, she bathed him. It was both sensual and nurturing, the prefect description of this new dimension of their relationship. She was familiar with most of his body, but she found new spots she'd never explored. Touching him in places that made him wiggle and groan, and she understood what he meant about liking to hear her pleasure, because hearing him lit her up inside.

The water cooled, but their desire for each other reached a rolling boil. Every kiss, every touch, every stroke leading them further and further up an erotic path. All these years she had been yearning for something she could not fully define, and here she'd found it in the kind eyes of her best friend.

All along.

It had been Ranger all along.

The sweet humming in her head sang the Song of the Soul Mate, and she swallowed the fable like a starry-eyed homebuyer clutching on to the belief of the perfect dream home. In her head, in this moment, the fantasy was real. He *was* her beloved. The other half of her.

Nothing had ever felt so right or sounded so true.

Loving him changed the physics of her emotional universe and redefined the borders of reality. So many new possibilities. Together, they were discovering a new frontier.

"Let's get out of here." He stood up, water sluicing off him, exposing her to the full, glorious view of his proud male body bathed in candlelight.

She gulped. He had a lot to be proud of.

He reached out his hand to her. She took it and he pulled her up beside him. From the corner of her eye, she saw their reflections in the mirror. It struck her what a handsome couple they made. She, fair, blue-eyed and redheaded; he, dark-haired, dark-eyed, darkly tanned.

Opposites attract.

But it wasn't opposition that drew her to him. Rather, it was his familiarity that called to her. Their shared history. Their deep knowledge of each other's habits and foibles. The landscape from which they'd both sprung.

Taking her with him, he stepped from the tub and slowly dried her off.

Oh the waiting!

His restraint was phenomenal. Her heart knocked so hard she could feel her ribs pressing against the walls of her chest, hungry, desperate, aching. When he finished, he didn't speak a word, just handed her a fresh towel and turned his back for her to dry him.

Buffing his muscular butt dry was the highlight of the bath. She could get used to doing this every single night of her life.

Getting ahead of yourself. Slow down. One step at a time.

Good advice, but she could not ignore the thrill that shot through her as she knelt to pat his legs dry.

"All done," she said sadly, and got to her feet.

Ranger hugged her.

She looked into his eyes and was rewarded

with a smile so big it burned her like the sun. He tilted her chin up and kissed her lips, taking possession of her mouth as the humming took possession of her head.

And she was lost. So sweetly lost.

He bent to scoop her into his arms, and he carried her to bed. She didn't protest, just slipped her arms around his neck and let him be her knight in shining armor. He draped her over the mattress and eased down beside her.

The room was dark, the only light coming from tea candles shining through the open bathroom door.

"Do you have any idea how hot you look?"

She lowered her eyelashes and smiled, not coyly, but not quite believing that he thought she was sexy.

Scents drifted in the air — the vanilla fragrance from the candles, the velvet smell of lavender, the coconut sachet on her nightstand, his woodsy masculine aroma. They lay on their sides on the mattress, heads propped on their arms, face-to-face, staring at each other and grinning like kids.

He stroked her cheek with the knuckle of his index finger, moved to her bottom lip. She caught his knuckle between her teeth, bit down lightly.

"God, you are amazing," he said, his voice

filled with the same awe and wonder as when he talked about stars.

Scooting closer, he kissed her again, fusing their mouths in a searing brand of lips, teeth, and tongues. It was an I-found-the-love-of-my-life kind of kiss. A kiss that made promises Ember prayed he could fulfill. She'd been so unlucky in love. Could she bank on him?

Her head buzzed. The song that told her yes, yes, yes, she could count on him. Forever and always.

Should she tell him about the humming? How would it change things if she did? Would she be better served to wait until later? Or should she just spill it and see what happened? Her spontaneous personality, the part of her she'd spent a lifetime suppressing, shouted, *Tell him, tell him now.*

But how many times had those impulsive urgings gotten her into trouble with other people?

"Ranger, I —"

"Shh." He placed that enticing index finger to her lips. "Just let me look at you and savor this moment."

Got it. Spontaneous side checked. Shh, indeed.

He looked her up and down, shifting and moving to take her in. Like a good research scientist, he got to know his subject. Nibbling her earlobes, nipping her chin. Tracing his tongue down her neck to her breasts.

And so it began in earnest, their first time together. The first time these two best friends made love. Because even if neither of them wanted to say it out loud, that's what they were doing. Not just having sex or hooking up, but making love.

Ember focused on every little thing about him. Each touch. Each kiss. Each sound. Each smell.

In making love to Ranger, she felt as if the world had cracked right open and unfolded into a new and exciting territory she hadn't even known existed. Mundane life gave way to magic and she bathed in it. She felt fairy-dusted, light and beautiful and at the same time grounded and earthy, sexy and horny, revered and ravaged.

They took the normal precautions. Ranger got up at one point to retrieve condoms, but they felt so safe with each other, it seemed there was hardly any need, she was on birth control pills after all. She confessed she hadn't been with anyone since Trey, and he reminded her he hadn't had sex since he'd broken up with Tonya two years ago, about the same time Ember had started dating her ex.

"We're a couple of weirdos," she said.

"I like to think we finally got our timing right."

"If you haven't had sex since Tonya, how old are those condoms?"

"I bought them before I came looking for you tonight."

"Feeling that sure of yourself?" she murmured.

"I was going to do my best to convince you."

"I'm so glad you did," she whispered.

He pressed his face into her hair, took a deep breath, and murmured her name like a prayer.

Her head hummed so loudly!

And when they were at last joined, her entire body hummed with the beat of him. There was no awkwardness between them. She was wide open and totally vulnerable, and yet it felt so right. Safe. She felt safe with him in a way she'd not ever felt totally safe in bed with any man.

Need claimed them both.

They rocked together, shooting for the stars, clinging to each other, breathing hard. It was everything she'd ever dreamed it would be and more. So much more.

She cried out first, reaching her peak, but he tumbled soon after, calling her name, holding her close. She shivered. He shuddered. They gasped. Rasped. Drifted.

When they finally caught their breath, he pulled her to his chest and combed his fingers through her hair, petting her as if she were a precious commodity.

"You've got the cutest orgasm face." He chuckled as if he'd just taken a ride on his favorite roller coaster, pushing the tip of her nose with his index finger as if pushing a button to make the ride start up again.

She splayed a hand over her nose and eyes. "Please don't make fun of me."

"I'm not. I mean it. You are something else, Sparky."

Heat warmed her cheeks and she curled into his side, inhaled the potency of his sex. God, he smelled so good.

"Hey," he murmured. "Are you hungry?"

"Starving."

"Got anything to eat?"

"Fruit," she said. "And chocolate sauce."

He rubbed his palms together. "Now we're talking. You hang loose. I'll go get the food."

"Ranger?"

He stopped at the door, turned, looked back at her. "What is it, Sparky?"

"You are a thoughtful lover."

He laughed, delighted. "Meaning?"

371

"You took your time and . . . well . . . I just wanted you to know that's the first time I ever had an orgasm without my trusty vibrator."

He clutched both hands to his heart, staggered back as if Cupid's arrow had shot him through the heart. "Honey, that was just round one, and you ain't seen nothing yet."

CHAPTER 20

"She was one of those, who, having, once begun, would be always in love."
— Jane Austen, *Emma*

They sat up in bed naked, feeding each other fruit dipped in chocolate sauce and talking about so many things — the adventures they'd had as kids, their families, the things they'd done in the past year they'd been apart. He regaled her with tales of New Zealand, and she recounted hilarious home-buyer stories.

"So now that the film is finished, Luke should be doling out the endowment to the observatory. That's good," she said. "You're one step closer to getting your dream job."

"Yeah, I hope so. I can't shake the feeling that Wes was using the competition between me and Sheila to pry the money out of Luke."

"You don't think Wes is going to give you

the job?"

"Honestly? I don't know."

If Ranger didn't get the job, that meant he'd take the position in New Zealand. Her pulse quickened. If that happened, what did that mean for their future? She was afraid to ask. Afraid to ruin this awesome night with questions that could wait until another day.

"Here you go." Ember speared a slice of honeydew melon with her fork, dipped it in melted chocolate, and held it out to him.

He opened his mouth to take the bite, but a drop of chocolate dribbled on his chin.

"Wait, wait," she said. "I'll get it." She leaned in and licked his chin.

"I love how outrageous you are." He laughed a low husky sound. "No one in my life is as fun as you."

"Right back at you, big guy."

He tickled her lightly in the ribs. She giggled and tickled him back.

"I'm not ticklish," he said staunchly.

"Oh, you liar," she said, and tickled him until he flipped her on her back and pinned her down, wrists over her head.

She stared up into him. "That was a sexy move."

"Oh yeah?" His eyes sparkled like starlight.

"I've got more moves like that up my sleeve."

"I can't wait to see them."

"Pace yourself," he said. "It's a long time until dawn."

"Ooh, we're going to stay up all night?" She snuggled closer to him.

He relocated the fruit bowl and chocolate to the bedside table, plumped up the pillows against the headboard, and tugged her into his arms. They sat side by side, surrounded by pillows. "You bet your sweet butt. This is the first time we're doing this. We're going to make it last."

"I ever tell you that I like the way you think, Lockhart?"

"Ditto."

"It's nice," she said. "Already knowing so much about each other. We don't have to play games."

"Ah damn," he said. "I was looking forward to playing pin the tail on the —"

She tickled him again.

"You wanna get flipped?"

"I'm not opposed." She wriggled her eyebrows.

"Settle down, Sparky. We'll get there." He slung his arm around her shoulders, and ruffled her hair with his palm.

"I forgot how you like to take your time."

"You're welcome."

"Sometimes faster is better."

"Sometimes it's not."

"You know, if things go too slowly, I'm in danger of falling asleep."

"Calling my bluff?"

"You're the gambler," she said. "You tell me."

He leaned in to kiss her again, and she was getting all wrapped up in the humming when something jostled the bed.

"What the hell?" Ranger asked, and they both startled.

Samantha leaped up on the mattress between them, gave Ranger a dirty look, and meowed.

"If you're here to protect my honor," he told the cat, "you're too late. Ember has already deflowered me."

Ember playfully swatted his shoulder. "You big doofus. You're in her spot."

"Well, excuse me, Miss Samantha." He wriggled closer to Ember, leaving a berth for the tabby.

"She sleeps with me every night."

"I think I'm jealous."

Samantha kneaded his leg with her paws.

"Now I'm the jealous one." Ember got up and snapped her fingers, pointed at the door. "Out Miss S."

Samantha rolled over on her back, gave Ranger a pleading look. Smart cat. She knew who was the soft touch.

"We could go somewhere else," he offered. "Leave Miss S to the bed."

"Spoiled cat." Ember scratched the tabby behind the ears, setting off a purr-fest. "Where shall we go?"

"Your couch is pretty comfy," he said. "And might set us up for some interesting positions."

"I like the way you think, Professor. Grab the pillows, and we'll leave Miss S to her beauty rest."

They trooped into the living room. The blinds were open, and moonlight spilled across the couch. He plunked down, took her hand, and hauled her into his lap. "Anyone every tell you that you look beautiful in moonlight?"

"Corny." She rolled her eyes.

"Truth."

"Anyone ever tell you that you look beautiful naked?"

"All the time," he teased.

"I'm always the last to know."

He kissed the tip of her nose. "It's better to be last."

"Why's that?"

"Because last is now."

"Good point."

He rubbed his thumb across her chin. "I remember how you got that scar. First grade, monkey bars."

"I challenged you to a chin-up competition."

"I won," he pointed out.

"Only because I busted my chin and the teacher made me quit because I was bleeding all over the monkey bars."

"They took the monkey bars out of school because of you."

"I have a way of ruining things for other people."

"That's bullshit. You do not."

"Seems like it." She reached for his right thumb. "What about this?"

"Oh yeah." He ran his index finger over the scar at the pad of his thumb. "You still remember that?"

"How could I forget?" she said, old guilt jabbing into her fresh and new. "I caused that too."

"Not really. We can blame it on Lucy."

"Lucy blamed me for sure."

"She was *pissed.*" Ranger chuckled. "I'd never seen her so angry, and she got pretty mad at Duke on a regular basis."

The memory floated up to Ember as vivid as the day it happened. It was one of the defining moments of her life, and a major ding in her psyche that had come full circle the day Trey told her so bluntly — *You're an unlovable freak.*

She and Ranger had been ten years old when it happened, and he'd been recovering from heart surgery to repair damage caused by the rheumatic fever stemming from unchecked scarlet fever he'd had when he was a toddler.

Ember's mother had actually been the one to recognize that the boy had scarlet fever after his mother had left and before Duke had married Lucy. Ranger and Ridge had been left in the care of a string of under-qualified nannies. If Bridgette Alzate hadn't taken Ranger to the doctor when she had, he very well could have died.

On that fateful day, Ranger had been trying to keep up with schooling from his sick bed and Ember, as she did every afternoon, dropped by the mansion with his homework.

"You're the only one who comes to visit every day," Ranger had said. "Even my own brothers avoid coming in here." He'd glanced out the window where they could see one of the corrals where Rhett and Remington were roping a bronze steer head mounted to a bale of hay, Ridge giving them the lessons.

"That's 'cause I'm closer to you than your brothers," Ember had said, crawling up to sit cross-legged at the end of his mattress.

"Too bad you can't be my brother," he mumbled.

"Well, I'm a girl, so that's out . . ."

"I don't think of you as a girl," Ranger said. "You're not prissy and giggly like most girls."

"You mean like Aria?"

"I don't want to say bad things about your sister, but kinda, yeah." He'd grinned and she'd grinned back.

"You know," she said. "There's a way we could be kin."

"How's that?" He straightened up against the pillow, winced, and placed a hand to his chest.

"You okay?" She'd scooted closer.

He scowled, and she knew it was because he hated looking weak. "I'm fine. What were you saying?"

"Blood brothers."

"Or in this case, blood siblings?" He'd been so smart, even back then. His bedroom was packed with books.

"Yeah," she said, and slipped her pocket-knife from her pocket. "That." She glanced around the room. "We need a bowl."

"What kind of bowl?"

"This'll do." She somersaulted off the bed and retrieved the yellow plastic emesis basin that had come home from the hospital with him. Bounced back onto the mattress beside him.

Ranger eyed the knife with curiosity. "How do you know so much about blood brothers . . . um . . . blood siblings?"

Ember tossed her flame-colored hair over her shoulder. "Don't let the hair fool you. I'm half Apache."

"I know," he said. "I've seen you on the warpath."

She playfully punched him on the shoulder. "Do you want to do this or not?"

"Sure."

She reached out her hand. "Give me your thumb."

Trusting her completely, Ranger had given her his hand.

She opened the blade.

"Do we need to say something?" Ranger asked. "A ritual?"

"You're gettin' ahead of me." She positioned his hand over the emesis basin, stared him in the eyes. "Do you, Ranger Lockhart, vow a solemn oath to this bond between us that runs deeper than brother and sister?"

Ranger's eyes locked on hers. "Yes," he

declared without an ounce of hesitation.

Ember pressed the tip of her knife into his thumb, meaning to make only the smallest of cuts, just enough to coax out a drop of blood, but at the same moment she pushed the knife against Ranger's skin, Lucy had come barreling through the door without knocking. A tray of lemonade and chocolate-chip cookies in her hand.

Lucy had taken one look at the wild red-haired girl child about to carve up her ailing stepson, and she'd let out a curdling scream and dropped the tray. Shattering and clattering plates and glasses.

Startled, Ember had slipped, the knife plunging deep into the pad of Ranger's thumb and coming out through his nail on the other side.

Blood bloomed, pouring into the cheerful yellow emesis basin.

Ranger let out a stoic grunt. Ember jerked the knife out, embedded deeply in the wound. More blood flowed. Lucy yelled. Grabbed Ember by her collar. Propelled her through the house and literally threw her out the back door.

"You wicked, wicked girl!" Lucy scolded, standing on the back porch, her hands on her hips, the afternoon sun shining on her fiercely angry face. "What is wrong with you? Ranger just had heart surgery and you're cutting him!"

Ember, who wasn't given to tears, couldn't keep them from tracking down her cheeks. She was so deeply sorry. She'd never meant to hurt Ranger. She loved him as much as her actual brother, Archer. Maybe even more. She would never ever do anything to harm him.

And yet, she had.

"You're not right in the head," Lucy yelled. "Don't you care at all what people think about you?"

"Leave her alone, Lucy," Ranger commanded from the doorway. His face was ghostly pale and he had a bandanna wrapped around his thumb but the blood was soaking through. "She only cut me so deeply because you interrupted."

Lucy whirled around to face him. "Thank God I did! If I hadn't come in, this little heathen might have scalped you!"

"Don't be stupid," Ranger said flatly. He wasn't usually so rude to his stepmother, but he was taking up for Ember, and he was in pain. "We were conducting a blood ritual."

"And here you are, spurting blood all over the patio. You got what you wanted. Happy now?" Lucy's cheeks flushed red, and her chin quivered.

Ember recognized then how upset Lucy was, saw things through her eyes. She ducked her head and apologized profusely to both Ranger and Lucy.

"No worries." Ranger winked at her. "We're bonded for life now."

But they weren't. She hadn't cut herself. They hadn't finished the ritual. She hadn't sworn a vow. Their blood hadn't mingled.

"You," Lucy barked at her. "Get home now, and don't let me catch you sneaking back over here. I'll be having a stern conversation with your mother." She whirled around to Ranger. "And you, go get in the car. That cut needs sterilizing and stitches."

Lucy had whisked Ranger away, and when Ember had gotten home, she'd gotten a spanking and had her pocketknife taken away, but worst of all, she'd been banned from the mansion, and from hanging around with Ranger. Ember's mother had grounded her for a week and told her she needed to learn to think about the consequences of her actions before she acted. Which confused Ember. How could you think about what you did before you did it?

She supposed Lucy would have eventually relented and let her see Ranger again, but not long after that bloodletting incident,

Ranger's stepmother had been diagnosed with inflammatory breast cancer, and she'd quickly succumbed to the terrible disease.

Ember shook her head, snapped back to the present moment, kissed Ranger's thumb again. "I caused a hell of a ruckus."

"You brought excitement into my boring bookish life. Thank you," Ranger murmured. "I'm glad now that we didn't become blood siblings. It was hard enough for us to get here even without that heavy symbolism."

"How hard was it?" she teased.

"About as hard as I am now," he said gruffly, and she could feel his erection growing against her leg.

"I'm glad you like me." She smiled as a warm, fizzy sensation seeped through her. "Apparently, I'm an acquired taste."

"All the best things are," he said, and pressed his lips to her forehead. "Champagne, coffee, olives, blue cheese . . ."

"So now I'm blue cheese?"

He nibbled her earlobe. "I love blue cheese."

"You sure know how to sweet-talk a girl."

"Not just any girl," he said. "You."

Another warm fizzy feeling started in the pit of her stomach and wriggled up into her heart. "You don't sweet-talk Dawn?"

Why had she said that? She didn't want to know about his relationship with Dawn.

"Dawn is sweet," he said.

"I'm not."

"I know." He laughed and kissed her again, slipped his hands down to cup her butt and they forgot all about Dawn.

Before Ember, Ranger thought sex was fun, enjoyable, a pleasant way to pass the time, but nothing in this world compared to making love to his best friend.

Who knew love could be like this?

Love. Yes. He was in love with her. If he hadn't known it before, he surely did now.

Ranger kissed her soft and slow. He'd waited a long time for Ember. He was damn well going to enjoy every second.

She squirmed in his lap, things heating up rapidly. She laced her fingers through his hair, covered his face in kisses. He grinned at her enthusiasm, the rapt expression in her eyes. Her hot little hands were all over his skin — sliding, caressing, kneading him in places that felt so good he groaned aloud.

Her tongue seemed to be everywhere at once — his lips, his throat, his belly button. His body throbbed and vibrated, alive with their combined energies. His temperature clicked from hot to cold and back again in rapid succession. Shivers and sweats. Like a pendulum swinging back and forth between extremes, sweeping him along on a current of sensation.

She delighted him in ways he had not ever been delighted. He tasted her, touched her, smelled her — lips, teeth, nose, tongue. Gliding over her body, those creamy breasts, her flat belly, her vibrant triangle of red.

Ember was on her back on the couch, and he was on the floor on his knees, her legs thrown over his shoulders. Moonlight shimmering over her bare skin, illuminating her like pixie dust. The moon had always fascinated him. Its pull on the tides. Its feminine mystique. And she embodied those moon qualities.

He stopped breathing. Spellbound.

Ranger wanted one thing. To please her. Whatever she desired, he would stop at nothing to give to her. He pressed his lips to that gorgeous red triangle, breathed in her essence. Her scent was spicy and exciting. Her skin, silky and smooth. Her taste on his lips, richly female.

She whispered his name, a prayer in the night, letting him know he was on the right track. He wanted to be her hero. Whatever she needed, he could provide. He would rocket her to the stars. Give her a light show unlike anything she'd ever seen.

His mouth found the most delicate part of her and Ember threw back her head, let out a strangled moan.

A wordless joy mushroomed inside him, growing like a thick Bavarian forest after long soaking rains. He was so grateful to be here. So happy to please her in this most intimate of ways.

Her whimpers guided him. He listened for every muffled sigh, every quick-caught gasp. She smelled of brine and bliss, her skin a hot, silken road. He navigated each buck and wiggle as he tamed his wild, red-haired pony.

She yielded to his tongue, giving him the reins, letting go of control. He recognized it as the gift it was. Ember trusted him completely. His pride shone like a polished medal.

He loved her as much as he loved the stars. The sky, and all that it encompassed, had been the salvation of a sick, lonely kid, and so had Ember. She'd always been his champion, his heroine, his best friend.

She tasted like stardust, otherworldly and surreal, spectacular and spacey, eternal and abiding. He could always count on her to be there.

As he savored her, Ranger thought happily — *comet, eclipse, binary star, gibbous, ephemeris.* In his head, he married the two things he loved most, astronomy and Ember. Her flavor taunted him, haunted him.

His erection grew, but he ignored his needs, focused solely on her. This was her playground. Her turn. For right now, only she mattered.

He closed his eyes, saw a shower of meteors and a trillion light-years stretching out before them. Felt every atom, and every cell vibrating. The cosmos was inside them and they were the cosmos. In between her soft moans and his own heavy breathing, he heard the sacred silence of space, endless and all encompassing. Tying them together with all there ever was and all there ever would be.

Through loving her body, he drank the history of the universe. The Big Bang of creation. The birth and death of galaxies. Swallowed radio bursts of pulsars, got swept up in those furiously rotating neutrons. Flared with the force of five hundred million suns. Tingled like a supernova. She moaned his name and shuddered against him, clutched his hair in her hands, called his name again and again and again.

He groaned, clung to her, inhaled her, breathed in her sexy feminine scent, let it fill his lungs, and nourish him with her essence. He tightened his arms around her as she burst in a blaze of quivering gasps, his beautiful woman, his shooting star.

Ranger was ridiculously overjoyed. Making love to Ember *was* making love to the universe, and with her in his arms, he felt as if he had finally found his home.

CHAPTER 21

"If I loved you less, I might be able to talk about it more."

— Jane Austen, *Emma*

Dawn — the sunrise, not the Kiwi astronomer — was peeping through the window, shining a wan stream of pinky-orange light over Ranger and Ember as they lay, arms and legs entangled, on her bed, Samantha curled up at the foot of the mattress.

Ranger's bare chest was level with Ember's face. Fascinated, she watched that muscular chest rise and fall with his low, deep breathing. She snuggled closer, smiled dreamily. She had known this man all her life and now he *was* her life.

Wow, okay. That sounded like something her sister Kaia would say, not fiery, independent Ember. What about real estate agent Ember? Movie director Ember? Matchmaker Ember? The sides of her that didn't need a man to have an identity.

Right. She didn't *need* a man, but she wanted one. She wanted *this* one.

Forever and ever until the end of time.

"What are you thinking?" Ranger asked, and lazily drew a heart in the flat place between her breasts.

"You. Me. Us. The end of time."

"I like the way you think." He propped himself up on his elbow, leaned over and kissed the tip of her nose.

A satisfying hum skimmed from her nose to her brain, singing that now-familiar soul mate song.

"Could I ask you a question?" He caressed her hair.

"Sure."

"You don't have to answer if you don't want to."

"For you? I'll answer anything."

"I know." There was a sweet smile in his voice. "But you don't have to."

"Just ask the question, Lockhart."

"Why did you marry Trey?"

"Truth?"

"No, lie to me."

She playfully punched his arm. "You were with Tonya, and it was looking like you were going to get married and you were just starting your second PhD and you didn't have

392

time for marriage, for me, and everything . . ."

"I will *always* have time for you." His tone turned fierce, and he reached over to squeeze her hand.

"I know," she said. "That's why I couldn't get in the way of you and Tonya. She was good for you. I thought you two had a chance."

"So you thought, 'hey, let me take up with the biggest asshole I can find'?"

She shook her head, glanced away. "Never mind."

He reached out, cupped her chin in his palm, drew her face back to his. "Ember." He paused a beat. His gaze held hers, strong as a bear trap. He wasn't letting her off the hook.

"I picked him because he was the opposite of you, okay?"

"Why?"

"Because if I picked someone just like you, it was as if I was marrying a pale imitation of the real thing. Like buying a print because you can't afford a work of art."

"Hmm. I guess that makes an odd kind of sense."

She stared into his eyes. "You think so?"

His nose crinkled. "Hell no. It makes no sense at all."

"Well, of course not to you. You've never let your emotions rule your head."

"I wouldn't say *never.*"

"Please. There's a reason you're the best poker player in the Trans-Pecos. You learned a long time ago how to shut down your emotions and not feel a thing. I blame your asshat mother."

"I don't, why should you? Sabrina did what she had to do to survive."

"She sold her kid for money."

"That's harsh. It wasn't like that. It —"

"It was exactly like that." Ember folded her arms across her chest.

"Look, she did what she did. I can't change it."

"And I did what I did. I screwed up and married Trey. I can't change it either."

"I don't blame you for marrying him any more than I blame Sabrina for leaving. We're all human. We all screw up. Blaming doesn't change things, it only creates un-happy feelings."

He had a point. He kissed her, and she hummed and they luxuriated in the sexy feeling of being in each other's arms.

"You know what I was thinking about?" he asked a few minutes later.

"The existence of life elsewhere in the universe?"

He inclined his head. "For once, no. I'm thinking eggs over easy."

"You cooking?"

"God, yes. You can't boil water without burning it."

"Haha. For all you know I learned how to cook while you were in New Zealand. A year is a long time."

"Did you?"

"No."

"So, eggs?"

"That would be great except you'd have to go to the store. I've been so busy with directing the film I haven't had a chance to go shopping."

"Whatcha got?"

"I think there might be some slightly stale pretzels in the top of the pantry."

"Breakfast at Eggs and More?"

"Now you're talking."

"Ugh, that means we have to get dressed. It was my plan to spend all day in bed making love to you."

"I do have cat food if you're feeling adventuresome."

"I'll pass on the Fancy Feast."

"You know," she said, wrapping her arms around his neck, "food is overrated."

"There *is* science to back up intermittent fasting." He kissed her, his mouth warm against hers.

Samantha woke up, stretched, and meowed for her breakfast. She was having no part of intermittent fasting.

"I'll just open a can of food for her and be right back." Ember slid off the bed and pranced naked into the kitchen, Samantha following right behind her. She knew good and well that Ranger was watching her walk away.

She wriggled her butt for his benefit.

He applauded. Loudly.

Grinning, she fed the tabby, went to the bathroom where she grabbed a box of condoms she'd bought right after her divorce but had never opened, and headed back to the bedroom.

Ranger was lying on his side, giving her the full monty, letting her see for herself that he was more than up for using the condoms in her hand.

"Great minds think alike." He crooked his finger in a sexy "c'mere" gesture.

And she went, springing onto the bed and into his arms.

They were just heating up the sheets when his cell phone, which was sitting on the dresser across the room, buzzed.

"You're getting a call," she said.

"Ignore it."

"What if it's family?"

"They'll call back."

Second buzz.

"What if it's an emergency?"

"You're the only emergency that matters," he said, and nuzzled her neck, nibbled her skin.

"You say that now . . . ooh, what are you doing?"

Third buzz.

"You like that?" he murmured in her ear.

"Mmm."

Voice mail picked up the phone call.

It was Dawn — the Kiwi astronomer, not the sunrise — and her voice came splashing into the room as welcome as an ice-water bath. "Ranger, are you there? Pick up! Pick up!"

Silence deafened the room for a nanosecond.

"You wanna answer?" Ember asked.

"Why?" He ran his tongue along the outside of her ear.

She shivered against him. "She sounds excited."

"You *are* excited." Lightly he pinched one of her puckered nipples.

"Ranger?" Dawn's voice again, pleading from the cell phone. "Call me as soon as you can. I'm at the observatory and I've made a breakthrough. I think I've found a way to prove what FRBs really are!"

He jerked his head up, dropped his hand, bulleted it out of bed, and snagged up the phone. "Dawn, I'm here, I'm here. What did you find out? Tell me everything."

Leaving Ember naked, horny, shivering from the loss of his body heat, and feeling like an old shoe tossed aside on the trash heap.

Ranger's loyalties were torn right in two.

On one hand, he had his beloved Ember lying naked and sexy as hell, waiting for him in bed, and on the other hand, he had Dawn on the phone telling him she'd made a breakthrough in their research project exploring fast radio bursts, one of the most perplexing mysteries in astronomy.

If Dawn was correct, not only would the discovery make both their careers, he could cherry-pick any job he wanted — no having to raise funds to please a board of directors — because it could potentially solve the enigma that had been plaguing astronomers since 2007 when a five-millisecond radio burst showed up from an unknown source billions of light-years away.

He and Dawn would be legendary in the annals of astronomy.

"I'll be right there," he told Dawn.

Turning to Ember, he saw the light go out of her eyes, and his stomach fell right to the floor. Talk about horrible timing. Dawn's call coming right when he and Ember had finally hooked up after years of waltzing around each other. This was a tender time he should be nourishing, cherishing.

But Dawn had made a breakthrough on one of the biggest astronomical puzzles out there.

He tried to explain it to Ember, going into detail about what a big deal this was. He talked fast as he dressed, jamming his legs into his jeans, feeling the excitement pump through his veins. He tried to temper his thrill for Ember's sake, but he just couldn't do it. He'd lived and breathed this stuff for over a decade. His life's work had culminated into this moment.

If Dawn was right.

"Astronomers are not sure what causes fast radio bursts," he said, zipping up his jeans and searching for his shirt.

"Um . . . okay."

He could tell she didn't understand. "FRBs are powerful but very short radio waves that last no more than a millisecond. They've only been observed by astronomers twenty-five times to date."

Ember frowned. "Are you saying that you have discovered life-forms elsewhere in the universe?"

"That's one theory, yeah, but there are many theories. It could be a neutron star with a very powerful magnetic field — surrounded by debris from a stellar explosion. Or jets of material shooting out from the rim of a supermassive black hole. Dawn thinks she's found the answer."

"Which is?" Ember held her breath.

"I can't say. Not yet. Not until I've seen her evidence, not until we're ready to go public."

Ember sprang to her knees in the middle of the mattress. "This is huge! Oh my gosh, Ranger, I got goose bumps. This is everything you've worked for."

"I know!" He was lit up from the inside, on fire with possibilities. He stepped toward the bathroom, stopped, spun around, came back, pulled her into his arms, and kissed her so hard neither one of them could breathe. "Thank you, thank you for being so understanding."

"Why of course." Her dear face was a wreath of smiles. "You're my best friend in the whole world, hell the whole universe. All I've ever wanted was your happiness. Astronomy makes you happy. Go, go." She made shooing motions. "Don't feel like you need to hurry back to me. Keep your mind where it belongs. On your work."

"That's going to be pretty hard to do." He hissed in a breath through clenched teeth. "When the image of how you look right now keeps popping into my brain."

"Get out of here." She splayed a palm on his chest and pushed him away. "I'll be here whenever you get back, no matter how long it takes."

"You are the best girlfriend in the whole damn world. How did I get so lucky?"

"Because *you're* amazing. Now go, find out if E.T. has been trying to phone home."

And with that, she pushed him out the door.

With all her heart, Ember was happy for Ranger. She didn't resent him leaving their bed to go running up to the observatory to stare through a telescope with Dawn, or whatever it was they were doing.

Honestly, she'd barely understood a word Ranger had said. It made her feel dumb as a fence post. She'd always known he was a brainy guy, and she tried her best to keep up with all the science-y stuff when he patiently tried to explain it, but astronomy just wasn't her thing. Oh, sure she liked looking at the stars with him, but he was doing that just to indulge her. His mind was light-years beyond hers.

To keep from dwelling on her inadequacies, she took herself to breakfast at Eggs and More. She settled into a booth with Belgian waffles and six strips of bacon. Don't judge. Her boyfriend had just left her bed to go frolicking with his research partner; she was entitled to bacon and waffles if it cheered her up.

It was still early, not quite seven, and the diner was gearing up with customers. The bell over the door jangled, and Ember glanced up to see Fiona stroll in with Palmer. They were looking mighty cozy, walking arm in arm, as if they'd just spent the night together.

So much for her matchmaking skills. She'd tried her best to keep those two apart and look at them. Their faces were sunbeams.

The last thing she wanted was to bathe in *their* afterglow, when her own afterglow had been cut tragically short.

Okay, not tragically, that was just feeling sorry for herself. She caught the server's eye, made doggie-bag motions over her plate, kept her head ducked down, and prayed Fiona and Palmer didn't see her.

She needn't have worried. They had eyes only for each other, and by the time the server wrapped up her food in a to-go bag, Ember had completely lost her appetite.

Ranger did not come back that night or the next. The day after that was his birthday. Ember had gotten a special present for him, but it would have to wait until she had him in her bed again.

He called her of course, and sent texts, and had the local florist deliver a massive bouquet of stargazer lilies, with a sweet note that said, "When you gaze on these, think of me, because I'll be thinking of you — Ranger."

Yeah, right. He was thinking about fast radio bursts, and she knew it. Not that she was jealous. She wasn't. Not of his career. Not even of Dawn. She just felt . . .

Left out.

While he couldn't fully discuss the breakthrough with her, it wasn't quite as earthshattering as Dawn had made it sound. Apparently, she'd figured out a piece of the puzzle of the FRBs, not the whole enchilada. Still, even that small piece was a big deal in the astronomy world, and renowned scientists, the world over, were flying in to investigate the discovery.

With all the brouhaha going on, Ember didn't know if Dawn had remembered about Ranger's birthday, but Dawn texted her to say that the party had moved from Wes's house as they'd originally planned to a star party at the observatory because it had a lot more room for the visiting astronomers.

Ember dressed with care. It would be her first time seeing Ranger since he'd walked out of her bedroom sixty hours earlier. She wondered if he'd gotten any sleep and if he remembered to eat. He could forget about the essentials of daily living when his mind was fully engaged.

She wore his special present — a sexy black-and-red bustier with garters — underneath a sapphire sheath dress, knowing that the color played up her hair and her eyes. She applied extra makeup and put on a pair of catch-me-do-me stilettoes. She wanted him to take one look at her and forget all about fast radio bursts and smart research partners.

At least for a little while.

When she arrived at the observatory, she saw people in formal wear going in through the front entrance. Men in tuxedoes, women in ball gowns, and she felt distinctly underdressed. Dawn had not warned her that what started off as an off-the-cuff birthday party had morphed into a formal affair.

She should have figured it out. The place was chock-full of astronomy VIPs.

There was even valet parking, and her heart sped up when she turned her car over to a wide-eyed young man and realized she was going to have to walk into the building with strangers.

Not that strangers intimidated her. Not one bit. She was an outgoing extrovert. But the people walking into that building were some of the smartest people in the world. What did she have to offer in the way of conversation to the likes of them?

She glanced around, hoping to find someone she knew. Ridge or Rhett, any of her sisters, Palmer, Fiona, Zeke, Chriss Anne, Spencer, Angi, Andre. Luke. As Cupid's mayor, Luke should be here.

Finally, she spied Wes Montgomery and his wife, Sally, handing the keys to his Cadillac to the valet.

He smiled and waved her over.

Relief flooded her. At last, someone she knew. They exchanged pleasantries and walked up the sidewalk together.

"That friend of yours and his partner have turned this observatory on its ear with their research," Wes said proudly. "I always knew

Ranger was going to make a big splash."

"It doesn't hurt that he's so handsome either." Sally leaned in close as if revealing a secret.

"You'll be giving him that job now," Ember said with the force of a real estate agent fighting to get her client the best deal possible. "Right?"

"Ember." Wes shook his head. "Don't you get it?"

"Get what?"

"I don't stand a chance of landing him now. The world is Ranger's oyster. He can go anywhere in the world. The McDonald is mostly a teaching observatory. He'll *want* to go someplace where they're doing cutting edge research on FRBs. I wouldn't be surprised if he and Dawn both end up at CHIME."

"CHIME?"

"Canadian Hydrogen Intensity Mapping Experiment."

"Oh," she said, because she didn't know what else to say. It was fully starting to sink in that Ranger was a rising star and he was not long for the Trans-Pecos.

"I'm sorry now that I made him jump through those hoops, and that Luke coerced him into doing that silly film." Wes seemed to suddenly realize who he was talking to, made a quick forgive-my-faux-pas face and said, "No offense."

"None taken." She knew the film was inconsequential in the grand scheme of things. She also knew Ranger was special, had always known it. That's why she'd wanted to be his blood sibling when she was ten. She'd been hoping to absorb some of that specialness.

Didn't happen.

A tuxedoed waiter passed flutes of champagne to Ember and the Montgomerys. Another server passed through with savory puff pastries. A third carried figs wrapped in prosciutto and held together with a toothpick.

Someone had doled out a lot of money for this shindig, and Ember knew it couldn't have been Dawn. She was a poor student on a fellowship.

And since she still hadn't seen any of Ranger's friends or family, she concluded that Ranger's party hadn't simply been moved from Wes's house to the observatory. Rather, someone with big pockets and a lot of pull had hijacked it from Dawn.

The kind of pull that could magnetize Ranger right out of Cupid.

Feeling sick to her stomach, she waved off another waiter carrying skewered chicken satay on a tray. The party sprawled from the indoor air-conditioned building to the grounds around the telescopes. It felt like people were speaking a foreign language — quasars, distant dwarf galaxies, megaparsecs, dark energy, and y-ray bursts.

Some groups were engaged in heated debates about confirmation biases, and speculation that FRBs were proof of alien space travel. It made Ember's head spin unpleasantly.

Ranger had talked to her about such things before. But he'd given it to her in small digestible doses with easily understood explanations. Here, everyone else was already up to speed. No need to dumb it down for the guests, except for her, and no one was paying her any attention anyway.

A couple came up to greet Wes and Sally, giving Ember a chance to break away from them. She needed to get off by herself. Needed time to absorb this new information, this startling knowledge that there truly was not a place for her in Ranger's high flying world.

CHAPTER 22

"I always deserve the best treatment because I never put up with any other."
— Jane Austen, *Emma*

Ember tried chatting up people, but they weren't the friendliest bunch. Scientists, she'd discovered, were generally introverted deep thinkers, with no disposition for idle chitchat. She introduced herself around the room, told a few jokes, nothing off-color, but she got strange looks for even trying.

Okay, tough crowd. She was starting to feel like gum stuck to the bottom of their shoes when she spied Dawn standing on the sidewalk outside the Visitors Center surrounded by a group of tuxedoed men who were hanging on her every word.

Dawn made eye contact, smiled, and lifted a hand in greeting.

An inordinate amount of happiness flooded Ember at seeing someone she knew, even if Dawn was one of *them.* At least she was a friendly face.

Breaking away from her group, Dawn rushed up to her. "You came!"

"Of course I came. It's Ranger's birthday. Congratulations to you, by the way. Apparently, you are responsible for all this hub-bub." Ember flapped a hand at the well-heeled group surrounding them.

Dawn crinkled her nose. "Ranger is just as responsible as I am for the breakthrough. He started the research project. This posh stuff is maddening, but it's part of it."

"What is it exactly that you discovered?" Ember asked, a small part of her holding on to the hope that if she could just understand this stuff she still had a place in Ranger's universe.

Dawn started spouting a whole lot of stuff Ember didn't understand, but the gist of it was that Ranger and Dawn's research had accurately predicted when the next FRB would occur, and it had happened just as their calculations forecast. No one had been able to do that before. It took the astronomers one step closer to figuring out the source of the fast radio bursts.

"That's awesome. I know you are so proud of your work."

"And I know you are so proud of Ranger."

"He told me," Ember said. "About his plan to make me jealous."

"Did it work?" Dawn winked.

"It did." Ember couldn't help grinning.

"Go on with you, then." Dawn poked her in the ribs with her elbow. "That's why he's smiling so much."

"I'm sure you're the cause of that."

"Don't sell yourself short, Ember," Dawn said. "You mean a lot to him."

Dawn was such a sweetheart that Ember couldn't believe she'd been jealous of her.

"I've got to entertain this bunch." Dawn jerked a thumb over her shoulder at the group waiting for her to return. "After all this ruckus dies down, we'll all go for a drink."

"That sounds nice," Ember said, and meant it. "Have you seen Ranger?"

Dawn turned her head. "He was here a bit ago. You want me to text him?"

Ember held up her phone. "I did when I first got here, but he hasn't answered."

"Some gasbag probably has him cornered somewhere. He'll text you back." Dawn gave Ember's shoulder a friendly squeeze and went to rejoin her colleagues.

Leaving Ember alone once more.

The place was getting more and more crowded, but still, there was no one that she

411

knew. She wished she'd asked Dawn where Ranger's friends and family were, almost went back to find out, but a bulky man in a reflective vest that read SECURITY came over to escort Dawn off to a private wing of the building.

So much for that.

It was starting to get dark, and more people were moving from inside the building to the telescopes outside. The migration drove Ember indoors to get away from the crowd. Really, if she wasn't going to get to see Ranger, she might as well go home. She was standing in an empty corridor trying to decide what to do when her cell phone dinged.

Her heart leaped, and she wrestled the cell phone out of her purse. Turn around, Sexy.

She stopped breathing, turned to find Ranger standing there, looking drop-dead handsome in a tuxedo, red bow tie, three-days' worth of beard scruff, and cowboy boots that matched. Her slightly rumpled, dapper, cowboy professor.

Her heart skipped a beat, two. Not her professor. Not anymore. He belonged to the world.

He pocketed his cell phone, cocked his head. Winked.

412

She meant to tell him how good he looked, how happy she was to see him. She meant to ask him how he was feeling, if he was eating enough, if he'd gotten any rest. But looking into those dark eyes, she got swept up in his pulse-stopping grin, and she couldn't say a word. Instead, she flew across the corridor to him, her heels clattering against the tile floor.

The minute she grabbed hold of his tie, Ember knew she shouldn't do it, was yelling at herself not to do it, but there was an unstoppable part of her, that Lucy Ricardo part of her, that wild redhead DNA that simply could not be suppressed.

This was dumb. This was stupid. This was that night, with Trey in the wine cellar, all over again. Why did men in suits at fancy parties cause her to lose her mind? What was wrong with her?

With that bow tie stretched out as her leash, she opened the nearest door without a combination lock keypad on it and pulled him inside.

It was a janitorial closet.

Not the most romantic place in the observatory, but on the plus side, it did smell like soap.

In the pitch dark, her hands were all over him and his were all over her. Fingers combed through hair. Mouths fused. Legs trembled.

He picked her up and she locked her legs around his waist, and he did a little half-circle in the tight enclosure to find an empty wall and pressed her against it.

"God, I missed you." He showered her with hot kisses, ran his arms up and down her body. "You are so hot."

"Me? You're the hot one."

"We're both hot, how's that?"

"Very democratic."

"Did you get the flowers I sent?"

"I did. I loved them. Thank you for thinking of me."

"I'm always thinking of you. So stargazer lilies, were they too on the nose?"

"They were perfect, just like you," she murmured.

"I hate that I got stuck up here. Especially right after we —"

"Screwed our brains out?"

"You're incorrigible."

"And you love that best about me."

"True." He kissed her forehead, sending a low vibration buzzing through her head.

"C'mon, this is me you're talking to. Be honest. You're loving every minute of this star stuff."

"I didn't love leaving you behind."

"But you love what you're doing."

"Well, yeah, Dawn's discovery is monumental —"

"She told me it was your research that was the key. She just noticed the pattern."

"She's downplaying her role. I gotta tell you, Em. I think I might be the luckiest man in the world. Having an amazing woman like you in my life, being on the cusp of uncovering one of the biggest astronomical mysteries of *my* time. Hell, it makes up for my mother packing up and leaving me, for my hard-ass father, for the scarlet and rheumatic fevers, the heart surgery. It was all worth it to be where I am today."

The tone of his voice was just about the sexiest thing she'd ever heard. She captured his face between her palms and kissed him so fervently, he let out a groan.

His hands were up her dress, burning hot against her skin.

She was so happy to be here with him, to be loving him, to hear the strong, steady humming in her head when his lips touched her. In this moment, they were completely on top of the world and she forgot that they were in a closet at the McDonald Observatory, and that world-renowned dignitaries had gathered, that the man she loved was doing world-changing research.

Right here, right now, it was just Ranger and Ember, two best friends who had fallen in love making out in the closet.

And the darkness was sublime.

Until the door jerked open, and the light got in.

"Dr. Lockhart." The burly side of beef hired as a bodyguard stood in the doorway of the closet. "The governor is waiting for you."

Ranger eased Ember to the floor and slipped behind her so he could quickly zip up her dress, and his trousers.

"The governor?" Ember gasped. "Of Texas?"

"Yes, ma'am," the bodyguard said, averting his eyes.

Ember touched Ranger's arm. "Did you know about the governor?"

"I just found out a few hours ago that the governor was flying in for the party to meet Dawn and me."

"And you let me pull you into the closet?" Her voice was an angry whisper.

He knew she was having flashbacks to that incident with Trey. He wanted to reassure her and tell her he wasn't the least bit ashamed, and in fact had enjoyed himself immensely and they would still be enjoying themselves if the guy at the door hadn't

416

interrupted.

"Doctor," the bodyguard said, "the governor is on a tight schedule, if you could just come along with me now."

"You ready?" Ranger took Ember's arm and they started for the door.

"I'm going to meet the governor?" Amazement tinged her voice, and he could feel goose bumps dot her skin.

"No, ma'am." The bodyguard held up a palm. "Access to the governor is by invitation only. You are not invited."

"Then I'm not going either," Ranger said. "I'm not into this VIP nonsense."

"Doctor," the bodyguard said, propping the door open with his foot. "*You're* the VIP the governor has come to see."

It fully hit Ranger that his life was about to change in a major way. He'd been so busy verifying Dawn's discovery that he hadn't had much time to think about it. But now, with the governor of Texas waiting on him, reality sunk in, and he wasn't sure that he was prepared for this.

"You have to go see the governor," Ember said. "I'll be fine. You can tell me all about it later. I'm going on home, and I'll see you tomorrow."

"Can she wait for me here?" Ranger asked the bodyguard.

"In the janitorial closet?"

Ranger glowered at the guy. "At the party."

"There's a lot of demands on your time," the bodyguard said. "I'm guessing."

"Really." Ember beamed at him. "It's fine." She reached up to brush off his shoulders. "Oh, you've got a little lipstick on your cheek." She rubbed it off with the pad of her thumb.

They left the closet escorted by the bodyguard. Dawn was in the corridor along with a dozen other astronomers visiting from around the globe. Men and women he'd only dreamed of meeting.

This was his time to shine, but he couldn't do it because he was worried about Ember. How was she feeling? Was she really okay? Why the hell couldn't she come with him to meet the governor? Seemed like bullshit to him.

The bodyguard herded everyone toward a private elevator at the back of the building. Ranger stopped. No, he was taking a stand. If Ember couldn't come, he wasn't going. End of story. He turned to go back for her . . .

But she was already gone.

Moving as fast as she could without calling attention to herself, Ember went back the

418

way she'd come, past partygoers, who like her, had not been invited to meet the governor. People were lining up to peek through the telescopes. Others were lying on blankets staring up at the stars. Still others were seated in various places inside and outside the building.

"Canapé?" asked a passing waiter, extending a tray with fresh puff pastries.

Why not? She hadn't eaten, and she didn't get to spend time with Ranger. If she hadn't been driving herself back to Marfa, she would have gotten a glass of champagne. There was so much to celebrate tonight.

Except it didn't feel much like a celebration. At least not to her.

Don't be jealous, she told herself. *It's petty and it's not you.*

No, she wasn't the jealous type; she was the type to pull men into small spaces at parties and make out with them.

She closed her eyes against the memory of the bodyguard interrupting them right when they were about to get something seriously started. Would she never learn? If she was going to be Ranger's girlfriend, she would have to control herself. Her outrageousness wasn't going to cut it. It hadn't worked with Trey and . . .

Actually, Ranger had seemed amused that

they'd gotten caught. He'd smiled and sent her a wink, and when he zipped up the back of her dress, he'd planted a humming kiss to her nape.

Ember reached back to finger the spot that still tingled, and walked out of the observatory. She headed down the sidewalk toward the valet stand, her mind and emotions churning.

Two women were already standing there waiting. She didn't know either of them. Ember hung back because she was not in the mood for casual conversation. She'd wait in the shadows until the valet brought her car around.

She heard the women mention Ranger, and she pricked up her ears. Eased closer in the darkness.

"I don't know what Ranger sees in that crass redhead," said one of the women — an older, bejeweled, bleach-blonde in a white summer dress. "Honestly, he'd be better off with no escort at all than that one."

"Can you imagine having her at your dinner party? She's quite outrageous," replied the second woman, another blonde who was slightly younger but not quite as attractive as the older woman.

"Someone needs to pull him aside and straighten him out about her. He requires someone befitting his station in life, and that redhead certainly does not fit the bill."

"She is pretty though," said the younger woman.

"All the more reason to get rid of her. Beautiful women are such a distraction. He needs his mind one hundred percent on his work. Ah, here's our car now."

It was a black, new model Bentley. The valet held the car doors open for the women. They slid inside and drove away, leaving their poisonous opinions behind them.

To fester inside of Ember. She heard Trey's chiding voice in her head, *Don't you care what people think of you?*

Yes, of course she cared. She didn't want to, but she did. So why did she keep making the same mistakes over and over? Why couldn't she learn not to be so much herself? Why couldn't she just toe the line and be what everyone expected her to be?

"Don't let them define you."

Ember jerked her head up. Heath Lumley was standing there, flashlight in hand. She offered up a weak smile. "Hey, Heath."

"I'm serious, Ember. Who are they? A couple of rich snobs with nothing better to do than gossip. Why should you care what they think?"

"I need to pay more attention to what

people think of me."

"Which people?" Heath's teasing tone was kind. "All three-hundred-plus-million people in this country? Or the seven and a half billion globally?"

"It does sound pretty stupid when you put it like that."

"Even when it comes to people you love and who love you, which ones are you going to carve yourself up to please? Your parents? Your siblings? Your grandmother? Ranger?"

"Ranger accepts me for who I am."

Heath grinned at her like she'd gotten straight As on a report card. "Exactly."

"Thank you, Heath, you've made me feel a lot better."

"Hey, you helped us buy our dream home."

At least someone had gotten their dream. Heath had gotten his house, Ranger had gotten his earthshaking discovery, and he was on his way to getting a dream job.

"Do not feel sorry for yourself, Ember Leigh Alzate, you hear me?" she scolded herself on the way down the mountain. "You are nothing but happy for Ranger, and I don't want to hear another word about it."

Tears burned the back of her eyelids.

"Oh hell no, you most certainly are *not* going to cry." She sniffled and turned on the satellite radio to drown out her troubled thoughts, punched around on the presets, but the airwaves were filled with too many love songs, so she switched it off.

In her rearview mirror, she could see the observatory, glowing white in the dark of night, until she rounded a curve and it disappeared from her view.

Ranger had eclipsed her. He didn't belong just to her anymore. Now the entire world would find out what she had known for thirty-three years. He was brilliant and funny and kind and complicated. He was a scientist and a cowboy, a cardsharp, and a man who'd donated bone marrow to a sick kid he didn't even know. He was a tender lover and crackerjack best friend.

And she was going to miss him so very much.

A single tear slid down her cheek, but she viciously slashed it away. *None of that, missy.* It was okay that she didn't belong in Ranger's world anymore. Really, when it came right down to it, had she ever belonged in his world?

She would get through this and support Ranger the best way she could, even if that meant from afar. Because that's what best friends did for each other. She only wanted him to be happy. It's all she ever wanted, and if that meant she had to step out of the picture, then so be it.

Vivid memories of the night flickered through her head like scenes from a movie. How handsome he'd looked in the tux. How he'd dove right in when she'd yanked him into the janitorial closet. How delicious he'd tasted. How warm and steady his hands had felt on her bare skin. How they'd gotten caught and she'd had that dark moment of déjà vu over her audacious behavior.

It hit her all at once why she'd repeated the mistake she'd made with Trey when she should have known better. It wasn't just because Ranger was so sexy and she couldn't control herself. In fact, this new theory would explain why she'd done the same thing with Trey eighteen months ago.

She'd *wanted* to get caught. Had courted the embarrassment and shame because, in both cases, her behavior gave her a way out of the relationship. With Trey, it had been about showing her real self to see if he could accept her, warts and all.

But with Ranger? Had sex in the closet really been about saying goodbye?

On a subconscious level had she courted the disdain of his community? Had she wanted to justify the snobby gossips' opinion of her?

It was a stunning idea. She didn't belong in Ranger's world, and deep down, she knew it, so she'd done something outrageous to prove she wasn't worthy of him.

CHAPTER 23

"The most incomprehensible thing in the world to a man, is a woman who rejects his offer of marriage!"
— Jane Austen, *Emma*

As soon as the private helicopter whisked the governor away, Ranger left the observatory. He was a man on a mission. Get to Ember, tell her how much he loved her, and ask her to marry him.

The logical part of him argued that he should wait, buy a ring, take his time, and do this up right. But another part of him, the part of him that asked WWED — what would Ember do — whenever he started overthinking things, yelled loud and clear.

Go claim your woman, dumbass.

He drove down the mountain, traveling as fast as he dared at night on the narrow country road, his hands gripping the wheel as his imagination toyed with several different scenarios, playing out how best to tell Ember that he loved her and wanted to spend the rest of his life making love to her.

His heart was a piston, pumping hard and fast.

Thirty minutes later, he finally reached her house, it was after midnight, and he was utterly breathless. He hesitated at her door, fist raised to knock, head spinning, a lump lodged in his throat.

The house was dark. She was probably already asleep. Should he wake her up, or would it be more prudent to wait until morning? WWED?

Screw morning. He wanted to be with her now.

He rapped on the door.

No answer.

He waited a minute, knocked again.

Nothing.

Restlessly, he shifted his weight and knocked a third time.

He thought he heard movement in the house, but the lights didn't come on. It could have been Samantha moving around.

Just go.

No, no. He was here and this was happening. He took out his cell phone and called her. It rang and rang and rang and then went to voice mail.

It's a sign. Go home.

From inside the house, he heard another sound, like someone whacking into a piece of furniture in the dark, followed by a muffled curse.

She was in there, awake and hiding out from him. Why?

"Ember," he said, raising his voice slightly. "Let me in. We need to talk."

Nothing. No light. No opening door. No response.

He rested his forehead on her door, whispered, "Please."

Finally, the porch light came on and she opened the door a crack, blinked up at him. "Ranger, it's late. After midnight."

"I know."

"Call me in the morning. You can tell me all about meeting the governor then." She moved to close the door.

His stomach scrambled up to his throat. Ember was shutting the door on him? Before she could get it closed, he jammed his foot inside. "I didn't come here to talk about the damn governor."

"What did you come for?" Her voice was high and taut, bordering on shrillness. This was not like Ember. Not at all. Something big was eating at her.

"I came here to see you."

"Now is not a good time."

"It might be the only time I have to see you for a while. Things are moving really fast. There's some things about the future I need to discuss with my best friend." Yes, he played the best friend card, but it was true.

She stepped aside, opened the door wider. "Come in."

He walked into the living room, turned to face her.

She shut the door, folded her arms over her chest. "What is it?"

"Can we sit?"

She inclined her head toward the couch. He sat down and she took the chair opposite him. Crossed her legs to join her crossed arms. Well, that was significant body language.

He knew what she was doing. Things were moving too fast for her, and she was putting up roadblocks. He didn't blame her. She hadn't signed up for any of this, but he sure as hell prayed she'd want to come along.

Ranger cleared his throat, spread his legs, leaned forward to rest his elbows on his knees, pressed his palms together in front of him, a gesture of entreaty. "I had fun tonight."

"I bet you did. You got to meet the governor."

"That's not what I meant. I had fun with you in the closet."

"I embarrassed you."

"No you didn't. How many guys can say a beautiful woman dragged him into a closet to have her way with him? I call those bragging rights." Immediately, he realized how that could be misconstrued, and she seemed to be in a misconstruing mood. "Not that I would brag."

"You didn't need to. Half the people at the observatory could've seen us coming out of the closet."

He laughed. She frowned. He winced. "Oh, you weren't making a joke."

"It's not funny. You should be mad at me. Why aren't you mad at me?"

"Um, because I'm not Trey." He scratched his head. "Wait, you *wanted* me to be mad at you?"

She shrugged. "I don't know what I want."

"Well, I know what I want." He sent her a piercing stare, put all the emotions churning around inside him into that stare.

"And what's that?" She was jiggling her right foot so hard that Samantha, tailswishing, came over to swat at it.

"I've been offered a position at the University of Waterloo."

"Waterloo? That's in Canada, right?"

"Yes, Ontario. They're doing cutting edge research on FRBs, and it's very possible that I could be one of the astrobiologists who proves that there is intelligent life in the universe beyond Earth, and even if that never happens, I get to spend my entire career investigating the possibility. I can't dream a bigger dream."

Her face was impassive; a stone-cold poker face.

"It's a visiting professorship they created just for me and Dawn, but it could turn permanent."

"I'm truly happy for you, Ranger. You did all the hard work and it's paid off." No emotion in her voice either. He couldn't get a read on her.

He was mangling this. Making a mess. *That's what you get for barreling in here after midnight, unprepared.* "But I won't take the job unless you agree to go with me."

"Why would I go with you?" she asked flatly.

Wow, okay, he had not expected that response. All he wanted to do was pull her into his arms and kiss her until neither one of them could breathe. "Can we start over?"

"In what way?"

"This conversation, can we start it over?"

"You're the one who came to my door."

Why was she acting so weird? Had he done something to offend her? He blew out his breath. He was just going to come right out and say it.

"Ember, I love you." He slid off the couch and onto one knee. He was still in the tux, so that was fancy.

"Get up, Ranger." Her voice sounded panicky. "Please get up before you say something —"

"I love you not just as my best friend, but as my lover, and —"

"Please, please," she begged, hopping to her feet. "Get up."

"I'm hoping you'll be my wife." He reached for her hand. "Marry me, Ember."

She pulled her hand away, staggered back, looked shocked. "I . . . I . . . I can't."

This was not what he expected at all. The intimacy they'd shared, the pillow talk, the great sex. He thought it had been leading up to this. Discovering that Ember was not on the same page was a complete blindside.

"Why not?"

"My life is here, my family, my job."

Reeling from her rejection, he started babbling. "I was hoping you could move your life to Canada and we could start our own family and there's plenty of real estate to sell up there."

"Where is this coming from? This isn't like you."

On the drive over, he'd had pictures of her flinging herself into his arms, declaring, *Yes, yes, I'll marry you.* It never occurred to him that she would turn him down.

"You're a cautious guy. A planner. You are not impulsive."

"You're right. It's not like me. I didn't plan it. I don't even have a ring. But after I was offered the job in Waterloo, I knew I couldn't leave Texas without you. So I asked myself, what would Ember do?" He heard a tremor run through his voice. "And here I am, making a fool of myself. Telling a woman who clearly does not have the same degree of feelings for me as I do for her that I want to marry her."

"Now see," she said softly, kindly, like telling a child Santa didn't show up on Christmas Eve. "That was your mistake, asking yourself what I would do. I'm not you, and you don't get to make the biggest decisions of your life based on me."

Ranger clenched his jaw, hurting to the very marrow of his bones. He searched her face, looking for a crack, a way in past this concrete barrier she'd erected around herself. And he caught a flicker of it. An uncertain light in her eyes.

"I have one more question for you."

"Ranger, please go home."

"Just one last question and I'll be on my way."

She sighed, the sound heavy and dark in the room. "What is it?"

"When I kiss you, do you hear humming?"

Yes, yes, she did hear humming. He didn't even have to kiss her to start it up now that they'd made love. All he had to do was touch her and *zing,* she was wired for sound.

He touched her now, his fingers around her wrist, gentle but firm. He wanted an answer, and her head was humming so loudly she could not hear herself think.

Neither could she tell him what he wanted to hear, even though it was true. If she told him she heard humming, he wouldn't take that job and she simply could not let him throw his future away for her.

She didn't want to lie to him, so she said nothing. Nothing spoke louder than silence, right? Let him gather his own conclusions.

"Ember?" His voice was barely above a whisper.

"It's late, Ranger —"

"Dammit, Ember, I'm baring my soul to you and you keep trying to throw me out."

"I . . . I'm sorry, I . . ."

It was all she could do to hold back her tears. She could not give an inch, or he would try to convince her that there was room for her in his world. But there just wasn't. She'd heard those women at the observatory, had tried to talk to those people who basically ignored her. She didn't fit, and she'd had enough of pretending to be something she wasn't in order to fill someone else's mold.

"You're killing me, you know that?"

She couldn't stop herself from reaching up to touch his shoulder. His muscles were steel cords beneath her hand. He looked so wounded, and she was the cause of it. Breaking his dreams of happily-ever-after so he could go after a bigger, more important dream.

"I know how much your career means to you," she said. "You've spent your whole life trying to get here. The last thing you need is to be distracted by romance."

"I don't get to decide for myself what it is I need?"

"You're not thinking straight right now."

"That's where you're wrong. I feel as if I'm thinking straight for the very first time in my life, and it's all because of you."

"Ranger." Why couldn't he just go and let

her sob herself to sleep? She was at her wit's end.

"Do you know how long I've waited to feel like this? My whole life, I wasn't like other people, or at least I thought I wasn't. I thought that I didn't need love, that romance was an overrated complication people got themselves tangled up in and then tried to make the best of."

She moistened her lips, caught by the intensity and passion in his dark eyes, gut wrenching and heart cracking.

"I didn't believe in that kind of love." He inhaled deeply. "But, now, with you . . . with you, I realized that isn't true at all."

"What part isn't true?"

"Any of it. All of it. Love isn't a complication. It's an enrichment. And here's the big kicker that I didn't even get until I walked into Susan and Bryant's wedding and saw you there after being away from you for a year. In that moment I fell in love with you in a way I never knew was possible and I realized . . . dammit, Ember, I realized that all this time I had been avoiding love because I'd secretly been waiting."

"For what?" she whispered.

"You," he whispered back. "I had been avoiding love with other people because I was waiting for *you* to love me the same way that I loved you."

Oh God, why hadn't he said something sooner? When she was younger and more selfish, and would have considered her own happiness over what was best for him. Dammit, being an adult hurt like living hell.

Ember shook her head.

"Don't give me that look." He fisted his hands at his sides, his voice rough and thick.

"Like what?"

"Like I'm Jack in *Titanic* and you're Rose floating on a piece of wood debris."

"You've got it wrong," she said. "It's the other way around. I'm treading water, and you're the one on your way to a great life."

"I can't have a great life without you in it, Sparky." Tears misted his eyes.

She was breaking him too. *Be strong. You give in now, he's the loser, the entire world is the loser.* "Rose did just fine without Jack. She lived to be a bazillion."

"One, there's no such thing as a bazillion, and two, she spent that bazillion years without the love of her life. How could that be just fine?"

"Now you sound like my logical Professor." She cupped his cheek with her palm. "A big brand-new world has opened up for you, and I'm not a part of it."

"What do you mean you're not a part of

it? If it weren't for you, I wouldn't be where I am today. Do you think I could have achieved any of this without you?" Ranger asked, his eyes brimming with shiny light. "Who brought my lesson assignments to me every day when I was bedfast? Who did homework with me and quizzed me for tests? Who was always there for me no matter what?"

She shook her head, wishing she could change the way things were. "You have to go to Canada. You *have* to leave me behind."

"Sparky . . ."

"Just go."

"This will end our friendship." His words came out like blood clots, thick and stringy. "Sex ruined us."

"I know, baby," she whispered. "I know."

CHAPTER 24

"Of all horrid things, leave-taking is the worst."
— Jane Austen, *Emma*

Like an exploded star, Ranger's hope collapsed into infinity, sucked in by a gravitational pull so powerful that nothing could escape it. Ember had left a black hole in his heart. Blotted out all light.

Ember did not love him the way he loved her.

And she hadn't heard the humming.

Not that he truly believed in the humming, but the human brain was capable of mysterious things, and everyone was different. Who knew? Maybe there was something in Granny Blue's DNA that could set off a humming noise in the head under times of stress, because wasn't that what falling in love was? Stress. Chemical reactions.

Aw shit, aw shit, what was he going to do

without Ember? He'd never been completely without her. They'd been apart at times, but they'd never been separated. Always friends. Never broken.

Until now.

He peered through the telescope of his life and found it utterly empty without Ember in it. What did anything matter without her?

"You still with me?" Ridge asked.

Ranger blinked; he was standing beside Ridge's pickup, the last of his bags clutched in his hands. His brother was giving him a ride to the airport where he was catching a plane to Waterloo.

It had been three days since Ember had taken a wrecking ball to his life, and he was still in a daze. His professional world was whirling like the speed of sound, and he'd been fielding calls and texts and interview requests and job offers and he hadn't had a spare second to absorb what was happening to him.

"What?" Ranger asked.

"Where did you go?"

"In my head."

"Oh, that damn place."

"Yeah. Ridge, what if I don't go?"

"Meh, nothing much. You miss out on the biggest opportunity of your life."

"Ember is the biggest opportunity of my life."

"Hey, I agree with you. I've had the big career and I've got my own family, and I have to tell you family trumps career every time."

"Your career was about making more money than Duke. My career could change the world."

"Well la-di-da, ain't someone full of himself," Ridge said, affecting a deep drawl.

"It's not about my ego, it's the truth. I could be on the forefront of finding life elsewhere in the universe."

Ridge cupped his hands around his mouth. "Meanwhile, back here on Earth, he shoots, he misses the free throw . . ."

"Basketball analogics?"

"Why not?"

"Maybe I'm just not cut out for love."

"Wah, wah. Poor you. Shall we go into the childhood horror stories? Whose mom played it worst? Mine dumped me on Duke's doorstep and then killed herself. Yours sold you out for two million dollars."

"With our background, kind of a wonder any women want us at all," Ranger mumbled.

"Oh, women love fixing damaged men."

"Apparently not Ember."

441

"You don't think that's exactly what she's doing by cutting you loose?"

"Which means?"

"Cruel to be kind, baby."

Hmm. Dawn had said the same thing to him when he was trying to get Ember to notice him in the first place.

Ridge clamped his hand on Ranger's shoulder. "It's all gonna work out, I promise."

"How do you know?"

Ridge shrugged like it was a foregone conclusion. "Sometimes man, you just gotta trust the universe."

"You sound like Kaia," Ranger grumbled.

"I know," Ridge said proudly. "She's a wise woman, you should listen to her. Look how things worked out for us."

"It's different with me and Ember —"

"Yes, we know, you are God's gift to astronomy, but here" — Ridge tapped Ranger's heart — "you're just a man in love."

"Screw you," Ranger said, and threw the bag into the back of the truck to join the other six. Ranger was a minimalist, and most everything he owned besides furniture and vehicles was in those bags.

Chuckling, Ridge climbed into the driver's seat. "Get a move on, little brother. If you miss your flight, Ember will surely kick my ass."

After Ranger left, Ember kicked herself into high gear and handled her grief the best way she knew how. Getting her ass off the couch and hustling houses. She had two homes in escrow, and four more waiting to hear back on funding. It had been a productive three weeks, business wise, since he'd been gone.

No sitting around bawling through a box of Kleenex, eating Ben and Jerry's from the carton while she binge-watched Meg Ryan movies for this gal.

But even so, she still couldn't pull herself out of her emotional tailspin. Three whole weeks without a word from Ranger. At least not to her personally; Ridge had heard from him and Kaia passed those tidbits of information along to her, but it wasn't the same thing.

Hey, he'd asked her to marry him and she was the one who said no. What did she expect? She told him to go. He'd gone. End of story.

But what choice did she have? She couldn't inflict herself on him. Not with the career he had. She'd gone over it a million times. She simply was not astronomy-genius wife material. She was a pizza and beer kind of girl, in his champagne and massive vocabulary world. Their differences were woven into the very fabric of their upbringing. The Alzates served the Lockharts. How could she and Ranger ever hope to be on equal footing?

At least with Trey they had been birds of a feather.

C'mon! Was she seriously trying to compare Trey to Ranger? She was flipping losing her nut.

"God, just let it go, Ember," she grumbled, and it wasn't until Kaia gave her a weird look that she realized she'd spoken out loud.

"Sweetie," Kaia said, "we're in the middle of Jiminey's ice cream parlor."

Oh yeah. Ember blinked. It was Saturday afternoon, and the place was packed with families enjoying ice cream. Kaia had shown up on her doorstep that morning and announced that she'd pumped breast milk, and Ridge was staying home to watch his daughter and they were going out to shake off Ember's doldrums.

"You don't have Ingrid. Why are we at an ice cream parlor and not at a bar?" Ember asked.

"You wanted Rocky Road. Then you took two bites and started crying."

Ember glanced down at the melted choc-olate, almond bits, and marshmallows in the paper bowl in front of her. Oh yeah. "Rocky Road, Ranger's favorite."

Kaia sighed and pulled a Kleenex from her purse. "You wanna go home and watch *When Harry Met Sally*?"

Ember nodded.

"Come on." Kaia reached for Ember's purse and slung it over her shoulder with her own.

"You're a good sister."

"I know." Kaia smiled softly. "I understand how much it hurts when you think you've lost the love of your life."

"Kaia, I don't think it. I *know* I've lost him."

Her sister nodded kindly. "Uh-huh."

As they were headed out, the door to the ice cream parlor opened and Palmer walked in with Fiona on his arm. Fiona's head was resting on his shoulder, and they were both grinning stupid-in-love grins.

"Ember!" Fiona squealed. "There you are! The best matchmaker in the entire world!"

Dial down the enthusiasm a little, sweet cheeks, Ember wanted to say, but she knew it was just sour grapes. Seeing a couple happy together made her think about Ranger, and thinking about Ranger made her cranky.

"I'm a lousy matchmaker," she said. "I tried to hook you up with Ranger."

"Yes, that was bad." Fiona laughed. "I mean, if you're not good enough for him, which of us mere mortals is?"

"I'm a mere mortal too," Ember said.

"You are so funny." Fiona laughed as Palmer slipped his arm around her waist. "Honey, she thinks she's a regular person."

"Um . . ." Ember backed up out of the doorway. "I *am* a regular person."

"Seriously?" Fiona inclined her head. "You really don't have any idea how amazing you are? You're a real estate agent who has sold property to rich and famous people."

"I'm not rich and famous."

Fiona waved a dismissive hand. "You've directed a movie."

"An hour-long film for the Chamber of Commerce tourism."

"I know." Fiona's smile was evangelistic. "Isn't that amazing?"

When Fiona put it like that, it sounded prestigious. Maybe Ember didn't appreciate her own accomplishments the way she appreciated other people's.

"You're classy and refined."

Ha! Tell that to the snobby knobs at the

446

observatory.

"You were so sweet to Dawn even when it looked like she was trying to steal your man."

Well, that was true.

"You're a natural leader," Palmer added. "You give confidence to the people who work for you."

"Looky there." Kaia nudged Ember with her elbow. "Your bossiness comes in handy once in a while."

"You're always helping others. The way you helped me and Palmer."

"But I tried to keep you guys apart."

"We know." Fiona slid Palmer a sideways glance and fluttered her eyelashes. He leaned in, and they exchanged butterfly kisses and Ember tried not to roll her eyes. Apparently, she had caused this. "It was genius the way you got us to sneak around. The taboo. It's so exciting and forbidden. You're a brilliant matchmaker."

Yeah, that had not been her plan at all; she deserved zero credit and had, in fact, caused a lot of trouble with her meddling. "I guess love wins out."

"It does," Palmer agreed. "We're getting married next summer and you have to be there."

Ember blinked, stunned by their news. "I will."

"Yay." Fiona clapped her hands. "This is on the down low, but in case you are keeping score for matches made, Chriss Anne and Zeke are seeing each other."

"Another match made by your wicked clever method." Palmer winked.

Oo*kay*.

Fiona put a hand on Ember's shoulder. "You're a very special person, Ember, can't you see that?"

"She's got this hang-up that she's unlovable," Kaia whispered loudly to Fiona. "Ex-husband did her dirty, and a few other things. There was a pocketknife and a bloodletting."

"What?" Palmer looked startled.

"Ancient history." Ember stepped lightly on Kaia's foot.

"You can't let a bad apple take the shine off your light," Fiona said. "Right, Palmer?"

Palmer pointed at Fiona, his eyes aglow as he studied the woman beside him. "What she said."

The two of them did make a good match. Why hadn't she seen that right off the bat?

Why? Because she'd been too busy trying to find the perfect mate for Ranger so he could be happy. That was all she'd ever wanted for him.

But when she'd actually had the opportunity to give him what he really needed to make him happy, she'd taken it away and sent him off to Canada without her.

wanted for him.

But when she'd really had the opportunity to put into what he really needed
to take him happy, she'd taken it away, and
sent him off to Canada without her.

CHAPTER 25

"It was foolish, it was wrong, to take so active a part in bringing any two people together."

— Jane Austen, *Emma*

Following her epiphany at seeing Fiona and Palmer together, Ember was a changed woman. Despite what Fiona and Palmer thought, it was not her cleverness at match-making that brought them together, rather a happy twist of fate.

Who was she to tell people how to live their lives? What did she know about the mysteries of the human heart? There was no rhyme or reason. No perfect theory. No one right way. Sometimes opposites did at-tract. Sometimes birds of a feather flocked together.

Maybe Granny Blue was right and it was all fated. Written in the stars long before you were born. Maybe there *were* soul mates. Or maybe it was just two people who loved and cared about each other doing their best to make things work. Maybe it was all of those things and none of them.

The only thing that Ember knew for sure was that *she* was not in control. She did not know what was best for anyone, much less herself. She was just a woman who loved a man. Loved him so much that simply thinking about him filled her with a deep and abiding joy.

Ranger her friend. Her best friend.

And her lover.

Did she dare hope she could convince him to give her a second chance? She didn't know, but she did know she had to try.

He was a poker player, and the only way to prove to him she was serious was to go all in. Ember quit her job at the real estate agency, broke the lease on her house, gave Samantha to Kaia, packed her bags, and bought a one-way ticket to Canada.

In Waterloo, Ranger tried to throw himself into his work, but he couldn't focus. Astronomy was a painstaking process, and a man could spend his entire career on a single project that ultimately contributed less than a drop to the total knowledge of the field.

Ranger was on the cusp of potential greatness, and he just didn't care. All he could think about was Ember. Without her, none of his achievements meant a damn thing.

And no matter how hard he tried, work didn't salve or save him the way it once had.

"You're missing her," Dawn said to him late one evening after they'd already put in a full ten-hour day, but still had a massive amount of work ahead of them.

"Yeah," he admitted.

"So call her."

"I can't."

"Why not?"

"She made it clear it was over."

"How did you get to be an astronomer if you give up that easily?"

"I didn't give up."

"No?"

"Ember gave up on herself."

"And you let her."

Dawn was right. He'd caved in. Rolled over. Because he loved Ember so much, he would do anything for her, even if it meant walking away.

Dawn's mouth dipped in a look of sympathy. "It can't be easy, losing your best friend and your lover in one fell swoop."

"I've known her all my life," he said. "Whenever anything happens to me, my first thought is . . . was . . . to call her and

452

talk about it. Whenever I have a big decision to make I ask myself WWED."

"WWED?"

"What would Ember do."

"That's really cute. You're adorbs, you know that, right?"

"I'm a man of thoughts and ideas. Ember is all action. I'm the introvert. She's the extrovert. I was her brake. She was the kick in my pants. Now . . ." He shrugged, took off his safety goggles, rubbed his eyes. "I don't have anyone to talk to or kick me in the seat of the pants."

"You could talk to me," Dawn offered. "I'll even kick you in the ass if you like."

"Guess it couldn't hurt." He plunked down on a metal stool, hooked the heels of his cowboy boots over the foot rung.

"What are you sitting down for? I was going to kick you."

"What am I going to do, Dawn? Work was the only thing that's ever always been there for me besides Ember. But now that I've lost Ember, I've lost interest in my work. It's as if the two are tied together."

"Maybe they are."

"Meaning?"

"Maybe she was your inspiration and without her you're no longer inspired. I'm an astronomer, not a psychologist, but do you want to know what I think?"

"Why not?" He opened his palms. "I'm grasping at straws."

"You've formed this mistaken belief that you don't need love. That you're somehow above normal human emotions, and if you just gather more knowledge it will ease those deeply buried feelings of inadequacy you struggle so hard to deny."

"Whoa, that's a mouthful."

"It means you won't ever find the love you do need until you stop running from your feelings."

"Is that what I'm doing?"

Dawn inclined her head. "Only you can say. What do you think?"

Ranger stroked his jaw, gave her assessment some consideration. "Do I sense a confirmation bias coming on?"

Her smile was filled with understanding. "It's just a theory."

"You've spent some time thinking about this."

"I've been watching you for over a year."

"Any thoughts on how to correct my . . . issue?"

"Reverse the order."

"What?"

"Love first. It's an essential human need. Love first, and then everything else will fall into place. Now stop being broody, ask for a leave of absence, and go straighten things out with Ember or I'm asking for a new research partner."

It was almost nine p.m. when Ember arrived at the University of Waterloo. She'd gone to Ranger's apartment first — she'd gotten the address from Ridge — but a neighbor who also worked at the University had told her he was still at work.

But of course, that was her Ranger. She should have gone straight to the university. She parked in the nearly vacant lot near the astronomy building and was just stepping out of her car when she saw him come out of the side exit, head down, walking at a furious clip.

Where was he going in such a hurry?

"Ranger!" she called.

He stopped and his head jerked up. The expression on his face told her he thought he was hearing things.

"Ranger!" She started running straight for him.

He opened his arms and she flew into them. He picked her up and spun her around until they were both laughing and dizzy underneath the street lamp.

"What are you doing here?" he asked, his

eyes shiny in the light. He was so handsome her breath caught in her lungs.

"I came to see you."

"Why?"

"There's something I have to tell you."

"I'm listening," he said. "Or should we go somewhere more comfortable? There's a coffee shop just down the street."

"We can walk and talk." She nodded. They could have taken her car, but her hands were so shaky over seeing him again she was not sure she could have driven. "How's the search for E.T. going?"

"Slow. You know science moves at glacier speeds."

"It sure moved fast that night at the observatory."

"Ember, about that night . . ."

"Shh." She put her index finger over his lips. "That's what I'm here about."

He wrapped his hand around her index finger, used it to haul her closer to him. It felt so good to be near him again.

"Bob Marley said that only once in your life do you find someone who can completely turn your world around," Ember told him.

"Big Marley fan are you now?"

"You have been gone almost a month. You can never tell about me."

"That's true." He smiled. "Your unpredictability is one of the things I like most about you."

"How's this? I came up here to tell you that you've not only turned my world around, but upside down and inside out."

"Ember . . ."

"Just let me finish. I practiced it on the plane ride up. I can share things with you that I can't tell another soul. You know all my flaws and all the mistakes I've made, and not only do you keep sticking around, you seem to like me even more because of it. That is" — she gulped — "you used to."

His eyes turned murky, unreadable. "You hurt me, Ember."

"I know, and I'm so deeply sorry. All I ever wanted was your happiness."

"At the expense of your own." His tone was soft, guarded.

"Don't you get it, Ranger? You *are* my happiness." She gulped again; how was she going to get through this if he'd decided they couldn't work? Was she too late? Had she lost her chance to make amends?

Rallying her courage — it was all she had left — Ember plunged ahead. "With you, I can share my hopes and dreams, my failures and disappointments. All of it. The messy parts and the inspiring ones, and you accept them both as gifts. And I do the same for you. How incredibly special is that?"

"Ember —"

She was on a roll and could not stop. She had to get this out or she'd collapse, and she was *not* going to do that. "When something wonderful happens, the first person I want to tell is you because nobody gets as excited for me as you do. When something awful happens, it's the same way. You're my great champion. You always have been, and I hope I do the same for you."

"Em—"

"You cry with me when I'm hurt, and you laugh with me when I'm happy. You've never intentionally hurt my feelings or made me feel as if my personality is a burden to you."

"That's because —"

She held up a hand, talking faster and faster to outrun the fear that she was making a terrible mistake confessing everything like this. "You make me feel special and included and talented and desirable."

"You —"

"No, *you.* You build me up and make me shine. You give me courage and hope. You make me feel beautiful even when my hair is a mess and I'm not wearing makeup."

He clamped his lips together, held out his hands in a sweeping, you've-got-the-floor-filibuster-away gesture.

"There's never any competition or jealousy between you and me." The way it had been with her and Trey. Everything in their relationship had been about winning. With Ranger, there was none of that. Whatever she had, she would give to him gladly, willingly without hesitation and vice versa. "With you, there's no stress. You're my calm, soft place to land."

His dark eyes were obsidian mirrors, and inside him, she could see herself.

"Ember," he said kindly, patiently, "could you let me get a word in edgewise?"

"Huh? Yes. Okay." She bobbed her head. "Please speak."

"I've been waiting thirty-three years for you to come to this conclusion. I've known all along we were meant to be," he said.

"You did?"

"I just didn't know how deeply and surely I felt it until that night at your house."

"Which night? The night we did it or the night I sent you away."

"Both. Dawn tells me I didn't think I needed love, but she's off the mark a bit. I only need *your* love. That's why I could never commit to any of the women I dated. None of them were you."

"Oh Ranger." She stopped on the sidewalk

and went down on one knee and took his hand. "Will you marry me?"

"No." He shook his head.

Terror hit her heart, downing her like an airplane plunging from the sky. Oh God, it was exactly as she feared. He did not want her anymore.

His voice and eyes softened. "We're not doing it like that."

Her pulse thumped crazily, pounding through her temples, twisting up her brain. "I know this is outrageous, I know I'm outrageous —"

"Hush," he said, his eyes brimming with humor. "I *love* your outrageousness. It's part of what makes you you. With me you can fully be yourself and not have to worry that I'll ever stop loving you. I said no because we're going to do this right. I'm buying a ring and I'm asking you again to marry me and you're going to say yes and we're going to live happily-ever-after. What do you say to that?"

"I quit my job and gave up my lease and bought a one-way ticket to Canada."

"All in."

"I'm thinking this is a game we both can win."

"Sweetheart, I know it is." He took her in his arms and kissed her, and her head hummed.

"Oh by the way. I lied."

"About what?"

"Not a full lie, more a lie of omission."

He arched an eyebrow.

"That night you asked me if I heard the humming and I never answered you." Her eyes met his, and he was staring into her as if she were the answer to all his prayers. "I heard it. I still hear it whenever you kiss me. I hear it right now."

"Really?" He squeezed her tight.

She nodded. "I was afraid to tell you before. Afraid you'd stay if I did."

"Ember, the humming has spoken," he teased. "We were meant to be."

"I love you, Ranger. As a friend and a lover. I love you in all the ways it's possible to love another human being. I can't say it enough. I'm going to say it every day, multiple times. I love you, I love you, I love you."

"I love you too, Ember Leigh Alzate."

"Soon to be Ember Leigh Lockhart. Ooh, I like the sound of that."

"Me too. I can't wait. But why the sudden change of heart?"

She explained to him then about Fiona and Palmer and how they'd made her see that what she'd viewed as her flaws were also her strengths.

"I've been telling you that for years. Your family has been telling you that for years."

"I know, but I think it's one of those conclusions you have to reach on your own."

"Thank God for Fiona and Palmer."

"Thank God for you."

Ranger stared at her, his dark eyes so full of love that she couldn't absorb it all. He brushed her hair from her cheek, tenderly hauled her into his arms and kissed her for a very long time.

And there, just off campus, near an adorable late-night coffee shop, Ember realized her struggle was finally over and she was at peace. She'd learned that she was lovable and the only opinion that mattered about the way she lived her life was her own.

Eagerly, as they walked into the coffee shop packed with students submerged in papers, books, and electronic devices, she breathed in a happy sigh. So many brilliant minds in one area, and they all needed a place to live. Oh my, but she was going to make a killing in this real estate market.

And, as Ranger pulled her into a back booth and kissed her until her entire body hummed, she fully understood that she had made the match of a lifetime.

ABOUT THE AUTHOR

Lori Wilde is the *New York Times* and *USA Today* bestselling author of over 80 romance novels. She is a three-time RITA award nominee, a four time Romantic Times Reviewers' Choice nominee and has won numerous other awards. She earned a bachelor's degree in nursing from Texas Christian University and holds a certificate in forensics. She is also a certified yoga instructor.

Her books have been translated into 27 languages and featured in *Cosmopolitan, Redbook, Complete Woman, All You, Time* and *Quick and Simple* magazines. She lives in Texas with her husband, Bill.

The employees of Thorndike Press hope you have enjoyed this Large Print book. All our Thorndike, Wheeler, and Kennebec Large Print titles are designed for easy reading, and all our books are made to last. Other Thorndike Press Large Print books are available at your library, through selected bookstores, or directly from us.

For information about titles, please call:
(800) 223-1244

or visit our website at:
gale.com/thorndike

To share your comments, please write:
Publisher
Thorndike Press
10 Water St., Suite 310
Waterville, ME 04901